the
Double K Ranch

To a Wonderful Friend and Special Leader!

PATRICIA COTE

TATE PUBLISHING & Enterprises

Published by Tate Publishing & Enterprises, LLC
127 E. Trade Center Terrace | Mustang, Oklahoma 73064 USA
1.888.361.9473 | www.tatepublishing.com

Tate Publishing is committed to excellence in the publishing industry. The company reflects the philosophy established by the founders, based on Psalm 68:11,
"The Lord gave the word and great was the company of those who published it."

Book design copyright © 2010 by Tate Publishing, LLC. All rights reserved.
Cover design by Leah LeFlore
Interior design by Lynly D. Grider

Published in the United States of America

ISBN: 978-1-61663-977-8
1. Fiction, Romance, Western   2. Fiction, Romance, General

10.08.04

DEDICATIONS

To Bob, my husband and best friend, Lois, the original "Florida Girl" and friend, Joan, a great friend with about 20 teakettles for a hot water tank in the woods, James, my editor that helped plow through the tons of ideas to come up with the jewels, Leah, fantastic artwork! Thanks for the encouragement, knowledge, help, and love!

THE DOUBLE K RANCH

ONE

Cade hated parties. But he was invited to the town's Halloween party, and this year he was using it to find a cook. Mrs. Dietrich, the town banker's wife, had promised him an opportunity to meet a candidate for the position. He'd been looking for quite some time, and skipping the party would cost him the chance at finding a good cook. The only thing left to do was suck it up and get ready.

His major interests were in his ranch and along with all his other investments; he had people to run every aspect of them. He could socialize all day and night with his ranch hands or CEOs that worked for him, but the idea of going to town and this particular party was enough to make his stomach muscles permanently tie themselves into knots.

Currently, his only headache was the absence of a good cook. Over the past several months, he'd been hiring and firing one cook after another. Since he was planning on expanding, he would have to hire some more men and eventually he would have to hire another cook, but for now he was after one good cook. He had exhausted every avenue of advertising and felt that he was getting a reputation for being a tough boss to work for, so he hesitated putting another ad in the paper.

He never dreamed finding a good cook would become a nightmare. One cook was the now infamous Delilah Willglen. He feared he would find her at the party, if for no other reason than to be an irritant.

Delilah was a liar, a thief, great at starting fights, insulting, mean, vengeful, had a vicious temper, held a grudge, and treated everyone with disdain. Her meals were never on time, and occasionally his crew went hungry unless someone went to town and came back with a load of pizzas or hamburgers. Her theft and laziness still riled him.

After finding her in the pantry late one night, sitting cross-legged on the floor with store-bought cookies piled like poker chips around her and eating herself into a coma he felt himself snap. Her face and fingers were covered and smeared with chocolate crumbs, her mouth was stuffed with so many Oreos that she couldn't swallow, and yet she attempted to stuff more in as though she were in an Oreo cookie–eating contest. It seemed she couldn't eat them fast enough. He gave her all the cookies and sent her on her way knowing that she would cause him all the trouble she could.

If he didn't hire tonight, he would call the cooking schools around the country looking for a graduate cook that wanted the Western atmosphere.

He was praying that Mrs. Dietrich was his "ace up the sleeve." She had lured him to the party with a lead for a good cook. No amount of begging, whining, threats, or pressure forced the information from her lips prior to the party. She wanted him at the party; he wanted the information.

Cade decided to treat the entire evening as business. If he could get his mind into business, he'd be successful tonight.

He scanned his closet and found the suit he had purchased in Mexico a couple of years earlier. It had caught his fancy and yet he had never worn it. It was tailored perfectly, made of suede and instead of black, brown, or tan in color, it was very light blue. Yes, this would fit his personality tonight. Bold in strength, daring with confidence, and a little flashy to prove he could be brash. He pulled it from the closet and held it up.

Oh yes! It'll fit this evening. Western, yet bold! It'll work.

Dressed in his aqua-colored western-style slacks and jacket, and black silk shirt, he pulled on his black western boots, rechecked the aqua-colored bolo tie with the silver and diamond tips, and headed downstairs with his black Stetson in his hand.

The colors enhanced his rugged good looks, dark short hair, and bronzed skin and surprisingly brought out the nearly aquamarine color of his eyes. He had confidence in himself and his success and strode from the house, climbed into his freshly washed emerald green new Toyota Tundra, and headed off to town.

The twenty-five-mile trip wasn't so bad in his new truck, but his stomach was in a knot at the prospect of yet another obligation he felt roped into.

Mrs. Dietrich, insisted on having this annual event under the guise of "town improvement." But the town never changed. Apparently, the rest of the town's population was of the same opinion as he, keep the town exclusively small.

With a prayer in his heart, he asked God for *success on finding a new cook that will last more than a month or two.*

Arriving at the parking lot of the local grange, he parked, and slid out of the truck crunching across the gravel, under the single light illuminating the lot. He was immediately greeted by the banker and his wife in the small entry decorated with huge spiders in webs and a pile of jack-o-lanterns.

He shook the banker's hand and gently hugged his wife. Mrs. Dietrich put her arm through Cade's and led him into the dimly lit, crowded hall abandoning her husband to the reception duties.

"Cade, I'm so glad you made it. I have that candidate for a cook you are looking for. She's a very nice girl, down on her luck, and I know she's desperate for work. I don't know what her background or experience is except she was working in the bakery before it closed several months ago. I also know she is an upstanding young woman, not taken with drugs or alcohol, has decent manners and morals and a high respect for other people. She's destitute, Cade. Please consider her for the job. She's scared to death of watching her last dollar disappear before she has a new job. She's been starving herself lately, too.

She's here somewhere serving with the catering company tonight. Oh, by the way, Delilah is here. I'm sorry, but I had to hire her as caterer because I couldn't get anyone else out here this year."

"Thanks, Mrs. Dietrich, for the lead and the warning. What's the girl's name?"

"Margo Benchly. Enjoy yourself tonight, Cade." She let go of his arm and turned back to the entrance door as Cade spoke his thanks.

After making his way through the line of couples around the edges of the room, he stopped to take a survey of the buffet, and hopefully discover the young lady looking for a job. Then he would depart the scene before the dancing and serious drinking, which he had no interest in or desire for.

Across the room, Margo, grabbed another tray of drinks and started weaving through the crowd. She was actually in a foul mood since she had discovered that her boss had lied to her. She was struggling to rein in her irritation and bad attitude. She needed a job in order to make enough bucks to stay alive. Delilah had portrayed the job as "quite busy as she had many customers out in Sheridan and Buffalo and even into Rapid City and her date book was full." However, Delilah must have figured no one would call her a liar and point out that her date book only had one day in it. Her antisocial attitudes, bipolar trends, and bullying habits usually kept her out of work. Margo had obtained the facts from Mrs. Anderson, one of the other "saloon girls" on the catering team.

Here she was, wearing stiletto heels, feet screaming in agony, a black lace and gold satin dress that had been altered so many times it was basted together. She had feathers in her long, light brown hair, which had been twisted up into a mass of curls at the crown of her head to fall down one side in huge sausage curls, and the party had just begun. *I'm five foot nine inches tall,* she thought as she pasted a smile on her face and wandered the room handing out drinks.

Cowboys and gamblers! You'd think it was a movie lot instead of Wyoming, Margo thought, never expecting to see so many cowboys and gamblers in one spot or grown men dressed like Bret Maverick; black dusters over gold vests over white shirts over black slacks and black boots. They all wore black string ties and black hats, and most wore a black gun holster across their hips as though they would know what to do with the toy gun it carried. Bret was a hit in this small town! *It was a costume ball, for crying out loud!* It was for Halloween, there was no theme, and yet most of them had elected to come as a gambler to this ridiculous attempt at adult, clean, albeit *boring*, party. When she served a drink to the town's bank manager dressed as a gambler, she was shocked! She thought he could have dressed as a banker from the 1800s. That would have shown some imagination. But here he stood, dressed like every other gambler in the place. Talk about boring! Somehow she knew no one should do their banking with Maverick!

At least the few cowboys had some imagination and taste, although most were of the same ilk—hats, guns, bandanas, boots, and scruffy, if not a bit dirty and dusty! She thought they looked more like bandits, but if the cowboy she was looking at had anything to do with it, the boring might change into some class! This one stood out from the rest; like Gene or Roy, even the Lone Ranger, there was nothing shy about him. Nothing quiet about his personality. The air around him popped. It was as though the power and confidence oozed from his pores. The fact that he was about six foot two or three, lean, and strongly built was only part of the equation. This one wasn't just a dude—some guy dressed like a cowboy but didn't know a horse from a soup can. This one had actually been out in the sun, and he was *stunning!* He was clean shaven, hair very dark and short, and his skin was golden from the sun. *I'll bet he has a horse, knows how to ride it, and actually pokes cows!* Margo thought. As she got closer to him, she noticed his eyes—light blue in color—nearly matching the intriguing suit he wore, to perfection! He wore no guns! Another intriguing concept! *He's perfect! A regular guy dressed like a city cowboy. Wonder if he can dance?*

He didn't seem to mind standing out in the crowd; it seemed he demanded the looks, the speculation. The envy!

As she wove her way toward him, she passed out drinks to others in the crowded room. By the time she got to this particular cowboy she was surprised she had any drinks left on her tray, as she hadn't paid any attention to whom she passed a drink.

"Hello. May I offer you a drink?" she asked the cowboy. Now she saw the diamond studded silver tips of his bolo tie. *A guy not afraid of wearing a little sparkle to liven things up!*

He smiled back at her and asked, "Could you tell me who Margo is?"

She stared at him for a moment and then finally answered with a slight question in her voice, "You're looking at her. Who might you be?"

"Mrs. Dietrich said you can cook and you were looking for a permanent, full-time job."

He was about to continue when he noticed her eyes dart to something behind him and turn to instant anger for just a flicker of a moment. He had no doubt that Delilah was behind him and on a fast track to cause him embarrassment or grief. Delilah flounced to a stop next to him, nearly knocking him over. He barely managed to keep from falling face first on to the boarded floor.

Delilah's perfume worked hard to cover an underscore of sweat and a layer of just-not-really-clean-clothing, and while she was only around five foot two or three, she was very much shaped like a beach ball. Her hair was a huge black ball, like something from the sixties, with the Goth look that Cade so detested. From his angle and height over Delilah, Cade could see much more cleavage in Delilah Willglen than he cared to see, and he stepped aside, giving her more room and enabling himself less of the disgusting view down the front of her dress and the opportunity to breathe easier. He glanced at Margo and saw a glitter of hate flash over her eyes and thought about how expressive her eyes were, like the window to her heart.

Margo was looking down on her boss—the temporary, part-time, lying boss that she actually hated with a passion.

What she really hated about her boss was her attitude toward other people. Delilah had a lack of respect for everyone. Margo's anger, along with her frustration, was rising dangerously and she felt helpless to change it.

Delilah's overpowering scent brought Margo's mind back to the moment. She could see the cowboy was irritated as his eyes grew black. The air snapped around him.

Cade held his anger in check and was thinking about the dreaded confrontation he knew Delilah was pushing for. Because Delilah was a person that you could go to war with, maybe even win a battle or two, but you never felt like you had won the war; since that was the case, he was making plans on a quick exit.

"What are you doing?" Delilah nearly screeched, instantly catching the attention of most of the guests in the room. Cade saw Delilah's eyes flash quickly around the room, ensuring she was the center of attention. "You're supposed to be passing these drinks around, not flirting with the guests! Now get your butt moving, girl. There are plenty of thirsty people around here." Delilah stood there, hands on her hips, causing her elbows to jut out on both sides and making Delilah look like a huge, round sugar bowl.

"Hold on, Delilah," Cade inserted softly. "She just offered me a drink, and I'd barely the chance to reject it before you nearly ran us down in your haste to take center stage. Throttle back, simmer down, and relax. You'll probably enjoy life a bit more. I know the rest of us will."

The room had grown quiet as the guests were all queuing into the heated discussion starting in the middle of the room and involving Cade and Delilah. And everyone knew what had happened between them.

"I'll do that!" Delilah threw at Cade, not caring if she was insulting. Then turning back to Margo, she looked her up and down, took the tray from her hands, and stated to Cade, "I'm going to enjoy myself immensely!" To Margo she shouted, "You're finished! Bring the dress back tomorrow before noon. Now get out." She reached up as she shouted, grabbed the shoulder strap of Margo's dress, and pulled with gusto, ripping the dress nearly off Margo and leaving her standing there grabbing at what was left of the dress in an attempt to keep herself covered. Delilah walked away from Margo, a dare apparent across her face.

"Oh! Cade, how typical of you! I think you should take her to a motel before ripping her clothes off! And, Margo, that dress will be costing you your night's salary!" Delilah shouted over her shoulder wanting to make a bigger scene then she had already constructed.

A huge smile on her face, a hideous laugh from her mouth, and confident in her self-appointed authority, sure she had offended and embarrassed Cade and hoping to have caused him any kind of financial and legal problems she could, she wondered off looking for someone else to harass. She didn't care a whit about Margo. Being totally ignorant that she was the one in legal offense, she strutted along with an over-enhanced hip sway, offering drinks to the guests while being totally ignorant of her arrogance and childish actions.

The dress Margo had worn as costume had been forced on her by Delilah. It was so close to a rag that Margo didn't really want to wear it, but she had no choice, except not to work, which meant she had no choice. Margo grabbed at what was left of the dress, trying to cover herself again, but she was too late and the basted dress fell apart and slid to the floor leaving her in nothing but stiletto heels and bikini underwear. Becoming more enraged by the second she stood back up, a boldness fused with the red-hot anger already burning inside. "That did it!" she hissed. She looked down at the black and gold saloon girl's dress at her feet. She was fueled by her anger and hate intensified her power. Delilah was a lone, rouge wolf. She was more than off balance mentally, her muscles were unconditioned from lack of exercise and indulging in too many starchy, sugary foods. She was uneducated and arrogant. In her anger, Margo reached out and quickly took the drink from a nearby cowboy, poured it on the floor, and dropped the glass, letting it roll across the floor making enough noise to be heard clearly by everyone. She put her foot on the torn dress and rubbed it over the spilled alcohol and around the floor as though she were wiping up the spill, never taking her eyes off the hated Delilah. She heard gasps of astonishment from men and women alike, but she didn't care. They almost made her feel righteous, which spurred her on. Margo stooped over, picked up the wet and filthy dress, and sang, "Oh, Delilah!"

Delilah turned to see what was going on, innocent and unaware. "You wanted center stage, you drama queen. Now you've got it!" Margo threw the dress as hard as she could toward Delilah. Anger gave her extra strength, and her aim was dead on as it landed in Delilah's face then wrapped itself around her head with its momentum ending in an audible "thwack".

The tray of drinks flew out of Delilah's hand, glasses crashing and sending glass shards and liquid everywhere. While people backed away from the flying glasses, the momentum of the dress-in-the-face caused Delilah to fall backwards, legs flying out, dress flipping up to expose her legs. Margo felt a twinge of regret, but her anger crushed that fledgling feeling instantly.

"There's your dress, Delilah, and well before noon tomorrow! You're nothing but a worthless bully. You care about no one except yourself; like all female bullies, you're just mean, nasty, and evil! I guess you're exposed now! Enjoy your newfound fame! Oh! Let me add to your fame. I guess I can't let your sterling lies and theft go unnoticed."

Mrs. Dietrich came up beside Margo to investigate the scene unfolding in the middle of the dance floor, and Margo said, "Mrs. Dietrich, if you check the refrigerator, I think you'll find another tray of food in there, set aside by this drama queen! She plans on 'discovering' it near the end of the party and will just take it home with her at your expense!" Margo's anger was an inferno now. "And while we're at it, 'Your Majesty'"—she turned back to Delilah—"everyone here knows you ripped that rag of a dress off me; Cade had nothing to do with it, so that's on you, too. If my night's salary is only worth that rag, it shows what a cheap employer you are. Of course, it's hard to pay your employees much when you only have one gig on your entire calendar. Nobody wants to hire you, Delilah. You've lied and stolen from everyone and the word's out! You should be left alone to finish this gig of yours, but Mrs. Dietrich would be the one to suffer. Since you seem only capable of poor taste and bad decorum, I'm sure the only muscles that get any exercise are your elbow, wrist, and jaw as you're constantly shoveling something in or out of your filthy mouth."

There was a squeal of rage from Delilah and some men started passing money back and forth taking bets on the outcome of the upcoming entertainment, which apparently was going to be a cat fight. There was even a short round of scattered applause from unknown sources, but Margo didn't care about anything. She was in a rage, and she was bearing down on the object of her anger with blood in her eye!

Suddenly, Margo noticed that Delilah was wearing tennis shoes instead of stiletto heels. Margo realized now that Delilah wore the long dress to hide those tennis shoes while all the time demanding that her employees suffered in the stilettos. She stopped her forward stalk on Delilah and removed one of those stilettos from her foot. Then holding it above her shoulder with the spike heel aimed and ready to sink into Delilah; she continued her forward movement. Delilah struggled to get up off the floor. Angry that someone dared to challenge her, hot tears slid down her cheeks leaving trails in the smeared white makeup. She roared like a wild thing. "How dare you come at me, you little trollop! I'm going to sue you!"

"You can't get blood from a turnip, stupid," Margo shot back.

Cade could see this was going to go nowhere. He needed to stop Margo from heading any farther into disaster.

Margo wasn't aware that everyone was watching her and silently encouraging her actions, she was moving toward her target without much concern of assault-with-the-intent-to-kill charge looming ahead of her. She did notice that no one came to the assistance of Delilah Willglen. *Everybody hates Delilah!*

Feeling something gently descend on her shoulders and a firm hand grasp her wrist and instantly reroute her from the room wavered into Margo's brain. It all happened so quickly she was outside before she realized what had really happened or even splutter a protest.

She followed where Cade led, which was into his truck. As soon as they were inside and the doors were closed, he turned on the engine and the heat. The realization that she could have murdered Delilah penetrated her mind and she started shaking in fear of what she could have done. Angry tears turned to tears of fear. She thought her pounding heart was going to explode.

"Well, now I'm really in a pickle jar!" she hissed out. "No job, no money, and no place to go! I don't have a clue where to get another job or money without robbing the bank." She lowered her face into her hands, and the tears ran faster and hotter, and her knees started to feel like soft wax as desperation sank in. She whispered, "Oh, God! How did I get here? What did I ever do to deserve this?" She started to sink into a vast canyon of despair, but Cade was there with understanding and compassion.

"Look, I'm sorry this happened. Delilah is a huge problem. I know because she used to steal from me. I actually came here to find you tonight. I have a cook's position open, and Mrs. Dietrich told me you can cook. Can you cook for thirty people?"

The voice, nearly unheard, finally penetrated her turmoil and reached her aching brain. She realized the cowboy was rubbing her arm, and when she looked up, she saw he was sincerely concerned about her. His jacket was over her shoulders, and she pulled it tighter around her arms to stop some of the shivers.

"What?" she asked totally lost.

TWO

I asked if you can cook."

"Cook; what are you talking about?" she asked angrily. She spun in the seat, turning her back on him. She couldn't look at him any longer as embarrassment scalded her face. Here she was in a stranger's truck in the parking lot in the middle of town, for crying-out-loud, dressed only in her underwear and stupid stiletto heels on a freezing cold night at the end of October; and a stranger, albeit a good-looking man, was asking her if she could cook!

"You need a job; I have an opening for a cook. If you can cook, the job is yours," he repeated.

He was not only gentle looking and gentle speaking, but he seemed gentle hearted, too. But fear and anger reared their ugly heads again and Margo was starting to wonder about her sanity. Was she really so hopelessly brain dead that she couldn't even catch a pick-up line when she heard it? Did she need to be committed to some quiet hospital for the insane?

"What luck!" her statement dripped with sarcasm. "I'm fired right in front of a cowboy looking for a cook. I can just imagine what kind of cook you want, too. Look, cowboy, I'm not sliding between the sheets as payment!" She sat up straight, pulled the warm, beautiful and soft jacket from her shoulders, handed it to the cowboy, muttered a "Thanks!" and started to get out of the truck in anger, but the thought of no clothes, no place to go and the freezing cold of November slowed her actions to a severely low gear. He put the jacket back on her bare shoulders. She spun around in the seat, her anger heating up again. "I'm not making a living anywhere, anytime flat on my back!"

"Hold it! Simmer down! Look, I own the Double K Ranch, it's about twenty-five miles out of town, but it's one of the biggest ranches in this state. And I will admit that the idea of you sliding between the sheets has its appeal"—he grinned and held up a hand to block a well-aimed fist—"but that's not what I'm looking for." He was still holding her fist at bay.

"Why?" she asked.

The question stopped him cold. He let out a frustrated sigh, let go of her fist. Normally, he would do an interview in an office or over the phone, ask specific questions to glean information from the applicant, then garner an application and resume, do a background check and then agonize over the decision and hope for the best. Now, his heart was full of compassion for the young woman in dire straits, with no prospects of anything better. He felt her pain, her fear, and wanted to help. He trusted Mrs. Dietrich to not put another washout in his hands. He needed a good cook and the alternative for himself was more wasted time, the alternative for Margo was death. He put his hands on the steering wheel then turned back around to face her and looked her cold in the eyes. "Look, my men are getting real loud about the meals they're cooking themselves, and I don't have the time or desire for cooking to make it better. I've been trying to hire a cook long enough that I've got a reputation of being a tough employer, but I think we can make each other happy with a lot of patience, some explaining, and a pile of listening and understanding. If you can cook, you've got a job with real US dollars for pay and that includes room and board and insurance benefits."

Margo finally heard what he was saying. "Did you say room and board? You just hired yourself a cook." She sniffed and heaved a huge sigh. "I only have one request."

"What's that?"

"Well, make it two."

"Okay," he replied.

"You can't hit me. I think you've seen my anger tonight, so you know I'd hit back."

"It was like watching a mountain lion attack. Absolutely terrifying but a thing of beauty! You were magnificent and I was impressed. So I promise not to take the first swing. But I also promise you that if you hit me, I'll hit back. I don't go around hitting woman, children, animals and employees, but I won't stand there and not return what's dished out. Clear?"

He was very aware that when he had let go of her fist moments before he suddenly felt he'd let go of something very important and valuable, and he was surprised at his feelings of loss and emptiness. He looked at her face and felt a tug of something nearly forgotten and buried deep in his heart. He never thought he would have that feeling again, and he was a bit surprised at finding it tearing around his heart with such speed that he was breathing faster than normal.

"You'd hit me?" she asked incredulously.

"Absolutely," he replied without a moment's hesitation. She believed him.

"What was the second request?" he asked.

"No stiletto heels!"

"Aw! And they look so good on you," he teased. He looked into her face, "Do you know how beautiful you look when you're ready to commit murder? And I have to say it, you do more justice to this fancy jacket than I do." He was trapped by the confines of the truck and couldn't put more distance between her fist and his face, and he was laughing at her. She took pity on him and didn't swing as she felt he deserved. Besides, she knew he was teasing and wasn't really mad at him. "Come on; let's get you to the ranch. We'll come back tomorrow for your things."

He turned the key in the ignition, and sat there staring at her. She was beautiful! Her golden brown hair was trailing down her back now that she had ripped the pins from it. Her eyes were emerald green and flashed in the available light from the building they had just vacated, and her skin took on a flawless ivory quality. She was tall and slender. He knew he'd seen a female warrior that would fight like a hellcat.

He reached out and gently wiped a tear from her face with his thumb then pulled the black feathers from her hair. Showing them to her, he said, "These don't quite go with the female warrior image I currently have of you." He put the truck in reverse but stopped suddenly.

"Wait, I have to go back. I forgot my hat and I like it too much to leave it behind." He opened his door, left the truck running so Margo would have the heater's comfort, and hoped she didn't bolt from town. It would be much too much of a waste to lose her now.

Inside he apologized to Mrs. Dietrich, stuffed a wad of money in her hand and while he found his hat stated, "That's for the girls you'll have to pay to stick around and help you after you send Delilah packing.

When he came back out to the parking lot, he really expected the worst and was pleasantly surprised to see his truck, still running, in the parking lot where he'd left it. The doors were locked, however, and Margo was asleep inside. He knocked on the window; she opened her eyes and unlocked the doors. He climbed in and instantly shivered for the temperature difference between outside and inside. "Are you all right?"

"I'm fine. I just locked it out of habit—something I learned a long time ago."

He looked at her in the light from the parking lot floodlight and wanted to stay there forever. "You are so beautiful!" he breathed. "Look, I'll understand if you decide tomorrow that you want out of this deal, but I have to warn you; you'll be the only female at a ranch with a herd of really decent guys that are extremely hungry for some good but simple food! I realize you don't know me from a prairie dog's hole and this is as sudden as a Wyoming blizzard in May, but I was telling you the truth; I do have an opening for a cook and I guess I wouldn't let you stand out there homeless and jobless anyway."

She rolled the window down and threw the stilettos out into the parking lot. "I really don't have any choice, and what idiot would turn down a knight in shining armor?" she stated as she rolled the window back up.

"Armor, shiny or otherwise, I don't have, but knight fits. I'm Kincade Knight. Most folks call me Cade."

He was driving down the road, rutty and bumpy, and she felt perfectly safe and finally warm.

He reached down and turned up the heat. "Let me know if you want more heat."

Her hands and feet were freezing, her head was spinning, and her stomach was turning. "Oh! I think I need to get out!"

She sounded panicked, and Cade made a hasty swerve to the side of the road as he quickly slowed to a stop. He reached over the back of the seat and pulled out a bottle of water, broke the seal as he unscrewed the lid and splashed a little water on his handkerchief and handed her the bottle, seemingly all at once. She took a couple of huge swallows and took deep breaths. Cade took the resealed bottle, held it against the back of her neck, and let her lean back until her head was against the headrest. He held the cold-damp cloth against her forehead.

As she calmed he turned the heater down and held her cold hand feeling her pulse thundering. He watched her continuously as her pulse slowed and she breathed easier. "Feeling better?"

"Yes. Sorry for the … problems," she replied.

"It's been a wild evening."

"One for the books, I'm sure." She was still leaning back against the headrest but she was looking better every second.

"Okay, do you want to sit here for a few more minutes?"

"I'm okay."

Cade suddenly remembered a blanket he always kept in the truck, found it and wrapped it around Margo's legs. She was shivering. He showed Margo the heater control and then drove back out on the road. "I just remembered. I have a candy bar in the glove box. Help yourself, if you're hungry. We're almost to the ranch gate now. If you want to know a little history of the ranch, I'll be happy to provide that service."

Margo grew sleepy and laid her head back on the headrest. Within a few moments she was sleeping. Awhile later Cade gently woke Margo with a soft hand on her shoulder, then slowly added pressure until she woke up.

He stopped in front of the house; the light was still on in the kitchen.

"Stay right there and let me come around and help you down. The truck's pretty high off the ground and you're barefooted and the ground has to be frozen by now."

She had one word for the ranch house—*huge*! It was at least three stories high, and the walls were made of logs. "Is this where they filmed *Bonanza*?"

Cade laughed and scooped her out of the truck and into his arms. "No, but that's what a lot of people think. Come on, I'll take you in through the kitchen entrance and show you the kitchen and your room and later you can see the rest of the place. We'll let Hop Sing cook again tomorrow, and then you can start the next day."

"Hop Sing? Is he here?"

Cade laughed and stopped dead in his tracks at the back of the truck. Margo was still in his arms, but she looked up and breathed, "Wow!" It was almost reverent. Cade had to look up, what he saw startled him and put wonder in his heart. A bright, small light seemed to pulse and stay still in the sky but there was a trail of stardust behind it. She'd found a comet. He looked back down at Margo and he saw her eyes looking deeply into his. His heart skipped several beats, and his legs felt weak. *I am really falling in love with her!*

She was beautiful, with the black velvet sky behind her, shooting stars flashing like diamonds. He couldn't resist another moment. He leaned a little, pulled a little, and kissed her lightly. She didn't resist or pull back. He kissed her again with more passion, and suddenly, as quickly as the fire had started, he threw water on it. "I'm sorry, Margo. I don't know what I'm doing. I'm really sorry," he whispered.

"It's all right, Cade. I don't know what I'm doing either," she breathed back.

He carried her over the wooden porch and into the house. He stood back and let her wander around her new work area. It was a huge kitchen.

"Two dishwashers and four ovens!"

He led her into her new bedroom and watched her eyes glitter
with surprise and joy. "Listen, I'll have to take you to town in the
morning to get you some ranch gear and your stuff. I can't let my
new cook work in her current attire. Until then, I've got some gear I
can lend you. They'll have to do until we get you to town." Winter
was coming, and she'd need some good gear for it so he'd just get it
now instead of later. He let her wander the suite, and he went up to
his room for a pair of jeans and a couple of shirts. Digging through a
drawer, a cold breeze brushed past his shoulder and fluttered a piece
of paper off his desk. When he stooped to pick up the paper he saw
the cedar chest against the wall across the room. *Kellie,* he thought.

Kellie's clothes were in the chest. It had been so long since he had
put all her stuff in there that he had forgotten them. He dropped the
paper on his desk and then went to the chest and sank to his knees in
front of it, his fingers shaking as they rested on the top of the chest.

The only thing he had done to this chest was dust it occasionally in the last several years. He shook off the feeling of despair and
opened the lid. The scent of cedar flowed out of it and inside where
Kellie's clothes. His love for Kellie bubbled up in his heart and the
back of his eyes burned with tears of grief. He had loved her like no
other. He didn't think he could love anyone else, but then, he realized,
he never thought he would take Kellie's clothes out of this chest and
give them to someone else. He shook off the memories and the feelings and pulled out her things until it was all on the floor in a heap
in front of the chest. When he reached the bottom of the chest, he
picked up the pile and carried it down the stairs.

The door to her room was now closed so he knocked lightly on
it, didn't hear anything, slowly opened it, and heard the water in the
shower running. He stepped in, dropped the boots at the foot of the
bed, laid the clothes on the bed, and left, closing and locking the door
behind him.

He climbed the stairs, pulled off his shirt and boots, changed
his clothes then sat on the bed feeling the cold sink in. A short time

later, a fire snapped in the hearth, and Cade was asleep on the couch nearby.

Margo finally turned off the water, wrapping her hair in a towel. Then she wrapped the other towel around her body and wandered out of the bathroom. She felt the coolness of the room engulf her, and she hurried to dress in the clothes Cade had left. She was surprised at the feminine look of the pink tee and over shirt, and was delighted with the flannel nightgown. She realized she was borrowing clothes, but was expecting men's attire, far too big for her frame, but beggars couldn't be choosy. She shimmied into the nightgown and looked at herself in the mirror. It was nearly a perfect fit. She had lost more weight, which bothered her, but she had no choice there either.

She turned out the light, pulled the spread back, and was astonished at the luxuriant sheets and blankets. She slid between them and snuggled down, hair still wrapped tightly in the towel. The bed felt like a cloud, and she was asleep instantly.

She was awakened by noise coming from the kitchen. The clock read twenty minutes after four. That had to mean that someone was starting breakfast.

She slid from the bed, pulled the towel off her hair, finding it still damp. She changed into the jeans, tee, over-shirt, and boots that Cade had left for her. Again she wondered where the feminine attire came from, more precisely, who it came from. She ran fingers through her hair, checked herself out in the mirror and determined that she was the best it could be. She was tired, but curiosity overpowered all senses, and she opened the door to a brightly lit kitchen.

There were three men in the kitchen instantly stuck in suspended animation when they looked at her. Finally, one of them found his voice again. "Well, who are you, gorgeous?" he asked in awe.

After introducing herself to the three men, they introduced themselves to her and continued doing what they had started. Steve was making bacon, Paul was making toast, and Henry was making oatmeal. She asked what they got to do around the ranch when they weren't cooking, and she found out that Steve was a wrangler and a surveyor and Paul was a wrangler and a heavy equipment operator. She was surprised, not knowing that a ranch would have use of much more than wranglers. Henry was the retired ramrod. He looked old enough to be retired.

Cade leaned against the counter in front of the coffee urns and smiled. He didn't think Margo would understand very many things about the ranch, but she was learning rapidly.

He moved over to the refrigerator and pulled eggs out and started cracking and dumping into a large bowl. Margo helped him. Five dozen eggs later Cade pulled a wire whip from the utensil drawer and started whipping the eggs. Margo was talking to Paul as he was making toast. It was the biggest toaster she had ever seen. It made eight slices at once. Then she moved over to Steve and talked to him while he made bacon. The water for the oatmeal was ready for the oats. Henry measured the oats, stirred, turned the burner down, and put the lid on the pot and checked the time. He had apparently made the oatmeal before.

Cade was now intently watching her, and she started to feel like she'd been caught with a hand in the cookie jar. She turned to him. "Good morning." She looked up into his blue eyes and saw the intensity of his look into her own eyes.

"I was wondering when you were going to collapse. I know you didn't get much sleep, and I remember telling you that you would not have to cook today. So why are you out here?"

"I'm okay. I'll probably hit the wall later this afternoon, but I guess I'm too excited to just lay there in bed while all this is going on right outside my door."

"Okay, but I don't want you working today. You look very pale, and I think you need a lot of food and rest. I am concerned about you, Margo. I don't want you sick." He reached up and slid his knuckles lightly down her cheek. "These guys have been doing the cooking for a while now. Henry has played Hop Sing for a long time. They are very good."

"I'm sorry; can I just have a cup of coffee and sit in a corner for a while?" She looked so hurt and pale.

"Sure. Come on we'll go up to the living room and I'll start the inspection tour for the day." He stepped to the huge coffee maker for a refill and another mug, filled it for Margo. She took it, added cream until it was full to the brim, and looked for the sugar.

They went up the stairs and into the living room that took up the entire second floor. Then up to the third floor where his suite was located. It took up about half the level and included his office and a master bath. Several bedrooms, smaller than hers, filled the rest of the level along with one bathroom. There was another floor full of bedrooms and bathrooms for someone but hadn't been used.

He told her that she had free range of the house and if she had time he wouldn't mind if she took up a dust cloth occasionally and chased the dust bunnies out.

There was a picture of a woman over the fireplace in the second floor common room, and Margo wondered who it was. She didn't realize she was studying it so closely until Cade, standing at her back, said, "My mother."

"She's beautiful." Margo nearly shivered but managed to push it down. She found Cade so haunting. He was very quiet in his movements like a ghost moving about. When he was near, she felt safe and secure and was grateful to him, but she found herself jumping constantly. Every time he got near, her stomach muscles tensed. Every time she looked up, she'd be surprised to see him there as he seemed to appear and disappear like a fog or mist. The thought made her shiver.

"Margo, you're cold," Cade stated and put his hands on her upper arms.

His warmth made her shiver again, and she shook her head and said, "I'm fine. I'm just very tired and shifting temperatures. And I should go back to bed, but I'm too excited."

He lowered his hands and walked over to the couch and sat down at one end. Margo sat beside him. She was definitely drawn to him, and he didn't seem to mind. He put his arm over her shoulders, pulled her closer, and took another sip of his coffee, and it made her feel very relaxed. His warmth seeped into her, and she was loath to move. He was so gentle and caring while at the same time exuding a presence that was extremely confident and in total command.

"You look good in those clothes. I must confess, they were Kellie's."

"Thank you. Who is Kellie?" She took a sip of her coffee watching him over the rim of the mug. He watched her, wondering what she was thinking until she looked up at him again. He saw wonder, awe, and fear wash over her eyes in an instant. "Will you tell me about the ranch, your parents, and Kellie?"

"Tell me about yourself," he said without answering her question.

"I have a tendency to be upfront with my feelings. I don't like games, mind or otherwise, and I like honesty. I have found that most people seem to like to hide a lot though, so I am constantly biting my tongue, usually too late, but I don't like being embarrassed so I hate to embarrass anyone else." She was quiet for a long moment. "I'm also very loyal and often get hurt by others that don't return my loyalty.

THREE

Cade decided it was his turn to put out some information, "My parents started the ranch. It was all land back then, a small house and barn, some horses, a small herd of cattle, and my dad started to expand, to utilize it instead of letting it grow trees. He hired Henry and Josh and a few others and I spent my childhood going to school in the kitchen while my mom cooked for the ranch and taught me how to read and write. She was a very patient woman and when I started to wiggle too much, she'd chase me out to the barn and let my dad and Henry deal with me. That usually meant cleaning stalls but finished off with a great horse ride.

"All of these guys have been with me here at the ranch for about four years. If it hadn't been for Josh and Henry, I'm not sure that I would still be alive."

"What do you mean about, 'if it wasn't for Henry and Josh, you're not sure you'd still be alive?'" she asked. When he grew silent, she looked up at his face and saw him looking far into the past. "And what is a ramrod?" she asked before he could answer her first question.

He flashed a quick grin. "I knew you wouldn't know what a ramrod is. A ramrod is a foreman. As far as your first question, long story, short version; when my parents were killed in a car accident about eleven years ago, it left me an orphan. I was so depressed that I didn't eat or drink; I had absolutely no interest in anything. The ranch started to fall into neglect and disrepair; the hands got fed up and quit. Josh did his best to keep it afloat, but I was sleeping all the time, uncommunicative, and frankly I didn't care. Henry became the 'Hop Sing' of the ranch out of necessity.

"One day, Josh literally picked me up and threw my stinking, neglected body into a tub of hot water and nearly drowned me. I guess he figured he'd end it all for me and make me happy in the hereafter or wake me up and make me happy in the here-and-now. I think he was past caring which choice I would take, but he and Henry were moving on.

"I cussed him up one side and down the other. Since it was apparent that I wasn't going to take the opportunity to drown myself, he grabbed a scrub brush and started using it on me. And he wasn't too gentle either. When I was quite red and raw from the scrubbing and worn out from yelling, he threw a bucket of cold water over my head, a towel in my face and left.

"I rinsed off, toweled off, and marched out of the bathroom to my room and put on the cleanest clothes I had. Then I stomped into the kitchen where the two of them were drinking coffee and sat down beside them. Henry handed me a cup of black coffee. Josh looked at me and grinned with some remark about how good I cleaned up, and then Henry put a plate of cookies in front of me. 'Eat the sugar,' he said. 'It will work like speed for a few minutes. When that happens, put a load of your clothes in the washer and clean the tub and the bathroom. Then you'll want to go to sleep, and I'll put your freshly washed clothes in the dryer. When you wake up, you can put another load in the washer and put away the dry clothes, and we'll get this place back on the road to working again.' I followed orders, with an attitude, and I don't remember anything after that until later in the early morning of the next day.

"That's when I heard yelling and banging and finally dragged myself off the bed toward the window to see what was going on. Just before I made it to the window, it busted in, and Josh was on the other side yelling my name. It was so hot in the house. He was breaking out what was left of the window and shouting at me to come out. I did without thinking and grabbed the boots I stumbled over on the way to the window. I walked over broken glass in my socks without cutting my feet and threw my boots out the window. Then I crawled out and stood there looking at Josh. The house was on fire. It burned to the ground with everything in it. Fire and rescue was far enough away that by the time they were notified and out here, the entire house was burned down.

"I was so angry and numb I couldn't function. Henry took me into the bunkhouse and put me to bed on one of the bunks.

"I lived in the bunkhouse with the two of them for over a year while Henry and Josh literally nursed me back to a functioning human being. They wouldn't let me sleep more than eight hours in twenty-four, and they had me on a schedule. The rest of the time they busted my backside with work, and when we weren't working on stuff around the ranch, we designed and built this house. During that time of rebuilding the house and ranch, I was rebuilt. I became a more caring person. Mom had always taught me to share and care. I guess she had to die to make that teaching flourish. Too bad really; she would have loved me this way."

"Don't you think she loved you?"

"Oh she loved me. She really did. She just didn't get to see her handiwork completed." He sipped his coffee. "I found that picture stored carefully in the tack room, and when this house was finished, the first thing I did was hang that picture."

They could smell breakfast and hear the voices from the dining area downstairs, and Cade stood up, pulling Margo up after him. "Let's go get breakfast." He led the way, holding her hand.

Cade stood near the head of one table and offered Margo an empty seat near his and introduced Margo to the hands. Margo looked down the lines of faces on both sides of the tables while Cade made announcements. The dining area had four huge picnic-type tables and each table held twelve people. There were several empty places.

Cade asked Gus to ask the blessing for the food. There was a prayer warrior in their midst, and he seemed to be appreciated. He stood and asked the Lord's blessing for the food, the ranch, Cade, and the new cook. She felt something warm run through her insides and marveled at something she never experienced before.

Several times during the meal, Margo glanced over at Cade and saw him discussing something with the man to his right. This prevented her from seeing Cade's beautiful eyes and face. What she didn't think about was the fact that the man Cade was talking to was noticing her constantly looking at Cade.

As soon as someone finished their meal, they picked up their dishes and took them to the dishwasher. Eventually, a couple of hands seemed to take over the task of filling the dishwashers, and before long a couple more were washing the pots and pans. Someone stopped and asked if they could take her dishes, and when she said yes they were scooped up along with Cade's and the other man's. She looked around and saw someone putting the butter and cream into the refrigerator; another was wiping down the tables, and another was sweeping the floor. As soon as everything was done, she was alone, except Henry who was rooting through the refrigerator. She sat there watching in awe. "That was fun!" she whispered.

Cade was watching her. *Usual stuff*, he thought, but he noticed that she was amazed. *Well, I guess she should be. She had no idea what to expect.*

"Kind of interesting, isn't it?" Cade stated.

"It's amazing! Who trained them?"

"It was definitely out of necessity, but if anyone trained them, it was Henry. He doesn't put up with much crap from anyone, and everyone helps everyone else or they stand before him."

"I feel like Snow White with the dwarfs."

"Okay, I'm going out with Josh to give assignments."

He opened the door and stepped down into the dusty yard with the men gathered there. While Cade watched, one of the men assigned each hand a specific duty for the morning. As soon as they received their assignments, they peeled out of the group and headed off in one direction or another. She was glad she had stayed in the warm kitchen and watched from the windowed door. It was far too cold without a jacket and gloves.

When it was done, Cade came back in the kitchen as the last hand headed toward the barn. That's when Margo saw the clipboard in his hand. She thought she recognized him as the hand that sat next to Cade at breakfast.

"Who is that?" Margo asked quietly and nodded toward the retreating hand when Cade was inside.

"That is the ramrod, Joshua Markham. Everyone calls him Josh. He supervises the hands, and he's very good at it. Occasionally he runs the entire operation for me as I'm away on business elsewhere."

"Is he my boss?"

"I wouldn't refuse to do what he says. But he's never taken a cook off the job before. I don't think he's going to have you herding horses, branding cattle, or painting the barn. He likes to eat too." He smiled at her, and she smiled back. "Let's go check out the pantry and make sure we've got everything we need. I've already got a list from Josh and a couple of movie rentals the hands want so we'll work on supplies and stuff for you. Ready?"

"Sure. They watch movies?" she asked as they moved into the pantry.

"Yes."

"When?"

"After dinner."

"Popcorn and beer?"

"Popcorn sometimes, beer never! I don't allow beer or alcohol on the property. As a matter of fact, anyone getting drunk and disorderly, on or off the ranch, is dealt with by immediate termination. I won't bail anyone out of jail or pay for court costs or legal fees. I don't think anyone needs to get drunk for any reason. I believe in God, but I don't herd everyone off to church every Sunday morning as the ranch still has to function."

Meal planning was Margo's job. Anything she wanted to make was perfectly all right.

"We'll go to the wholesale store once a month, which means a trip to Rapid City. Plan accordingly. If we run short of something, I'll go to town and resupply but grudgingly. Henry's good at this, so if you need help ask him. He'll be going with us, and we go the first Friday of every month.

"I try to give everyone a holiday here and there. Thanksgiving, Christmas, Labor Day, some others, but not everyone gets the holiday as the ranch still has to run and someone has to help. The hands usually switch off, so it's been pretty easy around here the last few years. I've finally got real good hands again so they get paid pretty well and stick around. It's helped me a great deal to have steady, reliable hands. I try to give them as many perks as I can."

Before they reached the pantry, Henry handed Margo a list of supplies needed. She asked him if the list was everything and he nodded. She gave it to Cade and he stuffed it in his shirt pocket and thanked Henry.

He took her out to the barn, the bunkhouse and showers, the stable and the tack room, even the pigs, hogs, and chicken houses, the herb and vegetable gardens and then they returned to the house. "I don't have time to show you any more today. Let's go back to the house and then go to town." He had been all business while showing off the ranch and she felt the need to pay close attention.

He came down the stairs with a jacket, gloves and hat. "Here, try these on. Kellie's clothes fit you, why not these?"

"You don't seem to mind. Does it bother you? I mean, me wearing her clothes?"

"Not a bit. Does it bother you?"

"No. Will it bother Kellie?"

"Not anymore."

She had slipped into Kellie's jacket and gloves and he set Kellie's black hat on her head. She adjusted it to where it felt right and looked up at him.

"Looks fine," he said. "Okay, let's head for town."

On the way to town, Cade asked Margo about her gear and where it was. "I don't really have anything, Cade. I mean a pair of old boots with a hole in the sole, an old white shirt that isn't white anymore and a pair of jeans that are more than well used. I was staying in that old motel not far from the Grange. There's nothing there I want or need."

Margo's mind continued on about Kellie, but she remained silent somehow knowing when the time was right, Cade would tell her about Kellie. But she couldn't stop thinking about her. *Who was she, where was she, why did she leave and leave all her stuff behind unless she died?*

Okay, if she died, would she mind if I were using her gear? More to the point, was she a person who would mind another female on the ranch? Doesn't sound like one has stayed very long since her time. Maybe she has something to do with that.

Margo believed in ghosts. She didn't know a lot about ghosts, but she believed in them anyway.

Nowhere Y, as the locals called it, felt hot and dusty for November first. Cade parked and rounded the hood to help Margo down from the truck. The high clearance of his truck was easily accommodated by his long legs, but while she was tall, she wasn't used to jumping in and out of the truck, and until she was he was playing it safe and gentlemanly. *Besides,* he thought, *it gives me a chance to hold her hand.*

When Margo was safely on the ground, Cade held her hand longer than expected. It was a pleasant feeling, and she was in no hurry to break the connection. However, when he did let go of her hand, it left her feeling like a child that just lost the last piece of candy. She'd never met a man like Cade. He was tall, good looking, a perfect gentleman with perfect manners and not the least bit lazy or afraid of work. Still, she wanted to keep her heart under control. She didn't think she should fall in love again.

Cade took her to the dry goods store. She walked in and felt like she'd walked into an old-time western movie set or gone back in time. There were some clothes in the back reaches of the store and a small changing room that was made from stacks of boxes holding supplies that hadn't been opened yet. The place was huge, and she wondered why she'd never been inside before.

Oh yes! No money! That would do it, Margo!

She picked out a pair of jeans, bathrobe, and an aqua-colored ribbon for her hair. Purple was her favorite color, but she'd suddenly fallen in love with aqua.

She stood next to him at the checkout counter, and he looked at her and smiled. "You look great in those clothes. How do Kellie's boots feel?"

"Like gloves. The socks are irritating, though."

"You'll get used to those. Keep them on. I got you a couple pairs of heavy wool ones. Those are for running through the house late at night so your feet don't freeze."

"Why would I be running through the house late at night?" she teased.

"Well, movie night for one. Never mind, I'll explain it later."

They locked all the stuff in the truck behind the seat then went to the grocery store. He took her to McDonald's where they bought two happy meals, complete with toys.

Delilah came in just as they sat down and any hope of enjoying a meal went out the window. As soon as Delilah saw Cade and Margo, she growled like a wild animal. Two state police officers walked in just in time to see her march across the room like a steamroller, rolling over anything that got in its way. She pushed over a highchair that some woman had just snatched her baby from. Now the baby was crying and its mother screaming. Delilah headed straight for Cade and Margo and the troopers were right behind her.

Delilah screamed as she swiped Cade and Margo's happy meals to the floor and then reached for Margo. But a quick trooper pulled Delilah's hand from its intended route, which was around Margo's throat. "I'm going to kill you, witch! I'm going to kill you!" Delilah screamed.

The store manager stood beside a trooper and over the noise Delilah was creating demanded that Delilah be arrested for whatever they could arrest her for. They agreed and pulled Delilah away from the table, then pushed and pulled her out of the store. She never stopped screaming.

"I'm sorry about that, folks. Let me replace your meals at least." The store manager was standing by their table surveying the mess on the floor.

Cade ordered new happy meals and the manager rushed off to get them. Cade waited for Margo to relax and look at him. She was currently watching Delilah being pushed into the trooper's cruiser. But it was a battle all the way. Delilah wasn't going easily in any case.

By the time she turned back to Cade, her face had some color again and she visibly relaxed. "Are you alright?"

"I am now. Talk about vindictive and relentless. Am I going to have to deal with that every time I see her again for the rest of my life?"

"Probably. You're in good company. That's what I deal with every time I see her. Just remember; no matter what, you can't win."

Their happy meals were delivered with apologies from the manager and Cade opened his and urged Margo to open hers. A store employee came along with a broom and pan to clean up what was left of the previous happy meals.

Margo relaxed and enjoyed lunch with Cade, and by early afternoon they were headed back to the ranch with their supplies. When they got back, Cade helped her haul in the goods and while she put things away, he took the movies out to the bunkhouse.

Margo ran upstairs to make Cade's bed but discovered it made already. She turned to go back to the kitchen and plowed into a hard chest. Reeling from the collision, she stepped back and felt strong, but gentle hands grab her arms to keep her upright and steady.

"Are you all right?" Cade asked. His voice was like a whisper, gentle and quiet.

"Yes. When you showed me around this morning, I noticed your bed unmade. I just came up to make your bed."

"Well, sit down before you fall down. You nearly knocked the wind out of me with that collision." He was teasing, but she didn't see it.

"Okay, sorry. I didn't hear you come in." Panic was evident in her voice.

"It's all right. You weren't doing anything wrong, and I appreciate your willingness to come help me out, but you need to rest. You're worn out, and your nose is bleeding!" He set her down on the edge of his bed and then dropped down on one knee in front of her. There was a red spot on her forehead where it had slammed into his chest. He figured there was a matching red spot on his chest, but wasn't worried about it. What he was worried about was her bloody nose and that she seemed to think she had done something wrong or was terrified of him and that bothered him a lot.

He handed her a tissue then went to the bathroom for a cold cloth. When he looked into her eyes, he noticed that they were a bit glazed and slightly unfocused. The red spot's edges were turning black and blue. Margo was going to have a huge bruise on her forehead. He gently pushed her back so her head rested on his pillow. He pulled her boots off, lifted her feet up and laid them on the bed then threw a light blanket over her.

"It's a long way to the doctor's office. But I'm considering the trip. Are you all right?"

"I'm fine. Just a little dizzy, that's all."

"Okay. Just take it easy and relax for a few minutes. Didn't break your nose, did you? Can I get you some water?

"No, and no thanks, I'm fine."

"Margo, you need to stay right there until you can stand on your own, which doesn't look like it will be anytime soon. You're pretty pale right now. I'm very concerned about my new cook's health."

"Well, you're right about me needing rest, but I feel so stupid going to bed now. I can't sleep here anyway."

"Don't feel stupid. You've been through a real tough time, let yourself get into a jam health-wise in order to survive, and it's going to take awhile to get back to normal. Just relax right there. I promise not to assault you or embarrass you. Shut your eyes, turn off your mind, and relax."

"Cade, thanks, but please let me up. I can't rest here. I feel like I'm in territory I don't belong in." She was falling asleep whether she wanted to or not. He could hear it in her voice.

He checked her bloody nose. It had stopped bleeding; the bruise was getting larger and darker. She was asleep. He sat at his desk and worked on payroll while she slept until dinner.

When dinner was on the table, Josh called Cade to tell him dinner was on. Cade tried to wake Margo but failed. He shook her gently, then a bit more rough. He called her name, he was starting to panic. He could see her breathing but he couldn't get her to wake up or even make a sound.

He pulled his phone and called the doctor. After giving a report on Margo he was told that the patient needed to be hospitalized. He was hearing probable brain concussion and malnutrition. He was even asked if she might be anorexic. He didn't think so, but how could he prove it at this point. He called LifeFlyte and as soon as he was done with them he called Josh.

Josh heard the panic in Cade's voice and was half-way up the stairs by the time he ended the call. Some of the hands and Henry became very aware of something amiss by Josh's body language and the room quieted rapidly as the attention switched from dinner to a problem in the making.

Chuck stood as he wiped his hands on a napkin then took his plate to the kitchen and quickly dumped the food in the trash. Henry took it from him and pointed to the door. Chuck thanked him and went to the door, swinging into his jacket and hat as he went through.

Josh knocked on Cade's door and when he heard "Come in," Josh opened it and stepped in.

"Anything I can do?"

"Yes, but I don't know what to tell you. My mind is in a panic and that's about all I know."

"Okay, you said you called LifeFlyte, right?"

"Right."

FOUR

W ell, let's get ready for that. You stay here with her and let me know of any changes. As soon as we get the helicopter down, I'll get the EMTs up here. You take some deep breaths. Do you want to go down and get the parameds up here? I'll stay with her."

"No. I'm too afraid to leave her. I feel responsible. Like I should have insisted she stay in bed and eat more. Like I should have taken her to the doctor whether she wanted to go or not!"

"Cade, don't start placing blame. You always tell us that it doesn't help. Get it fixed first then analyze the problem so it doesn't happen again. Take your own advise."

"Okay. You're right. Let's get Chuck out in the yard for the helicopter."

"Okay. I'm going down." Josh went through the door, leaving it open. When he got to the bottom of the stairs he looked for Chuck and Henry pointed outside. Josh went directly to Henry and told him what was going on. Henry nodded.

Henry climbed the stairs to ensure Cade had his wallet and documents to get the medical help for Margo and make sure he wasn't empty handed when it came to co-pays and other incidentals.

When he reached Cade he could see the panic in Cade's eyes. "She's going to be alright, Cade. Just believe that. You go make sure you have your wallet and ID and money for incidentals and insurance info, everything you need. Make sure you get some clothes for that girl. Pack something for her; don't forget her toothbrush and toothpaste, hair brush. You'll know, but you need to get moving. We don't want to hold up for you packing. I'll stay with her."

Cade knew Henry was right and he was galvanized into following those orders. He was in Margo's room packing her clothes and took the suitcase out to the porch as the parameds were climbing the stairs with a stokes basket and other equipment.

He followed them up the stairs and into his room. One was already checking Margo out. Another paramed started taking her pulse and writing notes while the third got things ready in the Stokes basket. Cade stood there while they did what they had to, then watched them pick her up and lay her in the basket, wrap her up in warm blankets and strap her down.

They carried her down the stairs with all their gear being carried in the basket or by the third man. Cade followed them out the door with her suitcase, jacket and gloves in his hand.

He climbed into the helicopter and sat where the paramed told him to sit. The last man stowed the suitcase under the seat and then jumped in. The door shut and he tapped the pilot on the shoulder. They took off, Chuck giving hand signals to the pilot, a salute was the last thing Cade saw of Chuck that evening.

She felt herself swimming to the surface when a cold, soft cloth was laid on her head, but before she reached awareness, she sank back down into peaceful oblivion. When she finally opened her eyes, she found Cade sitting on the edge of her bed.

During the next few days, doctors discussed brain surgery with Cade. The concussion was causing pressure inside her skull and if untreated it could kill her, but they needed to put it off long enough to fill her system with nutrients and get her strong enough to survive surgery.

Cade was beside himself. The thought of losing another person he was falling in love with was too much. He railed at God, then begged for forgiveness and Margo's life to be spared and to heal her.

He watched nurses and doctors come and go, wake her up and talk to her. Every time they lifted her head she would vomit. She screamed in pain several times.

Cade paced the floor as he silently prayed knowing he wouldn't be able to stand another loss.

She woke up and was watching him pace the room. "Cade?" she said with a weak voice.

"How's Sleeping Beauty this afternoon?" He looked tired; his eyes were dark with concern.

"My head is pounding a native war ritual. What happened?"

"We'll get to that. First I need to tell you something." He was holding her hand. "You are in the hospital." She immediately grew tense. "Margo, relax. You had to come here. I couldn't get the doctor to come to the ranch and he said I needed to get you to the hospital. He was right. You're not just starved, you have a brain concussion, and you are so malnourished they weren't sure they were going to be able to reverse the problem in time. I think they did pretty good, but you've been sucking up fluids and nutrients by the bottle full for nearly four days now.

"They wanted to do surgery to let the pressure out of your head. They were afraid they would lose you if they did surgery so they worked on getting nutrients into your system to get you strong enough to make it through surgery if you really had to have it."

"Surgery for what? What's wrong with me?'

"You have a concussion. You've got a bruise across your eye that makes you look like an adorable raccoon. But besides that, your brain swelled and it got a little tight inside your head, which is why your head is pounding. They wanted to do something to relieve the pressure. It could have killed you.

"I've had time to reassess my actions over those first days when you came to work at the ranch and I was wrong, Margo. I didn't do you any favors and I'm sorry."

She was in a panic. *What is he saying? Does he wish he hadn't hired me? Is he going to fire me? Oh! Please, Cade. Don't do that! Don't bring me here and then leave me stranded!*

He saw the panic and the tears and he wanted to scoop her up into his arms and just hold onto her, but he knew what lifting her head could do. "Margo, I'm not going to leave you stranded or fire you. I'm telling you that you have to stay here until they release you and no amount of begging, whining, or pressure about you leaving will change my mind. When the doctor feels you're good to go, you'll get dressed and pull your boots on and we'll walk out together. Understand?"

She nodded, wiping tears from her eyes with the back of her hand.

Cade felt Margo's panic and winced. He had his own panic attack. Kellie's face flashed through his mind and he felt worse. It was his fault she got this bad. He saw it coming and did nothing but let her have her way even though he knew it was the wrong way. He'd done that with Kellie, too.

"Margo, I love you. Don't leave me," he whispered.

He could see the fatigue in her eyes again and he urged her to close her eyes, shut down again and promised he'd be right beside her the whole time.

When she was asleep again, he stood in front of the window wiping his own tears away. He called Josh. He had to talk to Josh or Henry. Cade didn't know it, but Gus prayed constantly for Margo and for him.

Cade was good about calling Josh and telling him Margo's status. He was told that he shouldn't worry about anything, just make sure Margo was alright and bring her back because she was missed already.

When Sunday morning arrived, Cade missed Gus's prayers and short Sunday sermons. Cade wished he was a better prayer warrior but he didn't know where to start. A feeling pierced his heart and he launched into a silent prayer. He asked for forgiveness, for strength in helping Margo get past her medical problems and then he asked Jesus to heal her and himself. He realized he needed healing, too.

His biggest concern at that moment was that he didn't have the smarts or strength to help her get past her problem. *Lord, it has to come from You. I can't do it. I don't know what to do, so You will have to give me the strength, knowledge, wisdom, whatever is needed to make it so I can help her where You want my help, or show me how to sit back and let things alone so You can act on them without my interference.*

In the days that followed, Margo improved dramatically. He was with Margo most of the time. While she slept, Cade silently prayed without realizing it or would read a book he purchased from a candy striper that haunted the halls.

When her meals were delivered he watched her eat and would insist she take another bite of food when she said she was full. He counted the amounts of food she ate and wrote them down on a small pad he kept in his pocket.

By the time the doctor gave his release on Margo, Cade had educated himself on what Margo should be eating on a normal day and had determined that he would watch to ensure that she did eat that much.

He called a private helicopter firm in town and asked for helicopter service to take him and one passenger to the Double K Ranch. They arrived home Saturday evening.

The house was lit up and warm when they entered and both Cade and Margo were surprised to find most of the hands in the kitchen, waiting for their arrival. There was coffee and cake, a lot of laughter and enjoyment as the two were welcomed back. They made her cut the cake and she cut large pieces and placed them on plates.

When the hands left, Henry cleaned up the mess and Cade insisted Margo go to bed. She didn't protest or beg, whine or plead. She just followed orders. She was getting to start work tomorrow, with Henry's help.

Cade was terrified of losing Margo. For the two weeks she was in bed, he watched her mostly being pumped full of nutrients and watched the nurses watch her carefully for the concussion, but during her lucid times, they talked and learned about each other's past. Still, they had only touched a small portion of it and knew they had a great deal more to learn of each other. But maybe talking about it would help him get past it finally.

Cade remembered losing Kellie but kept it to himself, not feeling sure enough about his own feelings to dump them out for someone else to look at.

Margo had time to remember her past terror with Jerry and was nowhere near a point where she felt like pulling that time up from the depths of her private dungeon where she kept the worst of her life's experiences.

Sunday morning and Margo jumped out of bed, feeling energized and ready. She was in the kitchen and the light was on at four o'clock, the oven was on and she was pulling stuff out of the refrigerator. Breakfast was French toast, scrambled eggs, bacon, or oatmeal. When the dishes were in the washers, they went upstairs to the common room. Gus's sermon was short, very insightful, and encouraging; and Margo enjoyed it a great deal. She had not been in church for quite some time, and when Gus read from the Bible, she wished she had one.

There were no songs to sing, but Margo knew most guys didn't like singing or would not sing so that was totally understandable. Besides, they all had work to do; there wasn't time for signing. The hands departed after one more short prayer.

Margo was sitting in the dining hall when Cade came back in after assignments. He stopped at the coffee bar, poured another mug of coffee, grabbed a soda pop from the cooler, and came over to sit with her. "How do you feel?"

"Still a little tired, I guess."

"A couple more days of you resting between meals won't hurt anything around here."

"God is good! I never dreamed I'd find a job with a boss that cares so much about his employees. This place is like Shangri-la hiding in the middle of the mountains in Wyoming. I'm so lucky. Thanks. Thanks for everything."

"God *is* great! My mother loved me and taught me how to love everyone else. She always told me to treat everyone like I wanted to be treated; respectfully, thoughtfully, and with a bunch of kindness. She was a very good teacher.

"My father taught me how to run the ranch, financially and phys-ically. He used to call it 'leading with the two *f*s.' When I learned how to spell, I asked him why the two *f*s as one was a *p*. I remember him looking at me with this look of astonishment on his face. 'Are you sure?' he asked. Then with a twinkle in his eye he asked, 'Which one?'" Cade smiled at the memory. "I don't know why I thought of that." He reached for her hand and she took his into hers, joyfully.

"We had a lot of fun around here when I was a kid. At Thanksgiving and Christmas, all the hands would be in the house. We'd eat Thanksgiving or Christmas dinner, then everyone would go into the living room, and we'd sit around talking about Thanksgivings or Christmases past, and on Christmas we'd open presents. Then Mom would bring out cookies or pie and coffee, and we'd all eat our-selves into a stupor. There were a lot fewer hands then, and these guys weren't here when Mom was here."

"Do you usually decorate with a tree and all the trimmings?"

"Of course! There are lights around the house and on the barn. Tornado loves the lights."

"Tornado?"

"My horse."

"Zorro." She breathed.

Cade cocked his head to one side. "One of my favorite childhood heroes."

"Mine, too. Only mine is with the newer version—the one with the music in it, something about a mask?"

"I liked that movie, too. Exceptionally well done and the music was magnificent. However, for reasons I shall not go into, I'm not as fond of it as I once was."

Margo thought about his statement and wondered what had caused him to dislike the movie, but he had said he was not going to discuss it so she let it lay there. It was going to nag her, but she was going to ignore it.

"I want to see this Tornado. Is he black?" she asked.

"He looks like he jumped into a huge vat of black ink. He doesn't have a spot on him that isn't black, and he has some peculiar, lovable, and goofy traits."

She was getting all excited about a horse. "Like what?"

"Okay! Against my better judgment I'm going to do this one thing for you and then you're going back to bed or at least tucked onto a nice comfortable couch with a big book." She could hardly hold her head up, and she wasn't fooling him.

He left and strolled across the yard. The dust was settling into a hard concrete-like lumpiness, and it was getting colder out. *Well, it was the beginning of November. Life gets cold in Wyoming in the fall and winter.*

Cade came back and went into her bedroom. He came out with her winter jacket and asked, "Where are your gloves?"

"They're in the second drawer down." Her brain was in neutral.

He came out and handed her the gloves. While she put on her gloves, he knelt down and put her foot on his thigh and pulled a thick wool sock onto it and repeated with the second foot.

He grabbed her jacket and put it behind her and let her shove her arms through.

He carried her to the door. Margo assisted by opening it.

Cade set her on a porch chair. He stepped back and shut the door, then whistled. A huge-black stallion trotted around the corner of the house and stopped in front of Cade. "Tornado, this is Margo. Margo, this is Tornado. Say hello, Tornado, and be gentle; she's not real strong today."

Tornado casually moved over to stand in front of Margo, and put his head over the rail, blew air, then nuzzled the hand that was held out to him. He nodded and put his muzzle against the hand again.

"I think he likes you," whispered Cade. "He's not always real friendly with strangers."

Tornado shook his head briskly.

Cade disappeared for a few moments then reappeared beside Margo. Margo and Tornado were so busy getting to know each other that they didn't realize Cade had left. Cade watched the two things he had come to love so much—the horse for quite some time and a special lady in a very short time. The horse and lady seemed to have a great understanding for each other. All this realization hit him in the gut and almost knocked the air from his lungs.

"Margo, reach behind my back and take what I have in my hand. You can give it to Tornado."

She reached behind Cade and felt a carrot pushed into her hand. She took the carrot but was careful not to show it to Tornado yet.

She put the carrot into Tornado's view and watched him get excited, all the while she talked quietly to him. "Look, Tornado! Look what I have."

Tornado excitedly shifted his feet and swished his tail. He reached for the carrot, but Margo took a bite off the end and crunched on it, ignoring Tornado. Tornado quickly stepped back, blew air several times; he was insulted and stomped around in a circle then came back to the rail and wildly shook his head. His eyes bored into her, and she could hear his thoughts. "Oh! This is your carrot! How rude of me. I'm terribly sorry." She held the carrot out and as soon as his teeth had it, he pranced around the yard munching. Margo knew there was a smile on Tornado's lips.

"He'll probably come here every morning just to beg. He loves carrots." He watched Tornado carry on with the last of his carrot snack and then picked Margo up again. "Say good-bye, Tornado."

Margo said, "Good-bye, Tornado."

Tornado rushed toward the porch and pushed his muzzle into Margo's chest. She reached up and stroked his head a couple of times. Then Cade shoved Tornado out of the way and took Margo to the bed, laid her down on it, pulled off her socks, gloves, and jacket. He gently kissed her forehead and hung up her jacket.

"Go to sleep. I know Tornado wore you out, and you really need some more rest," he said as he pulled the blanket up to her chin.

He left the room without looking back. She was smiling when she fell asleep.

Pork chops were the main item for supper. Cade put a little of everything on her plate, and she didn't miss it. She felt like a child but knew Cade was taking care of her so she said nothing and let him fuss over her.

She cut off a piece of pork and bit into it. It was like biting into a piece of heaven. She was so impressed with the flavor of the pork chop that she really didn't bother with the potatoes, and veggies. She wanted to know what was on the pork chops. She took a second helping. Cade watched her and was glad to see her eating so well. But he wasn't letting her skip the veggies.

After dinner she took her dishes to the kitchen and was going to help, but Henry told her he'd do it and took her dishes from her. Cade was behind her and indicated with a nod to follow him. She did so and they went to the common room on the second floor. They sat on the couch in front of the fire and talked about everything. Margo wondered if there was a purpose to the quiet time or if it really had no consequence. Finally, Cade said he was tired, figured she was, too. He was going to bed and suggested that she go to hers.

She followed his instructions. She was tired, but since she had slept so long that afternoon, she wondered if she would really sleep much. She laid down and thought it was going to be a long night and was surprised when the alarm clock woke her up.

She had pulled a pan out of the cupboard when the backdoor opened and Henry, Steve, and Paul came in. They greeted Margo asking how she was feeling. They thought she looked much better.

While they worked and chattered around her, she made several loaves of banana bread to serve hot and use up some bananas that were getting soft.

After breakfast, it was back to her room to make the bed and clean up the bathroom, then upstairs to make Cade's bed and clean his bathroom. Then back to the kitchen to make lunch. She made harvest soup with homemade biscuits for lunch. She hadn't made biscuits in years and enjoyed it.

Lunch was a smashing success, and she was tired but feeling proud of herself. She let the guy's help her clean up the kitchen and went to her room, closing the door. She couldn't force herself to get in bed and sat on the couch, took off her boots, pulled the throw over her legs and snuggled down in the corner.

When she woke up, her head was on a pillow, but her neck was in a kink from sleeping wrong. She rolled off the couch, folded the throw, and put it on the back of the couch.

While making dinner, Cade came down the stairs and stopped in his tracks when he saw her.

"What are you doing?" he asked quietly.

"Making dinner," she answered with her head slightly cocked.

"I was going to get Henry in here to make it. You were sleeping so well, I was going to let you finish your nap up to dinner."

"That's sweet; I'm fine. What are you looking at?" she asked.

"What's wrong with your neck?"

"It's just stiff. I think I slept wrong."

He moved behind her and rubbed her neck and shoulders. It felt wonderful, and she didn't want him to stop. As he worked on the muscles of her back, neck, and shoulders, she stretched and twisted slightly. Her brain refused to continue a coherent thought while his magic fingers did their work. She was soft butter by the time he was finished.

"That should do it."

"I should thank you, but I'm irritated that the knot was so quick to unravel."

Cade just gave her a pensive nod and asked what she was making for dinner.

"Chicken."

Cade drank coffee and watched Margo put huge pans of apple strudel into the ovens.

"I feel like I'm watching some ballet or a well-choreographed musical. I just can't hear the music, but you're fun to watch and I'm looking forward to dinner."

The kitchen was clean and quiet, and she went to her room and practically collapsed on the bed. She wasn't even sure she had changed her clothes and slipped between the sheets.

FIVE

Three thirty a.m. started another day. When Henry and two hands arrived at four a.m., she had frittatas in the oven.

Henry busied himself with the coffee; the others unloaded dishwashers, put things away and set the tables.

After breakfast, activities changed to house cleaning. Cade had made his bed so she cleaned his bathroom and vacuumed the floor. Then she dusted the living room bookshelf that was near the stairs. She picked up a picture frame while dusting under it and looked at the picture. A beautiful young lady smiled out at her. It was only a headshot, but her eyes were amethyst and her hair was nearly the same as Margo's. She studied it for a few minutes, set it down and became aware of Cade standing nearby, watching her.

"That was Kellie. She was my best friend. We were going to get married about a month after that picture was taken. She loved this place, the horses, everything. I was so happy then." He was real quiet and seemed very distant to Margo.

"What happened?" As soon as she spoke the words, she winced and wished she could swallow them before he heard them. "I'm sorry. I'm prying and raking up coals that cause you unhappiness. I didn't mean to say that."

"It's all right. She's gone, and the fire died a few years ago."

Margo suddenly felt extremely sad. She turned to do more dusting to hide her tears.

"Are you strong enough to do housework?" Cade didn't really know how to talk about Kellie. Margo seemed to close him out. He thought she didn't want to know more, so he went upstairs.

Margo felt rejected and sadder. Why couldn't she control her heart?

Cade was in his office and had a pile of work to do and no time to get it done. He had to figure out a way to control his feelings for Margo, and until he did, he had to stay away from her.

Margo was so beautiful and reminded him of Kellie in so many ways. He never thought he would find anyone to love like that again, and he had accepted it. Any idea of getting married and raising a family had died with Kellie. Then Margo walked into his life. After getting her back on her feet, she had proved to be the best cook ever on the ranch. Now she was part of the ranch and his life.

Why can't people just be honest with each other and say what they mean and feel? I should go to her and tell her that I love her, and if she doesn't want my love, I'll just have to get past it! I don't want to get past it! I want her to love me back! If I love her, that doesn't mean she'll die. Either change your feelings, or tell her that you love her. Margo hates mind games! I love her. I have to tell her. I told her once, but she didn't hear it. I only had the nerve to whisper it.

He felt her presence and looked up to find her standing in the doorway. "Hi," was the only word that managed to make it out of his mouth.

"Hi." She stood there like a lost puppy needing attention and he had stray animal syndrome. She wasn't making life easy on him. His stomach was in a huge knot. His throat closed, and he could barely breathe. She was so beautiful, and he was so in love with her and hopelessly past speaking.

Now that he had admitted it to himself, he had to tell her. He raked his hand through his hair and moved around the desk forgetting the paperwork for later, again. "Margo, we need to talk, right now while I'm brave enough to get it out." He took her hand and led her to the couch in front of the fireplace. They sat side-by-side watching the flames for a few moments, Margo silent and waiting,

Cade thoughtful and quiet. Finally, he spoke. "I need to tell you about Kellie. I'm not sure I can get through it, but I've got to try. I loved her to distraction. She loved me and this place probably more than anything else. She was a girl from one of the ranches south of here. Anyway, we met somewhere and became friends, running into each other a great deal and then when I was too busy for her for awhile I discovered her on my doorstep. From that point on we were almost constantly together. I gave her a room down the hall and we vowed to stay apart, romantically, until we were married.

"That Zorro movie came out and I took her to Cheyenne to see it. We went by helicopter and spent the night in a hotel suite, keeping our vow of no romantic closeness until we were married. Anyway she loved that movie, I liked it a great deal, and when we got back here, we set the date for the wedding. She started making wedding plans and told me she wanted to get married sitting on horses. She was going to wear this very Spanish-style white lace dress and wanted me to dress like Zorro. When the preacher was done hitching us, we were going to ride off into the sunset to a place down ranch.

"I did a lot of work for that wedding. I fixed up number Nine–."

"Wait!" Margo interrupted. "Number Nine?"

"One of the range stations here on the ranch. They start at number one up at the beginning of the ranch road and it goes all the way around the ranch ending in number twenty back up by the ranch road. They are all about ten miles apart. The guys stay in them when they do the fence/property line work. I have to get back on the story or I'll give up and regret it. I'm losing my courage and I hate admitting that to anyone."

"Okay, go back to Kellie. I can learn about the range stations later."

"Thanks. Anyway she wanted to use number nine because it was across the ranch from the main house and as close to a lake as any of them are. I spent a lot of money and time at number nine getting it ready for our honeymoon. I wanted to take her to the Caribbean, but she wanted nothing to do with the ocean and 'boats' so I did as she wanted. I wanted her happy most of all.

"I spent time with a tailor in Cheyenne who made the cape and I found a store there full of western and Spanish-style men's ware. I bought a black outfit that was very Spanish—lots of silver work on it and, of course, the obligatory black hat with the flat brim. I was quite proud of myself for that little fete." He grew silent for a few moments and sipped cold coffee. Setting it down he continued with his story.

"She loved everything about this ranch. There wasn't a mean bone in her body, she was kind and loving and full of compassion for everything and everyone." He struggled with tears and finally had to wipe some away with his handkerchief. "She loved animals and children. I think she even had a soft spot for Delilah. Everyone loved her and I had settled down to spend a lot of years married to her. She went riding one morning and didn't return. I was in a panic and we rode out looking for her. I split the guys up and we all went in different directions. I was afraid she had ridden all the way down to Number nine and was stuck there for some reason. We didn't have cell phones then, so there was no way to contact her. We couldn't find her so I called the County Sheriff. He flew over the ranch with a helicopter and found her on the side of Mt. Nighthawk. When we got to her we saw her badly broken body not far from her dead horse." He stopped and swallowed, looking up at the ceiling. Margo waited holding her breath. She could feel his pain and hated it.

"Apparently she had ridden up the trail on Mt. Nighthawk and somehow the horse fell off taking her with it. They had gone down in a slide area and I don't know how long she lay there or if she died instantly. Anyway, we buried her up on top of the mountain. I figured as much as she loved this place, she'd like being buried there. Nobody goes up the mountain now.

"And to be honest with you—I don't know why I told you this story now. I guess I just needed to talk about it. Tell you about Kellie and what she meant to me. To let you understand why the fire burned out years ago and why it will never re-ignite. It can't. She's gone."

"But that doesn't mean you can't love again, Cade. It just means you can't love Kellie again."

"True. But will I be able to love anyone like that again?"

"I don't have an answer to that. But I believe you can love again."
Margo grew quiet, not knowing what else to say and not wanting to
hurt him or his memories of Kellie. "Cade. I'm sorry she died. I can
feel you loved her a great deal. I think she would have wanted you to
be happy, as happy as she was, especially if she loved you as much as
she loved this ranch."

"You feel like I do, but I don't know if I can let her go yet. She
still haunts my mind."

"I think she haunts your heart and I don't think that's what she
would want. I just think she would want you happy, no matter what."

They were quiet again and he looked at her and said, "I've got to
get back to the payroll or you and the rest of the hands are going to
lynch me when there's no money in your accounts. But first I have
to tell you," his throat closed again, for a moment. "I love you like I
never thought I could love again."

She was quiet, her head down, then she shook her head and whispered, "Cade, I can't." She jumped up, took both the mugs and nearly
ran from his office and down the stairs, but not before Cade noticed
her tears.

*Margo, don't be afraid. I love you. I need you. I want you. Why are you
afraid to love?*

Thanksgiving Day had finally arrived, and Margo had hit the kitchen
early to stuff the turkey. She had gone to bed late the night before
because of all the stuff she had made ahead of time, so she would
not be so busy on the holiday. She had made the stuffing and several
molded salads, pies, and rolls.

Henry came in at four to make the usual pot of coffee and stopped
to watch Margo stuff the turkey. "That's a big bird you're wrestling
with!"

"It sure is."

"You want some help?"

"Henry, thanks but it's Thanksgiving for you too, and I don't want
you working on one of your few days off."

"Margo, I'm retired! All my days are off!"

"Okay."

"I'll go make some coffee, and then I'll be right back."

He headed to the coffee bar, but before he could get there, Cade came downstairs and stood in front of the coffee urn and sleepily croaked out, "Mmm, coffee."

Henry stood there looking at Cade, silently laughing. "Son, the coffee has to be made before you can drink it."

"What am I smelling?"

"I don't want to go there. Just move so I can make the coffee."

Cade moved aside an inch, and Henry rolled his eyes and reached over Cade to drop the coffee in the basket, flipped the switch to start the brew.

Cade continued to stand in front of the urn for a few more minutes then he sat down nearby to wait for the pot to fill enough so he could pull a mug.

Henry went back to help Margo. She had the bird stuffed and tried to pull it out of the sink and get it into a roasting pan, but it was so heavy she couldn't budge it. Henry pulled it out of the sink and got it into the pan, but it was a struggle. "Are you sure this bird is dead? I'm not sure I'm going to win this battle."

Margo laughed. She opened the oven, and they each took one side of the pan and struggled to get the turkey into the oven.

Henry wiped his brow. "Are we going to get the oven door closed? I don't think I've seen the oven that stuffed before."

Margo shut the oven door, checked the oven controls, and giggled at Henry's humor.

"Margo, next time, let's stuff a couple of birds instead of one gigantic King Kong bird. Several are easier to handle than that monster we're roasting."

"I agree. Next year, three or four birds would be better. But you know, I'm worried that that monster won't be enough for all of us."

"Well, I wouldn't worry about it, there's always something that turns up every Thanksgiving around here."

"What do you mean?"

"You'll see." He turned away and went over to the coffee urn for a couple mugs of coffee. Cade was sitting there, looking like a heap of flesh holding an empty mug in his hand. He was asleep, and Henry marveled at the fact that Cade could sleep just about anywhere in any position. He slipped the empty mug from Cade's fingers and filled it, then held it under Cade's nose. A few seconds later, Cade's eyes flew open, and his head came up. "Mmm, coffee."

Henry set the mug down in front of Cade then turned back to the coffee urn and filled two more mugs, doctored one for Margo.

A short time later, breakfast was on the table, everyone was enjoying it, and there was a halt to the holiday cooking while the kitchen was cleaned up and all the dishes were stuffed into the washers and the cycles were started.

At breakfast, she'd heard some of the hands talking about what they were watching on the TV during the day. She handed a couple of bags of popcorn to Jim and told him it was for the TV gang. He thanked her, stuffed them under his jacket, and headed back to the bunkhouse with the rest of the hands.

The pots and pans were washed, dried, and put away, and Margo sat down next to Henry for a few more minutes of relaxing. Cade joined them, bringing coffee to Henry and a Cherry Coke Zero to Margo. While they drank their favorite beverages, Margo and Henry discussed the plan of attack on the holiday feast ahead.

With their mugs empty, Cade picked them up, took them to the sink and washed them out. Margo threw her can in the recycling, and the back door opened and two of the hands came in with six pheasants, four ducks, and a small pig. "We thought you'd like a bit more meat for dinner."

"Oh! Did you just bag these?" Margo asked in awe. They were beautiful.

"Yes. We'll clean them for you and bring the birds back. We'll cook the pig in the pit out back."

They went out the door, and Margo turned and ran into her room shutting the door louder than she intended.

Cade quietly knocked on it and asked if he could come in. When he heard her muffled reply, he opened the door and went in to find her sitting on the couch, crying.

"Hey, what's wrong?" He sat down beside her and pulled her into his arms.

"They killed one of the piglets. How could they kill one of those cute little pigs?" Somehow she started crying harder.

"Wait, Margo. They didn't kill one of the piglets. That was a wild boar. A small one, yes; but it was a wild one, and there's no reason to be crying over it."

"Are you sure?"

"Yes. They breed faster than rodents and rabbits. Sometimes I think we're going to be overrun by boars."

She dried her face, and he pulled her back into his arms and held her tight. "I love you, Margo. You're such an enigma and so special to me.

"I love you, too." She said it without thinking, then stopped and looked at him terrified of what would come if she gave him her heart. She looked into his eyes and saw nothing but love. "You really do love me or I'm reading the book wrong."

He smiled at her. "You're reading the book correctly. I really love you, Margo. I think I have from the very first moment I saw you. I was afraid Kellie's memories would get in the way, but I know they aren't."

She took in the smell of him and let her face cool off for a few more minutes then she pushed back and looked at him with a glint in her eye. "Cade, I have a turkey to check on, and you have ten birds to make sure have no feathers, fat, heads, feet, or guts included when I get them."

She was out of the room and into the kitchen in a flash, and Henry was getting things ready for another bird-stuffing round. Cade leaned back on the couch and smiled. *That's Margo! At least she knows I love her and I know she loves me. But there is work ahead yet.* He called the bird cleaners to ensure they cleaned the birds exceptionally well.

The pheasants and ducks were stuffed and in the oven, and Margo sat back for a few minutes surveying her battle plan with Henry, and they were at a point where there was nothing left to do. Everything else was done or getting there, and so Henry volunteered to watch the ovens so Margo could rest for a while when Cade wandered through with his jacket and gloves on.

Cade had made it as far as the door when Margo saw it snowing like crazy. "Oh! Look! It's snowing! Well, get out the Christmas decorations! Did we eat Thanksgiving dinner yet? It's not supposed to snow until after Thanksgiving."

"Well, it's certainly didn't wait. Looks like we're going to have a blizzard, Henry, and I think we are going to have to get some ranch work done today that we were putting off for tomorrow."

Henry looked out and agreed. Cade pulled out his phone and called Josh. After a comment or two with Josh, Cade closed his phone and headed out the door. Four of the hands departed the bunkhouse at the same time. Cade and the hands headed to the stables. After they went inside and closed the door, several more hands came out of the bunkhouse, all heading in different directions.

"Where is everyone going?" Margo asked.

"Well, you have gardeners going off to check the garden and do whatever needs to be done to protect what's going on out there, ensure the water valves are protected from the cold, stow tools and then you have a coop master checking on the chickens, a hog master checking on the hogs, a couple of guys are checking on the horses, and a few more are going out to herd the cattle closer to the barn so they're safe and easier to care for, and a couple more will be stringing up the snow line. This is the time of year where we have to feed the critters because they can't get it for themselves."

"So much to do. Will dinner have to wait?"

"Probably not. We have enough men to take care of all that in short order. If the herd is a problem, more hands will go out to bring them in."

Cade and four hands came out of the stables, wearing long black coats, heavy-looking chaps, and bandanas over their faces. They swung up in their saddles almost simultaneously and headed out of the yard to round up the cattle. Margo thought they looked like bank robbers heading out into the wilds with their freshly stolen loot. Another hand came out of the bunkhouse and headed off to the garden.

Margo went into her room, sat on the couch, and pulled the afghan around her and was asleep almost immediately.

A couple hours later, she woke up to the sound of the back door opening and closing. A cold blast of air found its way in, and she got up and went into the kitchen. Cade was back. He had his hands wrapped around a hot mug of coffee and his face was red from the cold. He was talking to Henry when she came in. "It's a cold one. I wouldn't be surprised if we have a foot or more by tomorrow if it keeps snowing like this. The wind cuts right through you."

"I've been playing with the radio while you were out. It should have come on automatically with an alert. I don't know why it's not working," stated Henry.

"They didn't put out an alert. This took everyone by surprise. I called the weather station to check on the short range in case this was just a little warning that might dry up tomorrow and leave us wondering if we were still sane. They were as surprised as we were. But they're sitting in nice warm offices and not worried about cattle and equipment, so a blizzard isn't a problem to them except during the commute."

"They said that?" Margo asked.

"No. Just that they were surprised, and it looks like it's going to be a full-blown blizzard already this year. Henry, I think that radio's all right. Just make sure it's set up correctly, and we'll leave it on now in case the weather station ever puts out an alert."

Cade finished his coffee and put his gloves on, and Margo asked where he was going. When he indicated that he was going to the bunkhouse, she asked if she could go along. He thought about it for a few seconds and then said, "Only if you put on your coat and gloves." There was a twinkle in his eyes as she dashed off to her room. When she came back, her coat was on and zipped shut over her sweatshirt with the hood up. She had her hat on top of that. She ran to the refrigerator, grabbed a carrot and then two bags of popcorn from the pantry. She was shoving her hands into her gloves when she got back to Cade.

"Margo, leave your hat here because the wind will have it to Nowhere before you get two steps out. You're hood should be all right." She hung her hat on a peg and opened the door; but before she went out, the radio crackled, and Cade pulled her back in and shut the door.

The weather station announced that a surprise Thanksgiving blizzard was approaching and gave the belated current details, indicating that things would change. Cade opened the door, and they went out onto the porch. "I should send them a bill for that information."

The cold wind cut through her face. She put her gloved hands on her face and felt the sting burning her nose. "Oo! This is cold!" she yelled over the sound of the wind.

SIX

Cade pulled her close and shielded her from the wind, and then he took her gloved hand and put it on the rope line that led from the house to the corral, pulled a large blue bandana from his pocket and tied it across her face like a bandit, then pulled a red one and tied it on his own face. She was surprised at how much the bandana helped keep her face feeling warmer. "See how this goes. It gets you to the corral. Then you take one of the rails to the next section of the snowline. When we get a blizzard, if you have to go out, you *must* use the snowline to get back and forth to the bunkhouse. Do you understand? It's too easy to get lost, and you'll literally freeze to death out here, ten feet from the door. I want your promise to use the snowline when it's out, even if there's no snow on the ground. Even if you can see your way across the yard and there's sunshine, use the snowline. It'll do two things for you. One, it will train you to use the snowline without thinking about it. You'll just naturally grab the rope. Two, you will get used to what to expect next. You'll know where you are and where the door is or the next rope, and so on. Understand?"

"Got it."

They walked along, Cade holding the rope and Margo following behind, holding the same rope. When they got to the corral, Cade's hand went along the top rail, and Margo's dropped down to the second rail. They stopped along the way and fed Tornado a carrot then continued on, ensuring the barn door was closed tightly.

Cade opened the bunkhouse door, and they rushed in and quickly shut and latched the door. A few noises from a couple of hands about the cold blast of air that came in with them, and then someone recognized Margo.

"Good afternoon, Miss Margo," was stated loudly to warn everyone a female was in the building.

"Happy Thanksgiving! Please don't let me intrude; we were just out checking things. Well, Cade was checking, I was following." She smiled at the few men that stood up and the rest were lying on their bunks, mostly napping. It was nice and warm in the bunkhouse, and the TV was on some old black and white movie. Margo recognized Lauren Bacall and Humphrey Bogart. It was on mute. She could see the remnants of the popcorn she'd given out and was glad they had enjoyed it already. She did hope they hadn't ruined their appetites for dinner.

She noted the clock on the wall and figured they would be hungry enough since it was about two o'clock and no one had wandered over for lunch.

"You guys going to be hungry this afternoon?" she asked as she placed the two popcorn packs on the shelves by the old refrigerator in the corner.

"Yes, ma'am. Thanksgiving is one of my favorites for sure," replied one.

Cade and Josh had completed their discussion, and Margo turned to wait by the door. Cade looked around the room, nodded at Jim, and then opened the door and let Margo rush out ahead of him. He shut the door and latched it tight. Margo was already down the snow trail along the side of the bunkhouse, hand on rail to rope. Cade followed. They made it all the way to the kitchen door without a misstep, and Cade was sure Margo would be all right if she had to come out in a blizzard.

Just before Cade reached her at the kitchen door, Margo turned toward the yard and leaped out into the snow already deep enough to make snow angels. She squealed as she landed on her back to make a snow angel. She grabbed a handful of snow as she got up and made her way to Cade and quickly stuffed it down the back of his neck. He yelped and grabbed her and tossed her out into the snow pile and then jumped in after her to hold her down in the snow. Then he easily pushed a bunch of snow down the front of her shirt. She was kicking and squealing, and he kept shoving snow down her shirt. She was laughing so hard she couldn't even stop him. When he couldn't get any more snow into her shirt, he stopped, leaned down, and kissed her. Softly, at first, then passionately, then deeper until he knew he'd lit a fire inside of her because she'd lit a fire in him.

"Cade, I figure you're all wet and cold, but I'm soaked and getting real cold, and that fire you just lit isn't going to win against this freeze. Can I please get up now?

"Are you saying I can light your fire but I can't keep it going?"

"Oh you lit it, all right. And I have no doubt that you can keep it going, but I'm saying it's freezing out here, and I'm going to turn into the ice queen if you don't get off me and let me go inside and change into warm, dry clothes!"

"I hear the music of Ireland in your voice. Are you Irish?"

"Aye, a bit. Now get off, ya great beast!"

She bucked, and he rolled, and she scooped a bunch of snow into his shirt. She tried to run, but he caught her foot and pulled her down on top of him. When she landed, snow belched out of his shirt and melted faster between them. Icy water ran freely down Cade's sides as it melted in their heat. He winced as the freezing water ran down his sides, soaked his shirt, and tried to refreeze.

"I think we've got an audience, and I want to go in and get warm, let me go," she said.

"You're as free as a bird, Margo." He laughed as he let her go.

"Oo!"

They both laughed as they stood up and went inside, not once looking back to see the faces looking out the bunkhouse windows.

Cade and Margo met back in the kitchen after a hot shower and dressing in clean, warm, and dry clothes.

The turkey was on the table along with all the rest of the dinner, and everyone was enjoying it immensely. Margo watched everyone enjoying the turkey, duck, pheasant, and pig and was happy it was so good. She stuffed herself, having skipped lunch, like the others, and was a bit irritated at herself for overeating to the point of pain. While the others wandered up to the living room to nap on the couches or just talk, Margo ran up and down the stairs a couple of times then went back to the kitchen to check on things.

She was back in the pantry checking supplies when Cade found her.

Henry dug out a huge punch bowl with cups and ladle and washed them, dried them and put them in the middle of the cook island. Finally he filled it full of bright red punch and ginger ale, and it looked so delicious, Margo could hardly wait. Green pistachio ice cream balls floated around in the center of the punch.

Eventually all the hands returned to the dining hall, and Henry ladled out the punch, and a couple of the hands started passing cups of Christmas cheer around.

It was sweet, delicious, and loaded with fun. Margo loved it and thanked Henry with a hug.

Everyone thanked Margo for the fine dinner, and she said she enjoyed cooking it and thanked those responsible for the pheasant, duck and pig contributions, and a special thanks to Henry for his help.

"And you were worried that there wouldn't be enough food for everyone." Henry laughed.

Margo laughed and nodded.

Finally Josh got up and pulled on his jacket, hat, and gloves. The rest followed. It was lightly snowing and happily without any wind, but it had piled up quite a bit of snow during the day. Margo was standing there looking out the window, and Cade put her jacket on her shoulders.

"Come on, My Love. Put this on, your gloves, and hat, and let's go outside. You'll want to be part of this."

So she did as she was told, and Cade opened the door and took her outside with the hands. It was freezing, and Cade had turned out the lights in the kitchen so it was totally dark in the yard. Cade stood behind her and wrapped his arms around her, as he had a habit of doing.

"What are we doing?" she whispered.

"Wait for it," someone said.

"Getting used to winter," someone else added and some laughed.

Cade looked at his watch. It was exactly nine o'clock, and Christmas lights winked on the giant hemlock that grew between the corral and the house. A moment later, lights winked on all the way around the house, to the stables and the barn and the bunkhouse. It was Christmas!

There was a cheer and a Merry Christmas chorus from everyone, and Margo was nearly jumping up and down like a little kid. "Oh, Cade, this is beautiful."

She heard Tornado scream from the stables, and Cade went over and opened the stable door and Margo could see a string of Christmas lights around Tornado's gate in the stable. The hands started moving back into the bunkhouse and the others followed, shutting the door to keep the heat in and the cold out.

Margo went to the stable to be with Cade, and Henry went back into the house to make sure everything was put away and clean.

Cade was talking to Tornado who was shaking his head. "Well, you're going to have to live with it, pal. I'm not leaving them on all night. They'll be on for a while tomorrow night and many more nights for a while. So settle down and behave yourself, or I'll tattle to Santa about this and you won't get any more carrots for a while.

Cade and his horse, thought Margo with a smile. *He so loves the animal.*

Tornado settled down instantly, and Margo just shook her head in disbelief. Tornado whinnied quietly and moved over to Margo. "I didn't bring any carrots, Tornado. I didn't expect to come this way. I'm sorry. I'll give you some tomorrow. Be a good boy now."

Tornado shook his head and set it down on Margo's shoulder.

Cade took Margo's hand and led her to the door where he turned out the lights, shut the door, and locked it closed. Then he took Margo's hand again and led her to the house. The Christmas lights were still on, and they were beautiful. All white like glistening ice, except the huge hemlock that was twinkling in multi-colored lights and holding a silver Ⓧ on top.

Days went by, and Cade never seemed to find the opportunity to tell Margo how much he loved her and wanted her. She seemed to never be alone these days. He wasn't going to chase her around the ranch so he kept waiting to catch her alone.

He went down to the kitchen one afternoon to see if he could catch her alone. The desire to ask her to marry him was very strong. The kitchen had several guys in it drinking coffee, and he knew the wonderful aroma of cookies had lured them in from the deep freeze going on outside. He could hardly declare his love for Margo with the kitchen full of people, so he poured a mug of coffee and went back to his office.

Finally, on a the first day of December, when nature and man had drastically collided with each other, Tinker was injured when his horse fell and broke its leg on an icy patch near the house. Tinker's leg was pinned beneath the horse, the horse was screaming in pain; and the longer the horse writhed in pain, the more bone you could hear breaking, and it was Tinker's bones that were breaking.

Margo heard the horse scream, then she heard feet pounding across the yard and someone screamed in pain. She knew it had to be bad. Voices shouted, and the commotion in the yard took on its own life. Then she heard the one sound that made tears roll down her cheeks.

Josh pulled a revolver from his holster, took aim at the horse's head, and pulled the trigger. The horse died instantly. While the men worked to get Tinker free of the dead horse, Josh pulled his phone and called the emergency squad.

Cade came out of the house as soon as he heard the gunshot. He slammed out the kitchen door, pulling on his gloves, jacket, and hat. Margo went to the door's window to see a knot of men working on a downed horse. She knew instantly that they had killed the horse, but she couldn't see what else was happening. She moved to the window at the end of her private entrance. From there she could see everything as it was only a few feet away.

Cade scanned the situation, went to his truck, fired up the engine, and moved it closer to the dead horse and the knot of men. He backed it into a position directed by Josh, stopped, and they pulled the cable from the winch mounted to the frame of the truck under the bumper. It was attached around the saddle horn, and then Cade pulled the truck forward. The horse was pulled over to its other side, and that's when Margo could see Tinker laying on the ground and, through the glass, heard Tinker's bones breaking as the horse was pulled off his leg.

She ran into her closet and pulled out a blanket, threw on a jacket and ran out the door. She wrapped the blanket around Tinker as others worked to put a long wooden splint on his leg. While they did their work, Tinker lay there on the frozen ground, wincing in pain. Margo sat down on the ground and put her thigh under Tinker's head.

"Hold my hand, Tinker!" She reached out to comfort the fallen ranch hand and herself. She was so afraid. He held her hand so tight it hurt, but she wouldn't let go.

Finally, they picked him up and carried him toward Cade's truck. While the men placed Tinker into Cade's truck, Josh unhitched the winch cable from the saddle and ran the winch, winding the cable up. He and a couple of other hands leaped into the back of the truck, and when Josh banged twice on the fender, Cade drove off down the ranch road toward a field where the helicopter could land.

Margo stood up and gathered up the blanket, then went back into the house. She went to her room and cried. She cried for Tinker and she cried for the horse. Then she cried for Kellie and her horse and she cried for herself. They were tears to wash away piles of hurt and anger.

While a hand headed off to get the bucket loader, a couple of others took the saddle, bridle, and horse blanket to the barn. The farrier was already pulling the shoes from the horse's hooves. They could reuse the shoes for other horses. Everything that was possible was recycled at the ranch.

Josh and the hands returned in the truck without Cade. He went with Tinker. Margo felt alone but was glad that Cade had gone with Tinker. He did not leave her alone when she was sick.

When everyone was at dinner, Josh's phone rang. He stood as he pulled it off his belt and opened it as he stepped out onto the porch. When he came back in, his face was grim, and he was shivering. Margo wasn't sure if it was because he was cold or because of the news he'd just received. He stood by the door and repeated the news. "Tinker's leg is shattered. He might lose it. Anyway, they have flown him to Cheyenne so the doctors there can take a look at it and hopefully save it. Apparently Tinker won't let them take his leg. He would rather die than be without it."

It was deathly quiet in the house. Everyone had his own thoughts, and then Gus, the prayer warrior, lifted his quiet voice to God.

When he was done, a few quiet comments of gratefulness were whispered and most of the hands started cleaning up their dinner dishes without finishing their meals. Margo understood that they didn't want to eat.

They all did their usual work in the kitchen but in total silence, each one thinking about Tinker, and then they filed out to the bunkhouse. Josh told her that everything would be all right. Tinker was well liked, and everyone was a little upset about what had happened but they would survive and not to worry. "Just keep doing what you're doing, and it will work out," he said. "You have the cell phone Cade gave you?"

She nodded.

"You have my number programmed in it?"

"Yes," she stated.

"Don't be afraid to use it if you need anything," he instructed. "The house creaks at night, so if it gets too noisy, call and I'll come over."

Then he picked up his own hat, gloves, and jacket and went out to the bunkhouse.

. . .

Cade stayed with Tinker wherever they took him. He called Josh a couple of times in the night and the next day to tell him what was going on. Josh passed on the word about Tinker to everyone, and the ranch work continued. As the days went on, Cade was still calling the ranch on Tinker's status. Tinker was refusing all courses of action the doctors wanted to use, except pain killers.

Cade spent days trying to talk to him, to change his mind. The doctor was expecting blood poisoning soon and had no hope for Tinker's survival.

Cade was sitting beside Tinker as he slept one morning. He was reading a magazine and an article of some doctor in New York City caught his eye. Apparently he was doing great things with stainless steel bone replicas. Cade read the entire article and was impressed. He called information and obtained the doctor's phone number. He was surprised when the doctor answered the telephone.

After a bit of confirming he had reached the correct person, then relating the fact that he had just read an article about the doctor's success with stainless steel bone replacements he continued with the problem he was dealing with. He asked the doctor if he could help.

The doctor wanted Cade to bring Tinker to him, but Cade was afraid Tinker wouldn't be able to survive a trip that long, so he asked the doctor if he would come to Tinker. Cade would pay the fare and the expenses incurred by the doctor. The doctor accepted immediately and Cade thanked him; he ended the call and thanked God.

When Tinker awoke, Cade talked to him about the article and told him that he had made contact with the doctor. "Tinker, the doctor has agreed to come to see you. To look at your leg and all the exams and lab work and let you know if he can help you. If he can, will you go along with it?"

Tinker looked at Cade and closed his eyes. "If he can fix it. I'll do it, as long as I don't lose my leg. I don't particularly care if my bones are real or stainless steel but, I don't know, Cade. It seems like something out of a futuristic movie to me."

"I needed to know if you would even consider it. You haven't considered anything any doctor has said so far."

"Because they're all a bunch of followers. None of them has really looked at my leg. None of them has sat down and even contemplated a strategy other than to saw it off. They're all taking the easy way out. Just follow the leader mice. I won't do it. Now, I gotta say it, Cade. You keep pestering me about these lame-brain doctors they got here, you can go back to the ranch and let me die in peace!"

"Don't be so stubborn, Tinker. I'm not leaving you alone to die or for peace. I'm staying here and badgering you to keep you alive, at the very least. If you die, it's not going to be peaceful if I have anything to do with it. I need you Tinker. You're part of the family and I'm not going to lay down and let you go for no good reason."

Two days later, the doctor from New York arrived and walked into Tinker's room, unannounced and alone.

Tinker was asleep and the doctor introduced himself to Cade, then stated that he was assuming that Tinker was accepting at least the concept of something different since Cade had not called and put a halt on the trip from New York City.

Cade agreed and told him Tinker's stubborn ideas about the hospital doctors he'd seen so far and what he was demanding. The doctor did a quick examination of Tinker's leg then read his chart. Tinker slept through it all and Cade sat in the chair and remained quiet.

After Tinker awoke, a discussion and planning meeting took place in Tinker's room. The doctor explained everything to Tinker and waited for questions. When Tinker asked his question, Cade smiled. "When will you do it?"

The doctor looked at him and asked if he had a preference. Tinker laughed. "Do it as soon as you can. I'll clear my schedule for you."

Cade followed the doctor from the room and gave him his phone number.

The doctor took it and asked Cade if he would join him for dinner. Cade didn't hesitate and the doctor set the time and place. Cade went back to Tinker and the doctor went in another direction.

After dinner with the doctor and having learned a great deal more about the next few weeks as far as Tinker was concerned, the doctor went to his room for some rest and Cade called Josh. When he ended with Josh he went back to Tinker and gave Tinker some of the details of his near future. He was happy with Tinker's attitude and relaxed. "Tinker, he's going to fix your leg tomorrow morning."

"Good. I don't want to wait any longer."

SEVEN

Cade and Josh dropped out of the truck, and Cade was immediately surrounded by the hands. The happy faces that went back to work indicated that things were better for Tinker.

When Cade came into the kitchen, he stuffed his gloves in his jacket pockets and hung it up, then hung his hat on the peg above his jacket, and sat down at one of the tables. Margo brought him a mug of hot coffee. He sat there and sipped it for a few minutes in silence.

"How's Tinker?" she asked.

"He's doing real well. They removed his tibia and fibula and replaced it with stainless steel replicas yesterday. All seems to be going real well for him. Not much pain, high spirits, no infection or other complications, and he should be out of the hospital in a couple of weeks." He was silent again for several minutes, and then Margo couldn't stand it another minute.

"So how are you?"

"I'm okay but incredibly tired." He looked up at her and asked, "How are you?"

"Oh, I'm fine, just worried about you."

"Worried about me? I'm just tired; you don't have to worry about me."

"Well now, it's too late for that!" She turned and went back over by the stove and started polishing it. Even though she knew he loved her, her mind started a debate about his love for her, and with her heart, still timid and full of fear of her past, she started to believe that she had misunderstood his declaration of love. *What a fool you are, Margo!*

It wasn't long before Cade got up from the table, put his mug in the dishwasher, and then turned around and leaned against the counter. He watched her for a minute. She was so close he only had to reach out to touch her, and he knew the knot in his throat would melt and the tightness in his chest would ease up. He was swimming in a sea of hopelessness, and he couldn't see any help on the horizon. "Sink or swim," he breathed.

"What?" Margo looked at him.

"I love you," he whispered and, without looking at her, held his arms out to her and let her nearly leap into them.

She curled into him and just breathed in his scent. "I love the scent of you and leather." He felt her sigh, and he smiled, then she pulled back. The movement gave him a warning, and he schooled the smile from his lips.

"Did you just say I love you?" she asked.

"Yes, I said I love you. It's nothing new, I've said it before, remember?"

She buried her face in his chest and breathed in again. She was wrapped in his arms, listening to his heart beat erratically. Hers was beating just as jerky, and her mind was racing. She looked up at his face and his was smiling from ear-to-ear.

In one fluid motion, he picked her up and carried her up to the living room. There was a smile on his lips as he set her down and kissed her passionately. "I've been berating myself for not being able to say it so you understood it was for real, I wasn't just saying it for the moment or as in "I really like you" kind of thing. Then Tinker gets hurt, I fly all over the state with him to get him the medical attention he needed, and all I could do was think of you. I love you!"

"I don't understand what just happened," she whispered. "But I love it. I love you. A lot." She snuggled in deeper.

"Stay here with me and let me get my emotions under some kind of control. At least let me kiss you one more time. Well, make it twice, oh for … make it three times."

He held her against his chest and was so happy. He kissed her three times, passionately, and each time he let her loose, he grabbed her back to himself and kissed her again. He couldn't get enough of her.

They sat on one of the couches, and he pulled her into his lap and kissed her heatedly on the lips again. They held on to each other and talked about their love for each other for the first time.

He held her tight and just sighed. He was floating so high and he didn't want to come down. But he thought he'd better. They both had things they needed to get done, and this wasn't going to get them done. People were depending on them. Besides, there were the evenings alone in front of a fire that could be spent talking and learning about each other and letting love grow.

"Look. We both have things we have to get done. I'm so tired, I'm pretty punchy, but I suddenly don't seem to be thinking of a nice warm bed for sleeping anymore. How about we both go do what we have to do, get it out of our way, and make plans for this later?" He kissed her forehead. He kissed her lips softly but with an intensity that surprised him. "Margo! I love you!"

He put her aside, stood up, took two steps, and came back for another kiss, twice, then breathed out, "I've got to go take a shower!" and headed upstairs.

"I love you, Cade," she whispered.

"Ditto, Margo." He tossed over his shoulder halfway up the stairs and laughed out loud.

Margo was just finishing the last task in the kitchen before turning in. She was exhausted. She couldn't even think straight at the moment.

Cade had eaten a quick dinner and returned to his office. Payroll was due in the morning, and it wasn't ready. He couldn't stop thinking about Margo.

He was delighted that she loved him. But she was right. They had to slow down and make sure they really loved each other. They knew nothing about each other. How did they fall in love? Yet he felt going through the rest of his life without her would be torture. *I don't really care about her past. I love her, and what she did in the past is done, and I can't change any of it and wouldn't if I could because what happened is what made her the way she is and I love her.*

The house was dark when he finally shut the light off in his office and wandered the house to make sure lights were out, doors were closed, kitchen was turned off, but he had the payroll done.

When he got to Margo's door, it was closed, and he couldn't see any light coming out from under the door. "Margo?" he called softly. There was no answer. He climbed the stairs to his room, lay down, still dressed, and fell deep into sleep.

Cade sat beside Margo as she finished her dinner. "I called Tinker today. He's doing pretty good. Still no infections or complications. I thought I would go down to Cheyenne and visit with him for a few hours tomorrow afternoon. I'd like to take you with me, if you want to go. He asked how you were so I think he might like a visit."

"He asked about me? I'm surprised! Well, I'd love to go see Tinker. He's kinda special to me now. What time would you want to leave?"

"After lunch."

"Okay, will Henry want to handle the kitchen tomorrow night?"

"I already asked him and he said if you wanted to go, he'd run the kitchen. He just wants you to call him and tell him what's on the menu so he knows what to expect and when to get in here so it ready on time."

"Okay," she said as she pulled her phone and looked up Henry's number. "I'll get as much ready for him so he has as little work to do as possible. Cade left and she called Henry with the menu and her preparation plans.

Margo slapped the alarm clock off, went into the bathroom and showered then dressed quickly and was out in the kitchen on time.

She turned on the kitchen light just as Henry opened the kitchen door.

The morning was busy for both Cade and Margo; Cade didn't make it back down after breakfast until just about noon. By then the kitchen was cleaned up and Margo had discussed everything with Henry. She was dressed in her newest jeans and shirt and was anticipating Cade to have to beg off as he missed lunch.

Cade came downstairs and looked at Margo. "Ready to go see Tinker?" he asked.

"I sure am. Let me get my jacket, hat, and gloves." She went to her room. When she came back, she said, "Ready."

Cade opened the door and winter's cold blast hit her square in the face. She squealed with glee and astonishment at the frigid air. "Boy, is this cold or what?"

"It's cold!" stated Cade.

They climbed into a pickup and Josh drove them down ranch to a field where the helicopter was just coming down, Chuck guiding with hand signals to the pilot.

Josh stopped the truck near the machine and Cade helped Margo out of the pickup. He held her hand and led her to the helicopter, opened the back door and helped her in, then climbed in and sat next to her in the back seat. After he shut the door, he put a headset with mic on Margo's head then reached for one for himself. After he set it up, he looked at a switch near the place the headset cords plugged into. He flipped the switch and tapped the Pilot on the shoulder. The pilot flipped a switch and said, "Good afternoon, folks. What's your destination?"

Cade replied, "University Hospital in Cheyenne."

"Okay, if you're ready I'll give the signal."

Cade looked at Margo and she smiled and nodded. "Okay, good to go from back here," Cade told the pilot. Margo watched the pilot signal Chuck that he was ready to take off and Chuck looked down both sides of the machine and then gave the hand signals for straight up movement. Margo couldn't see Chuck after that, but the pilot spun the machine in a 180 and slowly picked up forward momentum across the ranch.

She looked at Cade when she heard him through her headset. He wanted her to know where she was. He was pointing and talking and she was getting a fantastic view of the ranch from above. She could see lakes, little buildings in a straight line and she guessed they were the range stations. Then they were over the fence line and Cade said they were off the Double K. They passed near a huge home nestled in some huge old oaks and Margo pointed at it and asked who lived there.

"The big house is Old Man Houk's. I don't have any dealings with him. The smaller house down here with the barn and out buildings is the Winters' place. He named it WinterHawk after my dad named that pile of rock on our ranch Mt. Nighthawk."

They landed at the hospital in Cheyenne and Cade told the pilot they would want to go back to the ranch around six that evening. The pilot acknowledged Cade's request and said he would be back at six.

They went down an elevator and stepped out, then walked down a hallway that separated nurse's stations and open waiting areas from rooms. Down near a corner, Cade checked the name on the little whiteboard near the door, then knocked on the door jamb. He indicated for Margo to stay put and stepped inside. She could see Cade all the time and hear him talking to Tinker.

"Hey, Tinker. How you doing? Feel like company?"

"Sure. Come on in."

"Okay. I brought Margo."

"You did? Where is she? There's another chair around here somewhere. Do you mind getting it, boss?"

"Be right back. Margo? It's okay, come on in here and I'll be right back," Cade said as he left the room.

Margo stepped into Tinker's room with a smile on her face. Tinker was in his bed, looking like he was there to overcome an illness, not having had a crushed leg and surgery. She expected IV's, monitors, traction, casts, a lot more than a happy face smiling back at her and asking her to sit in the only chair in his room.

Instead of sitting, she reached out to Tinker and he took her hand and held it tight for a minute. "I want to thank you for doing what you did that day. You knew I needed somebody to hang on to and you offered. Nobody else had time to hold my hand and tell me it was going to be okay. They all had work to do to get me out from under that horse. You provided your leg for my pillow and your hand for some extra strength that I needed and a soft voice of encouragement and I can't tell you how much that meant to me right then."

"Oh, Tinker. I really was scared. I wish I could have done more, but I was afraid of getting in the way and I never dreamed you would really appreciate me being there, dripping tears and asking you to hold my hand. Tough guys, silly girl."

"Margo, don't you ever think that way again!" he snapped at her. Then he softened and said, "Sure we gotta be tough. Lots of testosterone out there. Lots of hard work. We've got cuts and bruises all the time, no use complaining, just do what needs to be done to tend them and get back to work. But we would never refuse your help and we certainly don't think of you as a silly girl.

"You have no idea how glad we were when you came to the ranch to cook. We figured you'd be a little skittish for awhile. We were total strangers and you landed in the middle of us and didn't know what to expect. But you're a strong one and somehow, even though you were weak and ill at the time, we all knew you were ours from the start. You're one of the crew. You have nothing to worry about as far as we're concerned. We'll take on anything for you. I mean that."

"Thanks, Tinker. I appreciate the kind words and encouragement. So, how are you doing. You look so much better than I expected. You had us all biting our bottom lips for awhile."

"Oh! I guess I probably did. I just couldn't lay down and let them run over me. Already had a horse do that and I was pretty angry about it."

Cade returned with a chair he had confiscated from someplace. He set it next to the other chair and reached past Margo to shake Tinker's hand. "Miss me?" he asked with a grin.

"Margo and I had a nice conversation while you were out there foraging for that chair," Tinker teased.

They sat there for several hours and talked about Tinker's surgery and his future at the ranch and the near future of physical therapy.

The time came to leave; they hurried back to the heliport on the roof and got to the glass door in time to wait a few minutes. Finally, one helicopter landed and they stood out of the way as an emergency crew brought some accident victim into the hospital. The helicopter took off after that and another, smaller helicopter landed. Cade took Margo's hand and led her quickly out to the helicopter and they got in and buckled the belts. Cade tapped the pilot on the shoulder and indicated they were ready. He turned and handed a headset to Margo and took one for himself checking the switch on the box.

He put his on and Cade heard the pilot talking to someone over the mic, but it was to his company. He indicated to Margo to remain quiet. Margo nodded her understanding and looked out the windows. Finally, the pilot went straight up and slowly turned to the North and started his flight back to the Double K Ranch.

As they flew back to the ranch, Margo asked Cade questions about Tinker and learned even more about him. Seemed Tinker, one of the taller, thinner, wranglers, was also a "Jack-of-all-trades". He was very dependable and had a sweet tooth that was bested by no one else."

Margo laughed and asked if Cade would be able to get Tinker back to the ranch. "You know, Cade, I could move upstairs and Tinker could have my current room behind the kitchen. He'd be so comfortable in that huge comfortable bed with that gigantic bathroom. I'd be near him all day to get him food, do whatever I could for him. They guys would be going right past his room all the time and they could slip in and out for visits and I can't see any reason why it wouldn't work. Would it?"

"You have a great idea and a super point. I have to do some research on this *physical* therapy anyway so let me look into that idea, too. You'd move upstairs?"

"Yes. I've done all the cleaning up there. I can take one of the smaller rooms near the bathroom. It would work out well, I think."

"Well, let's see how it goes."

The next day, Cade asked Margo if she had time for a horsemanship class. She teased him and said, "No, but I can make time for a horse-womanship class."

He teased her back. "I'm not sure I can even get my tongue to bend well enough to say that word. But you're on anyway." No one was around so he kissed her quick. "After lunch, today?"

"Sure. I'll be ready," she replied. He kissed her quick again and went outside, slamming the door behind him and dragging his jacket and hat on, then his gloves as he crossed the frozen yard.

EIGHT

She called Tinker. "Hey, Tinker. Guess what were having for dinner." She laughed when he whimpered and begged to come home. She felt good knowing his spirits were high. They talked for a few minutes, then he had to get off the phone. "I'll save you a piece of cake tonight."

"Mean!" he laughed and ended the call.

Cade took Margo to the corral where one lone horse was standing to the back of the corralled area up against the barn. It was very docile looking, and compared to Tornado, it was asleep. She caught up to Cade, wanting to pay attention so she could go riding when she had time and not have to get someone to help her all the time.

Cade explained how to operate the gate and what to do around the horse. "Take this bridle and hold it like this in your hand." Margo took the bridle from Cade and held it as he had shown her and then put it on the horse as instructed. Margo had hands-on instructions, which she liked because she knew she would remember.

After learning how to put the bridle on and lead the horse with the reins, he had her take the horse to the rails and told her how to tie the reigns so the horse wouldn't pull free and wander off, but at the same time, she would have a quick release so she could just grab the reins and go, if she needed to.

Saddling the horse came next. He told her what to do and she followed, without any problems, including what seemed like a complicated knot on the cinch to the saddle. Once she had accomplished the knot, it no longer seemed complicated. Cade made her undo and redo the cinch without his prompts. No problem.

Now he told her to mount up and walk the horse around in the corral for a few minutes. While she was riding around in the corral, Cade went into the stables, saddled Tornado, and led him out into the yard.

"Margo, let's go for a ride," he stated and pulled the gate rails to the side so she could ride the horse out of the corral. He swung up onto Tornado and headed out of the yard.

They headed west toward the mountains, and Cade instructed her on how to sit straighter so her back wouldn't hurt. Posture was extremely important while riding a horse, how to place her foot in the stirrups, so the ball of her foot not the instep was in the stirrup. Then he grinned and reminded her that she was probably going to be saddle sore tomorrow.

Margo had forgotten that little item, and she winced at the thought of it. She also remembered that the best way to get past it was to get back on the horse. Since she knew that wasn't going to be the first thing she could do she would have to do a few exercises to try and chase out the tight muscles, which meant that she was going to have to get up earlier.

An hour later, Cade was instructing Margo on how to unsaddle the horse and where to put the saddle, blanket, and bridle, and how to care for the horse after it was ridden. She took it to the stables and put it where she was told, then groomed the horse, fed the horse and made sure it was secure for the next person.

It was time to get back to the kitchen to make dinner, and Margo headed off to the house while Cade made a call on his cell phone. She had just enough time to take a hot shower first.

So much of her days became routine. She would call Tinker every day because she knew it cheered him up. She always had some tease for him and she knew he looked forward to her calls.

THE DOUBLE Ⓚ RANCH

Henry was always in the kitchen for breakfast and dinner help. He loved to cook and he gave Margo some great tips along the way on how to cook on the grill or make some special dish for fun. Since she was so into cooking herself, she always enjoyed his company and his long tales of the good old days.

Paul, Steve and Chuck had become constants in setting tables and cleaning the kitchen after meals. Chuck was the best floor cleaner and liked doing the floors. They always shined after he was finished. Paul and Steve were experts at emptying the dishwashers and setting tables and they were quick putting leftovers away well protected and efficiently.

One character that surprised her with his kitchen skills was Mike. Mike, like the others, was a wrangler, but he was also the mechanic. He kept all the engines running and the vehicles clean inside and out and when Margo heard how many machines he kept clean, she wondered how he had time to do anything else.

Josh was very good at being a foreman and everybody seemed to like him a lot. She learned how to schedule her time so that she could go riding for about a half-hour every day. If she could squeeze and hour into riding a horse, the better, but she had to remember to include the startup and grooming, which is why she usually only rode for a half-hour.

Cade had taken the time to research Tinker's physical therapy location and it was determined that Rapid City was the closest set up. When Tinker was released from the hospital, he was taken to a Rapid City Rehab facility. It was clean and pleasant and he didn't mind it. Being on the edge of the city, he could look out his window while he was stretching and working his muscles into knowing who the boss was again.

Margo's daily calls continued to cheer Tinker, and he gave her details of his rehab. He was actually enjoying his routines and already had them memorized a week after arriving. He had to do them once daily, but he was usually out of his room and down to the treatment area twice a day. Once with the trainer, once on his own, but he knew the trainer was watching because occasionally the trainer would give him variations or assistance in a particular problem area. Margo was glad he shared the information as it made her feel part of his team. He always said he enjoyed getting her encouragement.

Cade had placed Tinker in a rehab facility in Rapid City that was very nice. It was very much like a beautiful old mansion. A large, wandering, single story building with ornate "ginger-breading" in many places. Everything was sparkling clean, inside and out and the staff were very pleasant and helpful. The grounds were spectacular and the sidewalks looked like they had just been swept. There was never a dirty corner or dusty table.

The entry hall was wide and stayed that way all through the middle of the building making the scattered common areas along the sides very inviting to sit and talk or wait, if needed. Tinker's room was accommodating for two people with a great deal of room to walk around in. Everything was polished and clean. There was no clutter anywhere. His TV was in a "hutch" type dresser along the wall opposite the foot of his bed. He was usually dressed in sweat pants and sweat shirts and sitting in a wheel chair in his room. Cade and Margo visited Tinker there a few times before he finally graduated to going home. They would go to a common area and sit alone to talk quietly and enjoy each other without bothering anyone else.

Because Tinker had an email account at the Rehab she would be able to do emails, at least, and there was always the phone.

She spent a great deal of time after breakfast washing and drying her clothes, and meal planning. She had started planning Christmas dinner right after Thanksgiving as she wanted to ensure she had all her supplies. They would only go to the wholesale house once the first Friday of December so she had to be ready then. She wanted it perfect and enjoyable.

Now she had organized it all so that she had things measured out and stacked together for different dishes. Anything she could do ahead, was done. It was going to be a huge dinner and it was going to take time to make it perfect.

Finally Christmas Eve day was at hand, and she had closed herself up in her room upstairs. Even Cade was shut out. While Cade spent a day missing Margo, he was busy off ranch, taking a lot longer than expected due to snow and ice down ranch with some cattle issues, which helped his case of missing-Margo.

She had talked Cade into taking her to town one day. She'd called the dry goods store, and they had her order ready for pickup, wrapped in plain paper. She got out of the truck, ran in, picked up the order, paid, and was back out in the truck in five minutes flat. Cade wasn't in the truck but came back a few minutes later with a package under his arm. Neither would tell the other what was inside the packages.

Cade then drove over to the Video store, the guys were returning some and wanting others, so it took awhile to hunt down the ones they wanted and get the newest catalogue for the guys. Margo jumped out of the truck and ran in with him to help find the movies.

While they were in the Dry Goods store, Delilah came out of the shop next door and saw Cade's beautiful emerald-green Toyota sitting in the parking lot. Nobody but Cade had a truck like that. She had been forced to park around the corner because the lot was full, but here's Cade's truck right in front of the door. It was amazing how well that man was treated. Like some kind of King or Emperor. It really irked her!

She got in her car with so much anger she thought steam should be pouring from her ears, at least. She sat there, grinding on the "perks" Cade and his little tramp got. While Delilah was mentally grinding on injustices to her, she saw Margo come out and get in the truck, then Cade backed out and drove down the street a block to the Video store. She followed after they got out and went into the store. She parked in back and walked around to where Cade's truck was now parked. Still grinding on the arrogance of "Cade and Company". She glanced around and seeing no one around, she keyed the passenger side of the truck. As she furtively watched around her, she took her key and scratched several circles around the door key hole, then wandered the key up scribbling little-endless circles around the door handle and finished with "Cade's Trollop" largely scrawled on the door. When she left, she had a smile on her face that beamed out like a neon sign. She got in her truck and drove across the street to the gas station and while filling her beat up red, white, and blue Datsun, she leaned against it and watched them come out of the Video store. Cade got in behind the wheel, and Margo jumped in on the passenger side apparently not seeing the keying to the door.

A new subject to grind on. "Stupid, blind girl! Can't even see something as clear as that ugly snoot you have on your face! What is wrong with you? Nothing short of dead brain syndrome!" she muttered to herself. She finished filling her truck, slammed the hose back into the pump, screwed the lid back on her tank and climbed in her truck. She spun wheels getting out of the gas station which caused the clerk to look out and see who was so stupid. He saw Delilah's truck. Nobody would own that thing except Delilah. Besides, he'd seen her getting in and out of it enough to know it was Delilah. He made a note of it for his boss in case there was anything in the future on the issue, checked the pump and discovered she'd left without paying. *Boss has to know about this,* the thought He wrote the amount down on the note. He figured he was going to hear about letting her leave without paying but, "Hey! Ya gotta update this old dump if you want people to pay first," which, according to his way of thinking, was the only way to get past having people skip on you.

When Cade and Margo got back to the ranch, they jumped out of the truck and went in the house. Cade had left the keys in it so someone could move it if they needed to and a short time later, Mike came in and found Cade in the kitchen getting coffee.

"Boss, you need to see this."

"What's up, Mike?" He followed Mike outside and around his truck to the passenger side. Mike pointed at the door and Cade moved closer and immediately saw the keying. The longer he looked, the more he saw and he was starting to see red. "I know this wasn't there when we left this morning. It had to have happened in town. Who did this?"

When he saw "Cade's Trollop," He knew in his heart who had done it. *Delilah!*

"Boss, I think I can fix this, without much trouble and cost. If not, we'll have to mask it off, sand it, primer it and repaint it. You might want to consider getting a can of paint from Toyota to match. If you want, I'll start work on it right now and let you know in about an hour."

"Perfect. Thanks, Mike. I'll be waiting on your answer before I make that call."

Within the hour, Mike had called Cade. They were in the "shop area" where Mike did all the repairing of all the equipment on the ranch. With a lot of rubbing and some grainy-compound, he had managed to "erase" about a third of the key marks from the door so well, that Cade had to really look for them and get the light just right. It saved all the extra work and expense for the alternative.

"I'll finish rubbing it out and put a couple layers of car wax over it, then every time we wash it, I'll do an extra layer of wax on the door. It should be alright. If we have a problem, there's always the alternative," Mike finished.

"Okay. I'll leave it to you. Thanks, Mike. Looks great!"

Many of the Christmas cookies Margo had made went into boxes, one box for each of the hands, and she had wrapped each one in paper and ribbon with a simple knot. Now she was putting them under the tree.

"Just in time for Christmas?" Cade was standing at the bottom of the stairs.

"Hi!" She moved to his side. He looked a little sad. "What's wrong?"

"I'm lonely, and I miss you. What have you been doing up there, locked behind the door?" He looked like a little boy unhappy because Santa didn't stop by.

"That!" she said and pointed to the tree. "It certainly makes the tree look grander."

"Are you ready for tonight?" Cade asked as his usual confident and strong self.

"Yes. How about you?"

"Oh, I'm as ready as I'm going to get."

"Sounds almost ominous," she commented.

He took her hand and led her to the couch near the fire and sat down, pulling her down beside him. He wrapped her up in his arms, kissed her neck, and then just held her close.

For weeks, Margo had been wracking her brain trying to figure out what to get Cade for a Christmas present. At some point, shortly after Thanksgiving, she had called Mr. Dietrich, the banker, and asked him if he could help find a bookkeeper for Cade; one that would do payroll and pay bills. She asked him to keep it quiet because if he found one in time, she was going to present it to Cade for a Christmas present.

Mr. Dietrich thought it an unusual Christmas gift, but then his favorite customer was Cade and he always thought of Cade with a lot of joy and respect. If Margo wanted to give him a bookkeeper for Christmas, well, alright!

She still hadn't heard anything and was disappointed but there was still hope. A small glimmer of hope, but hope nonetheless.

Margo was very aware of Cade wanting a bookkeeper for the ranch. She had gleaned from him, that all his other holdings were handled individually. He had never combined them into a huge conglomerate. Each had its own CEO, CFO, Personnel, Accounting, any department they needed to get the job done was there—except a bookkeeper for the ranch. He'd always just handled it, but that didn't preclude him from hating it.

When the first of the hands walked in, the kitchen was clean and smelling wonderful. "Merry Christmas, Cade. Merry Christmas, Margo!

"Merry Christmas, everybody!" Margo had put a fat column candle on each table and surrounded it with holly sprigs and holly berries. Someone lit the candles and the dining hall took on the look of Christmas.

The rest of the hands came in along with a blast of cold air. They hurried in so the door could be shut as fast as possible, but it took awhile for everyone to get through. Everyone got their drinks and sat down, wishing a Merry Christmas. And dinner was on the table.

Cade asked Gus to ask the blessing, and everyone stood during the prayer then sat and enjoyed a grand Christmas meal.

When the kitchen was spotless again, everyone had gone up to the living room to see the tree and all the decorations. Margo was getting coffee when Cade came looking for her. "Come on, beautiful. You're missing the fun."

Cade led Margo up to the living room. Two wingback chairs were side-by-side and empty, and he set her down then took the seat beside her. The furniture had been rearranged into a huge horseshoe on Thanksgiving and was still the same. A huge Christmas tree was in the corner where the wingback chairs had originally been. The living room was filled to capacity with all the hands, and Margo felt so comfortable she didn't want it to end. They were all talking and laughing and enjoying themselves.

Christmas dinner was over and the hands thanked Margo by giving her applause. She didn't know how to accept it other than with "Thanks." She felt it was a lame way to thank them for thanking her for making Christmas dinner, but she didn't know what else to do.

Some sat around and played board games, like Monopoly, Scrabble, Life, Pictionary, and a few played poker using candy mints for chips. After a while, Margo went down to the kitchen to make sure there was enough coffee and that the sugar bowl and cream thermos was full. All was well, and she went back up to the living room with the others for a while longer. When talk turned to work, she figured it was time for desert.

"Anyone for desert?" she asked.

Smiles and affirmatives were heard, without a single dissenting vote. She went down to the kitchen to get out the pies and cut them up onto dishes.

Henry started to get up, but Cade restrained him with a hand on the shoulder. "Henry, you sit there. I'll go help in the kitchen."

Henry got about four of the hands to run up and down the stairs to distribute pie, forks, napkins, and coffee. Pie was devoured and adored. Margo got many compliments on her pies, and it made her feel extra special and boosted her confidence by several miles.

"Merry Christmas, Guys!" Cade said. "Margo went to a lot of work wrapping boxes and setting them under the tree."

Margo got the ball rolling. "Jim, you and Tom are closest to the tree. If you don't mind would you pass the boxes out? And please, everyone, open them at the same time."

Tom passed two to Cade. Both were flat and obviously pictures. Cade leaned both against the side of the chair for opening later. "Okay. You guys, open your gifts first."

All the presents were the same size and covered with midnight blue heavy foil paper that was covered with tiny, shiny stars. Each hand tore off the paper and cord and opened the box, then pulled back the tissue paper inside. "Cookies!" a couple of hands spoke up. Everyone was grateful and closed their boxes to take back to the bunkhouse.

"Margo. There's a gift here from the guys to you. You should probably open it now." He handed her one of the flat gifts that had been set aside earlier. She pulled the huge ribbon bow off and then pulled the paper off, taking all the time in the world. "She obviously doesn't want Christmas to end." Cade sighed and a few of the hands laughed.

When she was done pulling the paper and ribbon away, she held up a picture to view it better. It was a oil painting of a beautiful white horse. The white horse was standing on lush grass somewhere on the ranch with the mountains in the background, a sunset over the mountains. The horse was so white it was almost mystical.

"It's beautiful." Margo was awash with emotions.

"Who is the white horse?" she asked.

Cade looked at the picture. "Let's see." He studied it for a long moment. "How about I open this one and then we take a walk out to the barn and see if we can determine who this white horse is?"

"Okay. Thanks, Mike." Margo kept looking at the picture of the white horse.

The second flat gift was from the hands to Cade and he opened it a great deal faster than Margo. When he saw it, he was delighted with it. Tornado; a head and neck shot. His eyes shiny like he'd just devoured a pallet of carrots. Cade loved it. "I think I'll put this on the wall in the dining room. It's so like Tornado. Thanks, Mike. It's great."

Mike mumbled his thanks.

Cade and Margo, Henry, Josh, and a few of the other hands trooped out to the barn, wished Tornado a Merry Christmas after he made his noises, and they wandered down the middle of the barn looking at the various horses in their stalls. Margo didn't see any white horse or even a cream colored horse. Finally, they went back to the door and just before getting to Tornado's stall a white horse poked it's head out of the stall next to Tornado's stall.

The horse was so white it almost glimmered in the lights of the barn. Margo petted the beautiful horse and was talking to it softly. She looked at the name on the stall door. STORMY.

Underneath it, in black paint on the wood, Love, Cade was painted in script.

Cade was standing next to her, Josh and Henry and the others standing nearby. "Margo, Merry Christmas. This is your horse. She has quite a bit of spirit. Please—I have one request. Don't ride her until we can go out together for a couple of times. I want to make sure you two are a good match before I let her loose with you. Understand?"

Margo just nodded. There was a knot in her throat. Stormy was beautiful and she already loved the horse, not knowing anything other than her name and that she was the whitest horse she had ever seen.

When she finally got her voice back she asked, "Does Tornado like her?"

"Tornado loves her. He's already asked if he can marry her and I told him it was up to you. He's got a few things he wants to discuss with you, urgently, I might add."

NINE

"Stay here Stormy. I'll be back. The guy next door wants to talk to me."

Stormy made muttering sounds as Margo petted her muzzle. Margo moved to Tornado. He put his head on her shoulder and tipped it against her head, then held it there as she stood still. "You like Stormy, Tornado?" He made muttering noises. "Okay. You can marry her, but you have to give me sons and daughters, I figure they'll be worth a lot because you are both so beautiful. Beautiful children have to follow you."

Tornado lifted his head, stepped back and nodded vigorously. She rubbed his muzzle and went back to Stormy. "Stormy, Tornado has asked for your hoof in marriage. I told him it was okay. What do you think?" Stormy muttered some more and then looked out her stall door towards Tornado who was looking Stormy's way. Stormy muttered some more and then whinnied her approval at Tornado. After a couple of pets, Margo stood back and thanked the guys.

When the hands went back to the bunkhouse with their cookie packs, Cade and Margo sat in the living room looking at the pictures, and Cade finally stood up and took the picture of Tornado upstairs to his room. Margo followed. "He's very good, you know? He captured both horses perfectly." She turned and found Cade starring as she had been doing.

They were getting ready to go to bed when Cade's phone rang. He pulled it from its holster and answered without looking at it. "Merry Christmas, Double K."

He listened for a moment then said, "Yes." And after another moment said, "Well, yes, I am looking for a bookkeeper. How did you hear about it?"

Margo sat there watching and waiting. After Cade had discussed the position with the caller he instructed the caller on how to find the ranch. "When can you start?

"That's perfect. We should be able to get you settled in and have you ready for work the first working day after the New Year. Thanks for calling and, Merry Christmas."

After Cade closed his phone and put it back in his holster, he looked over at Margo and said, "I wonder how Mr. Dietrich knew I wanted a bookkeeper."

"Merry Christmas, Cade!" she whispered it and wasn't sure he heard it.

He stepped over to her, gently took her in his arms, and just held her for a few moments breathing in the scent of her hair and learning the feel of her in his arms as though he had never felt her there before. He decided she was a perfect fit in every way. "I love you. Thank you for the Christmas presents."

She was loath to let go of him. His scent was one of leather and soap, and she took it in with gulps. How could she ever love this gentle and wonderful man enough? He had done so much for her, and she had done nothing more than make a telephone call to the banker. And she was as surprised as he was that the call had come on Christmas Eve. "I love you, Cade. Merry Christmas."

She looked up, and he kissed her sweetly, passionately, and deeply. He had her toes curling before he ended the kiss and even at that she was disappointed that it had to end.

Cade and Margo climbed the stairs stopping on the third floor long enough to kiss goodnight. Margo turned and climbed the last set of stairs and Cade settled for his room alone. *Margo was right!* he thought. It was best they had separate rooms. His resolve was getting weaker by the day.

There was a Christmas tree in the corner of Margo's room, and it was decorated beautifully. Margo knew instantly that Cade had ordered it. *He's so sweet. He loves to throw a surprise.*

The blizzard that hit full force in the middle of the night changed a lot of minds about a lot of things. No one went out except as absolutely needed to take care of the animals. The hands trudged in for breakfast and dinner, but Margo was advised they would stay out in the bunkhouse for lunch. She made sure before they all left after breakfast that they had a chance to take what they wanted from the refrigerator or pantry. Satisfied that they had what they needed, she tried to watch them make the snow trail back to the bunkhouse, but couldn't see past the end of the porch. Everything beyond the porch was white on white.

After Christmas, Cade and Margo spent their evenings in the master suite, usually in front of the fireplace with a warm fire burning brightly. Margo loved the spot on the couch next to Cade in front of the flames on the hearth. This is where they learned about each other and where one night they did "true confessions."

Cade had talked about his life as a child on the ranch. He'd been treated well by family and hands. He had a horse, a lot smaller than Tornado and not nearly so spirited and with a personality pretty tame compared to "the Big T," but it served its purpose, and he was glad he had it. He talked about his education, home schooling, taking his GED, and then going to college and majoring in business administration and biology. He'd always wanted to follow in his dad's footsteps, had always felt that he had any choice in the matter of his life and future, and had loved his parents totally.

He told her about a dream he had of buying the acreage across the main road and building a town site on it and sit back and see what would happen. He figured most of the folks from Nowhere would move there, and he'd name it Somewhere. It would cause the other ranchers to have to drive twenty miles to town instead of him. It was a joke because he didn't go to town that much, and when he did, it was usually to Sheridan or Rapid City, which was a lot farther away but bigger and offered many more services.

When it was Margo's turn to confess, she talked about her life as a child and how her parents loved her and she loved them, but the house was always full of strife and yelling and a lot of mental shoving by both her parents. She probably had quite a bit of resentment about it, but she couldn't do anything about it and hated dragging all the baggage around, so she dumped it as often as she could, which never seemed often enough.

Finally, she felt she could talk about Jerry. "I got married about two years out of high school. He was a nice enough guy, nothing spectacular and, looking back, not very ambitious. Also looking back and compared to my love for you, I don't think I loved him as much as the idea of being in love. At any rate we went to Vegas, eloped, and then went back to Tacoma. As soon as we got back there, his personality changed a hundred and eighty degrees. He first beat the crap out of me, and when I woke up, I was in nothing but an old T-shirt of his that barely covered me and chained to the stove in the kitchen. It was long enough for me to make it to the refrigerator and the sink, but that was it.

"Life for Margo at that point was waiting for him to come home, beat me senseless, fix his dinner, and beg him for a potty break. Often it was begging for another beating, but the only other choice was peeing on the floor which was grounds for more beating.

"My only friend at that point was a cat. Jerry hated the cat, and it stayed away from him. It was so smart that when Jerry drove into the driveway, the cat would hide and escape through a broken window in the back room. My jerk of a spouse was too lazy and stupid to fix the window, so the house suffered the extremes of temperature changes and most of the time I was too cold to really care about anything. Anyway, I loved the cat. As soon as Jerry would drive away in the morning, the cat would come in and be with me most of the day. I could reach the food, and so it was easy enough to feed him, and we'd sleep and play all day.

"One day, Jerry caught him and killed him, right there in the kitchen in front of me. I begged for the cat's life, but Jerry seemed to get great enjoyment from feeling the cat struggle for life and my begging, and it drove him on to killing the cat. My life after that was worse. I was always alone, except when Jerry was there beating me. He only came home to beat me and pass out.

"A few weeks after he'd killed the cat, I begged him to let me go to the bathroom as usual, he unchained me from the stove and pushed me into the bathroom then sat on the edge of the bathtub to watch. The sicko loved watching me pee. He'd sit there and hold the end of the chain in his hand and hit me with it occasionally. At the time I had several slashes to my legs from that chain. When I was done with the task, I pushed him backward and ran as fast as I could. I was sure he was chasing me and was so terrified he'd catch me that I couldn't even look back. I ran straight up the center of the street and ran right into the side of a police cruiser.

"They took me to a hospital and listened to my story, removed the chain from my wrist, and went back for Jerry. They found him, dead, in the bathtub. Apparently I had pushed him hard enough that he'd hit his head on the tile wall, broken the tiles, but also his skull. The DA was trying to get re-elected, and he was going to get there over me. Self-defense had no part in his scheme. Eventually, after being locked in jail for about three months, a newspaper reporter decided to take the DA to task via the newspaper and used me to nail the DA's rear to the wall. I was set free with an apology, a pair of worn out jeans, a new t-shirt, and a pair of dirty tennis shoes. No money, no life, no home, and no job. I don't know how they thought I would survive. I guess they didn't care.

"When I walked out of the jail in my 'new clothes,' the reporter was there and basically took me in. I lived with his sister rent free for a few months. He got me a job at the paper he worked at, and I survived for a few years. While I was there, I became friends with the lady that wrote the articles for the food magazine. She was friends with the fashion editor, and the two of them got me some decent clothes with the little funds I had and introduced me to several restaurant chefs. I got a job with one; I worked my tail off for that place. Eventually I needed to move on. I wanted to go east and someday make my own restaurant.

"I got a ride with a truck driver. He was heading east, and I thought maybe this would launch my career. I got in his truck and about the time we got to Montana, he figured I owed him a good toss between the sheets. I managed to get away from him, hide out between an old shed and an old house, and long after he drove away, I came out. I still had a few dollars in my pocket; and when I found myself in front of the bus station, I bought a ticket. I ended up in Nowhere, Wyoming, broke, starved, and lost. I passed out in the café, the bus driver left me and my stuff, and Windy, the waitress at the café, took me in. Occasionally, I helped out in the café, but mostly I did odd jobs around Windy's house, like paint, plaster cracks, seal windows, clean house, and she let me bake. She sold my pies, by the slice, at the café. The manager took no money for them so all the take on the pies was pure profit to Windy. She knew how to push those pies, too. Then I got a job at the bakery in town, moved to the rat and roach-infested apartment, and met Mrs. Dietrich one day at the bank. She's a nice lady. Likes parties, poor thing. Anyway, we got to talking, and she's good at getting one to talk. Nice thing is she seems to know how to put the pieces together to make it work. You were looking for a cook, and I was looking for a job. She made sure we met. Now I'll give you a choice."

"What's that?"

"You can be real honest and up front and tell me to get out and I'll leave with the clothes on my back and thank you for the time you've allowed me to live and work here and the clothes I walk away with; or you can put your arm around me and never let go of me again."

Cade looked at Margo, his eyes were swimming, and there was clearly anger on his face. Margo sealed her heart for the worst and prayed he wouldn't beat her while he chased her off the Double K. "Margo, if Jerry were still alive, I'd hunt him down and kill him, like the rabid dog he was. It wouldn't be quick; it would be the ugliest, longest, most painful death I could dream up. I hate what he did to you, the cat, and how he's blackened my heart. It's going to take awhile for me to get over his shadow. I am going to have to work real hard on getting rid of the anger and hate real quick. As far as you're concerned"—he put his arm around her and pulled her closer—"as painful as your past is, it's what's made you, and I love you so much more, and I thought I loved you as much as I could possibly love you already.

"Thank you for telling me about your past. Don't ever feel afraid that I'll tell anyone. It's your story to tell, not mine. Don't ever be afraid of me. I don't blame you for any of it, Margo. You have made me the happiest man on earth. Thank you."

Margo was silent for quite a while as her heart was stunned nearly to stopping. She loved this man with all her heart and could understand everything he had told her about his love for her because she was experiencing it also. How did she end up here? Only God could have made that little plan, and she was so thankful to Him.

Life with Margo was meant to be, and Cade thanked God for everything. He couldn't figure out why he had been given such a blessing as Margo and why his life was so blest because he never felt like he had done anything for God, but he wasn't going to tell God he thought He'd made a mistake.

The day the new bookkeeper was to arrive came and went and there was no sight of her and no call. Cade was disappointed, but angry, too. It told him she wasn't dependable and he kicked himself for just jumping into hiring her without doing the usual checks and balances he used with the men. He'd hired Margo quickly and wasn't disappointed, but he was lucky with her.

On New Year's Eve day, he called Everett, one of his CEOs from Chicago. Everett had a huge aircraft plant he ran for Cade. It seemed he always had a herd of young execs climbing the corporate ladder and he would tell Cade if he had one ready for "prime time" so Cade could utilize that executive somewhere in his empire. As it turned out, Cade was happy with the arrangement and looked to Everett as his "management personnel manager."

The only thing he owned that didn't have a CEO or GM and accounting department was the ranch. Having grown up with his Dad doing all the hiring, firing, and his mom doing the accounting, he never really gave it much thought. He was used to it that way so he just didn't think about it like he would a company.

He had spent a great deal of time thinking about making Josh the GM of the ranch. Let Josh handle all the issues and responsibilities and back away from running things on the ranch. It would give him more time and less stress, which he was inclined to want more than not.

So he had made up his mind to let Josh run the ranch and now he was going to ask Everett if he had an accountant that wanted a western atmosphere in Wyoming. He was expecting a long wait on the issue, but by turning over all except payroll and paying the bills to Josh, he have more time to do payroll and paying the bills.

While Margo was shoving the vacuum cleaner around in the common room, Cade shut the door to his office and did some research on his computer. Eventually, he had sent several emails to various Accounting agencies and all of the education centers he could find in the State that had a job board or offered their students placement help.

In Nowhere, Delilah was spending some time with a woman she had shanghaied from town. *Just like a fly in my web!* Delilah thought. *Another opportunity to hurt Cade and that little witch he took away from me.* Delilah, roaming around in town ran into a woman that asked if she could direct her to the Double K Ranch.

"Oh! Of course. You go out here to the main road–you know someone out there? It's a long drive from here."

"Oh! Well, I've got this map and it doesn't look that far from here. But I just got hired as bookkeeper and I'm in the process of moving my stuff."

"Okay. You go out here to the main road–wait, I'm going that way. Why don't I just show you how to get there. It's no problem, just follow me. This is my heap, right here. Your car near?"

"Sure. Just down a few spaces. Thanks. Hey, are you sure I'm not putting you out any?"

"Oh! I'm positive." Delilah jumped in her truck and backed out. *No more questions, moron. Just follow. Okay, think quick, girl. Where can I take her and... Oh! The service road on the ranch. There's that big old ugly Cell Tower down at the end that Cade let the phone company put up. Good spot! I'll kill her there and nobody will see or hear a thing. If this turns out the way I think it will, I'll get more money than Cade ever dreamed of having. Mr. Emperor! Oh! And if they pin it on you, well, won't that be a shame! You're gone, nothing will keep me from going after little Miss Margo then!*

Walter wished his customer a good day as she walked away from his counter and a movement outside caught his eye. It was Delilah talking with a female he'd never seen in town before. *Probably some stranger who asked her directions.* He thought. But when Delilah nearly jumped in her beater truck and left town with that same stranger following in her purple convertible, his thoughts changed. *What's she doing?* Warning bells went off in his head but then Mrs. Stewart was standing there waiting to be checked out and he had to get back to work. The stranger and Delilah forgotten.

The stranger followed Delilah out of town, down the main road towards the Double K Ranch and Delilah was making her plans. When she pulled off the main road down a gravel service road the stranger followed and Delilah smiled to herself.

She followed the winding and rolling road all the way to the end, leaving plenty of room to maneuver her little truck. She got out and walked back to the just stopping car. The stranger rolled the window down and said, "What happened? Did I miss something?"

Enough snow was still laying around, disguising a lot of territory so it was easy to indicate a missed side road with a wave of the hand in a vague direction. "Yes, there's the cutoff to the main house back there," Delilah pointed back down the road and when the woman stuck her head out the window a bit and looked back, Delilah was there to quickly and easily shove the woman's head against the back edge of the door. It only dazed the woman, but it was enough to enable Delilah the opportunity to slam Ms. Stranger's head against the bottom of the window, as hard as she could. She put a lot of her weight behind it and had the woman unconscious. She shoved her over so she was slumped towards the passenger seat instead of out the window. Now she pulled a pair of thin cotton gloves from her pocket, slid them into place and pulled the woman's purse out of the car, rifled through it and removed a considerable amount of cash from it. She threw the purse back into the car where it landed on the passenger seat.

She turned the engine off, leaving the key in the ignition and pulled a laptop from the back seat of the car and put it in her truck. Looking around, seeing no one, she climbed into her truck and drove around the end of the road. As she passed the woman's car, she laughed. She turned back around in the road and drove up behind the car, got out of her truck and went back up to the open car window. Leaning in, she put the gear in neutral, made sure the front wheels were straight ahead, then went back to her truck and maneuvered it forward until it was against the rear bumper of the car. With patience that Delilah never knew she had, she pushed the car forward until it was moving then she pushed faster until the car was pushed right over the end of the road.

The car in front of Delilah disappeared as it tipped over the end of the road into a gully. Knowing the end of the road was there, Delilah had stopped her truck far enough back that she didn't follow the car into the gully. She got out of her truck, walked through some brush and tall grass and little confer trees to the driver's door. Delilah opened the door and looked at the woman, now twisted forward beside the wheel. The car was facing down hill, the front bumper buried into the bottom of the gully. Delilah reached through the wheel and turned the key. The engine started. She managed to get her foot on the brake and pulled the gear down to drive, then pulled her foot out of the car, rolled up the window and slammed the door shut. One baby conifer's head was stuck in the door. Delilah bent over and ripped it out, now it was missing some of its top, but it would grown again.

She had popped the trunk open while she had messed with the gear shift and the key and now she opened the boxes and suitcases in the trunk and took everything of value and threw the rest around. Clothes littered the back of the car and the ground nearby, all too small for Delilah.

She went back to her truck, turned around and drove back to the main road and home, stowing the laptop in a pile of junk in the back room.

She pulled a two-liter of cola from the refrigerator, popped the top and set it on the cluttered coffee table in the living room then grabbed two packages of chocolate cupcakes with creamy stuff inside and sat down. She flipped on the old TV and watched, between flips and irritating "snowstorms" CSI. She loved CSI, CSI Miami, CSI New York, and NCIS. She thought as she dinned on cupcakes and cola. It wasn't long before she was asleep, the TV spluttering streams of shows to no one.

But back at the cell tower the car's exhaust pipe grew hot enough to ignite some pieces of clothing hanging down close enough and with a small amount of time, the entire car and contents was in hot rolling flames. Black, tar-like smoke billowing up into the sky to be dispersed by the cold winter wind.

TEN

Cade's chance on the job postings paid off as far as applications were concerned. He had several by the first full week of January. All of them were people looking for jobs, any job to apply on. Based on other information he gleaned, most of them wouldn't be happy working alone on a ranch in the middle of Wyoming, or anywhere else. Some were married, obviously not reading the job posting, not caring, or hoping he didn't mind them dragging their children and spouse into the job, or maybe filling out paperwork in order to account for collecting unemployment. He did get a couple of calls from the agencies wanting to know more information for sending a temporary-to-hire along for his review, which he wasn't interested in.

He kept up his search, widening the scope of where he posted his job opening.

The weather changed again and it snowed, then thawed just enough to make it all sloppy, then refroze and rained. Ice drops landed on everything exposed and then refroze into a layer of ice, too heavy for trees to endure, causing them to break or fall over. It was incredibly slippery and cattle learned quickly to just stand in one huge herd for whatever warmth they could create between them. Stepping outside the huge congregation of "buddies" was a huge risk of finding your face in the ice. Being a steer and then having to regain your feet, was difficult at best, but there wasn't a lot of help when you couldn't even get a foot to stay underneath you so you could lever yourself back to standing. Several critters were laying on the ground, some still trying to get up while others had given up and just lay where they had landed.

The cell tower five miles inside Double K property took a toll as heavy ice broke a support bolt and one of the arrays bent downwards breaking the connection between another cell tower precisely aligned with it, miles away.

A day later, it thawed good enough again and most of the downed critters managed to regain their feet and the engineers for the cell company made its way to the cell tower with the problem. Near its base, the engineers made a grisly discovery.

Of the two men, one made it well away from the scene to pitch his breakfast without disturbing anything in the area of the car with what appeared to be a badly charred body inside the charred car.

The other engineer backed away, having watched enough CSI episodes to remember to mentally mark his own footsteps and those of his coworker. He pulled his cell phone and called his supervisor who in turned called the state troopers.

Margo received a call from Mrs. Dietrich, the banker's wife from town. She stated she was wondering how Margo was doing. After Margo told her she was fine and happy, the woman asked her if she would be the caterer to a group of banking associates. Apparently, the group's headquarters was in Sheridan, but they traveled to a different town each month for a luncheon. Mrs. Dietrich had reserved the grange hall for the luncheon but needed a caterer.

"You see, dear, I wouldn't hire Delilah to run a dog fight. The woman is totally incapable of doing anything well. She is just too arbitrary. I refuse to deal with her," said Mrs. Dietrich.

"Well, okay, but why do you want me? I don't have a catering business and I've never catered an event before. Why are you asking me?" Margo was astonished at the woman.

"Some of your hands have been talking to a particular banker in town and he told me about it. Apparently you're tops as far as the

Double K hands are concerned. Margo, please help me. I've nowhere else to turn and it's my turn for the luncheon. I can't call it off and I'll lose face if I have to call Rapid City for a caterer."

"Who would know?" Margo asked.

"There are women in the group from Rapid City. Look, Margo. I know this is a strange request, but we've plenty of time to put it together. Get all the I's dotted and the T's crossed."

"I don't know, Mrs. Dietrich. I'd have to hire a crew, get a business license, make all the food. I really think you should find an alternative."

"There really isn't one, dear. Please consider it and call me back."

Margo was considering it. She couldn't get it out of her mind. She planned it over and over again. She called the county to ask about requirements on a business license, then calculated all the expenses, profit, and had filled a composition book with the details. She studied the issue for a week, continuing to do all the normal assigned duties in the house.

Margo went in to clean Cade's bathroom, she found him at his desk going over applications. He had a few he could call for an interview.

Margo did her work and when Cade came down for coffee, she asked if he had some time to spare. He sat down with his coffee and smiled at her. "What's up?"

She told him of the call from Mrs. Dietrich and all the calculations she had done. When she was done, he just looked at her.

"Cade?"

"Yes?"

"What do you think?" she asked, astonished that he seemed to think she had spoken in a foreign language he didn't understand.

"If you want to do it you can. You have a lot to do here, though. Will you have time for it after you get your work done here?"

"Yes. I've worked out a schedule that would work."

"Okay. Have you considered who to hire for this work?"

"Yes."

"Well, then I guess you better get it started."

"Okay, then. Guess I need to go to the county building to get my license going. Will you take me there?"

"Yes. Or you can drive my truck if you feel safe enough." She was shaking her head before he finished. "Okay. I'll drive. Let me know when you want to go."

"Is an hour warning enough time or do you need more?"

"An hour is fine. Anything else?"

"No. I think that just about covers it, from my point of view."

"I do have something I need to ask you."

"What's that?"

"Do you know my truck was keyed last time we went to town?"

"Yes. I heard Mike talking about it. I was surprised."

"You didn't know anything about it?"

"No. Not until I heard Mike talking about it." She wondered why he asked her that. A light in her head came on and her eyes grew huge. "Cade?" she was fighting to stay rational and calm. "Do you think I would do that to your truck? Do you think I would do anything to harm or ruin something of yours? Because if you do, if you can't trust me yet, I–."

"Margo! Stop! I don't think you did it, I don't think you would. I do trust you. I was just asking if you knew about it."

She cooled off as though having a bucket of ice water dumped over her head. "Okay, then." She turned and ran up the stairs.

She was standing in front of her window looking down into the yard and saw Cade walk across the yard towards the bunkhouse. Even from up here she felt her heart skip a beat. She pulled her phone and called Cade. Just before he entered the bunkhouse he stopped and pulled his phone, looked at it and then turned and looked up at her window. He knew where she was. "Hi, Margo! Through being mad at me?"

She wanted to wipe the grin off his face. "No, but can you take me to town tomorrow morning? I figure it will be quicker and easier if its first thing after they open."

"Okay. It's a date." He took a few steps away from the bunkhouse. "When is Mrs. Dietrich's party?"

"Not until April. I have a lot to do between now and then and the license will probably take the longest, since government is involved. Never seen a government anything move very fast."

"Agreed. Anything else?"

"No."

"Okay. Later."

"Cade?"

There was no answer. She watched him shove his phone back in its holster as he went through the bunkhouse door.

Now she was through being mad, or irritated, or whatever she had been feeling. Now she just loved him and needed to finish her work.

The next morning, Cade took Margo to the county building where she applied for her license. He left her at the table in the main office to do the paperwork and went to see an old friend down the hall.

She felt like she went through the paperwork like a whirlwind and wondered if she set a record for processing a caterer.

Margo went out to the truck and found Cade standing near it talking with some man. As soon as he saw her, he nodded to her and held out his hand. She moved to his side and looked at him. He introduced her to Carl Hodges.

Carl held out his hand and she shook it. "Nice to meet you," they both said simultaneously.

Cade and Carl talked a bit more then Carl nodded at Margo and departed. Cade and Margo got in the truck and this time, Margo looked closely at the door before touching it. She saw no marks and got in. "No marks on the door, Cade."

Cade looked at her and raised an eyebrow. "Are we going to get that report every time you get in the truck?"

"If you want it."

"I do not."

"Understood."

"Are you through being mad at me yet or is this going to go on for awhile."

"I'm not mad at you."

"You're sure? You seem to be."

"I don't understand why you were—"

There was a loud bang, the truck shook and Margo looked out her window. Delilah squeezed out of her beater truck, slammed her door shut, looked at Margo and Cade, laughed out a "Hi!" then stopped, opened her door again and slammed it into Cade's truck door. By this time he was out of his truck and rounding the hood. He stood there looking at her door putting dents and scratches in his door. He pulled his phone and grabbed the first person that walked by.

"You see that door making dents and scratches on my door?"

"Yes, Cade. I do. And I see it's Delilah Willglen doing the denting and scratching to your truck door with her truck door."

"What?" Delilah asked as she stood up and looked innocently at Cade and the witness. She turned and looked at his door, slammed hers shut and said, "Oh, My! Wait! Don't you go blaming me for that, Mr. Kincade 'High and Mighty' Knight. I'm not taking the blame for that or the keying to it. Now you leave me alone. I'm tired of your antics directed at me, personally. You've got no call." Delilah was in a rage and she was nearly charging like a bull.

"I didn't say anything about keying the door, Delilah, but I knew it was you because of the slander against Margo."

"I didn't key your truck, Cade. Don't you listen either? I already said I didn't key your truck."

"Then how did you know about it, Delilah?" asked the witness.

"You just mind your own cracklings Mr. Noisy!" she shouted at the witness as she moved closer to him.

Margo sat in the truck feeling helpless and astonished at Delilah. She was lying and going nuts right in the middle of town on a busy street! Delilah had the gall of something bullheaded.

Delilah swung her fist and caught the witness in the chin. He fell back a step putting his hand on his lip and jaw. "Delilah, you sidewinder. I'm calling the police. You need to be controlled again. You're way out of line." The witness was against the wall, still holding his jaw but ready to bolt if Delilah came any closer to him.

While Mr. Witness was yelling at Delilah, she turned and saw Cade dialing his phone. She slapped his phone from his hand and then popped Cade in the ribs. She couldn't reach his jaw or chin. Cade saw it coming and was in the process of moving back so her blow was more glancing than dead on and most of the strength was missing from it.

Margo pulled her phone and called the police. Somebody had to. Since the police were housed in the rear of the county building a couple of deputies ran out the front door of the building and right into the fracas going on in the street.

Delilah was restrained and marched off to the jail in handcuffs. A deputy asked questions of Cade, Mr. Witness, and Margo, taking notes, then calling for backup with a camera. A second deputy came out with a camera and took pictures of Cade's truck door, Delilah's truck door, Cade's broken cell phone laying in the gutter, and Mr. Witness' bruised jaw and cut lip.

Cade picked up his phone, climbed in the truck and sat there for a moment, breathing hard. Margo didn't know if it was because he was angry or hurt. She didn't know if she should ask or just disappear under the seat cover.

Past training made her sit there, looking straight forward, expecting the worst, but hoping for the best. At a time like this, doing nothing could be as detrimental to an angry person as doing something. But she couldn't do anything else except sit stock still and stare out the front window of the truck.

A minute later, Cade gently took her hand. When she turned her head to look at him, he whispered, "I'm sorry, Margo. I'm not angry at you. Please don't be afraid of me. I'm never going to hit you. You have to understand that. I'm not Jerry."

"You are definitely not Jerry," she said letting it stream out of her on the breath she had held in fear. "Did she hurt you?"

"No. She broke my phone and made a mess of that door. But she didn't hurt me. She is certifiably nuts and I'm going to push that she be locked up in a facility designed for the criminally insane."

"Really?" she asked.

Cade didn't answer. He sat up, turned the key in the ignition and looked back and around the truck then backed away from the slot and Delilah's wreck.

When they got back to the ranch, Margo went into the house to get a quick lunch ready for the guys. It had taken longer in town than anticipated and she was feeling bad about the guys having a late lunch.

Henry came in. "Margo. The guys had lunch from the bunkhouse chili pot. Not as good as yours, but we figured something happened in town that made you late. You alright? You look a little pale and Cade's hopping like a hot pepper out there. I haven't seen him this angry in a long time.

"Did you see the door on his truck?" Margo asked.

"Yes. What happened?"

"Delilah happened."

Her phone rang and it was Tinker. "Guess what?"

"What?"

"I graduated today. I'm on crutches and I don't have to use the wheelchair anymore."

"Oh! Tinker! That's wonderful. When do you get to come home?"

"Doctor says I have to stay here for about another week. Depends a great deal on the weather and how fast I learn how to use these things."

"Have you told Cade yet?"

"Yes. I called him before I called you. Sorry, Margo. Just thought I better give him a heads up first. In case there's a problem with me coming home to the ranch."

They talked for awhile, as they usually did, Margo telling Tinker everything new and Tinker telling her funny stories. When she ended the call she had to race awhile to catch up to her schedule but she made it.

A couple of weeks went by in a great hurry. Margo found herself so busy she never had time to stop. On top of all the work she was doing in the house, cooking and cleaning, she now found herself making and testing various dishes, using the hands as test subjects. She never had a bad vote on any dish she made. She always used ingredients she had on hand and didn't waste money buying fancy stuff she'd use once or twice, at best.

Finally, Carl Hodges arrived and did his inspection toward the first of February and as usual, Margo's kitchen was spotless. She had just pulled a huge pan of cookies and Carl was treated to several various kinds, chocolate chip with walnuts, peanut butter, almond rocco squares, and walnut balls, along with his coffee and a long discussion with Cade.

When he left, Margo waved with a shoulder and "bye" over it while she stuffed another huge pan of cookies into the oven. Cade came up with a piece of paper held so she could read it. It was her facility license.

She nearly slammed the oven door closed in her haste to throw her arms around Cade and hug him. When she let go he had her personal license in his hand and he watched her eyes light up with joy. She stuffed it in her pocket. "I want to hang onto it for awhile."

"Okay, but we need to talk. Come on, sit down and breath for awhile. If you need help to do something, I'll get a couple hands in here, so take a few minutes.

She sat and relaxed with a can of cola while he sipped hot coffee. "Margo, I've been keeping an eye on you. I was afraid you might overload yourself with this, and that's exactly what you've done." He put his hand up, palm out to stop her before she could splutter anything. "Hold on. Let me finish here." He looked at her and she settled down and nodded. "I think it would be extremely helpful to all of us if we hired someone to help you. A cook/housekeeper person. One with responsibilities that you hand out and one that's answerable to you, which would make you a supervisor. What do you think?"

"Oh! Cade! That would be great! It sure would take a pile of stuff off my shoulders. But what happens if the catering business doesn't go anywhere? There are no guarantees and we're so far out in the hills. This isn't the city where there are lots of people doing things that need to be catered and–."

"Hold it Margo!" He wiped his brow. "You get going like a huge tidal wave and I can't run fast enough. Okay." He took a breath and took her hand. "We'll still need a helper for you because I'm hiring a couple extra hands and eventually a bookkeeper for the ranch. We just need to hire another cook to make it all work well. So even if the catering business doesn't go anywhere, we've got someone here to keep it all working."

"Okay! That's great. I'm sorry if I swept you down river. I do get going sometimes."

He raised an eyebrow and then smiled. "I think I love you, Margo."

"Hope so. Love you back," she quipped as she stood and raced off to her room up the stairs.

Cade continued sitting at the table, sipping coffee, feeling like he'd just been through a dust storm after the tidal wave.

About that time, Josh walked in, poured himself a cup of coffee and sat down next to Cade. "What's up?" he asked.

"Is it wet in here, or dusty?"

Josh looked around didn't see any puddles of water or drips, no dust bunnies. "No. Did Margo miss something?"

"No, but I feel like I've been swamped by a tidal wave and then pummeled by a dust storm. That girl is flying. What's Henry doing? Can he come in and work the kitchen? Margo's making cookies." He was grinning and shaking his head at it.

Josh grinned, took out his phone and called Henry, and then drank some coffee. It wasn't long and they were into one discussion after another, as Henry arrived and tended to the cookies.

Now that she had her licenses, she could start calling people. First she called Mrs. Dietrich. "I just got my license so I can do your party. Let's get together as soon as possible so we can decide what you'll want. How many people should I be making this for? All the other things we need to nail down."

Mrs. Dietrich was ecstatic. She already had the numbers and while they may be a few people short, they couldn't be over because it was members only. She wanted something elegant but chicken, some kind of chicken roll or anything that looked expensive but was inexpensive. "Besides, we got several members with health problems and they just about live on chicken," she said. They got into details of profit for the caterer and the club so plate price was an issue, too.

When Margo was done with Mrs. Dietrich she called Missy, her friend in Beulah, a small town barely inside the Wyoming border. Missy was living with a sister as Missy had no one else, nowhere else to live, and without a job, she couldn't afford to live on her own. Missy took care of her sister's house and made all the meals and took care of the kids before and after school while her sister worked and supported all of them. Missy was always careful to keep her expenses to the smallest amount possible.

When Missy and Margo met at the Halloween party, they hit it off real quick and then vowed to keep in touch with each other. As soon as Margo got a phone she plugged Missy's number into it and called her about once a week.

"Hey, Missy. Margo. How's it going?"

They talked for awhile then Margo asked Missy if she was working other than for her sister. She knew the answer would be no as Beulah is one of the smallest towns at approximately 35 to 40 people, depending on who you ask.

"There's a job opening here, if you're interested."

"Okay, tell me about it."

"Missy, I'm offering you a job with me, at the ranch, room and board, insurance, benefits; it's great! Do you want it?"

"Do you think I'm stupid? Of course I want it. When do I start?"

"When can you get here?"

"Tell me where and I'm there."

Margo gave the phone to Cade who told Missy how to get to the ranch from Nowhere. He closed the phone and handed it back to Margo. "She'll be here tomorrow afternoon. If I let her live up there with you, will I get any sleep or should we separate the tribes?"

ELEVEN

W e better separate the tribes."
      "Okay. Tinker will be here on Friday afternoon. I'm putting him in the room behind the kitchen. Do not kill yourself or make yourself sick working to polish every nail head in that room. Understood?"

"Yes, sir. Thanks, Cade."

Cade turned back to his desk and the work on it.

Margo looked at her watch and made tracks to the kitchen. She had more to do, but riding on a high of adrenalin helped a lot.

The next day was a whirlwind day for Margo. She was so happy. Missy was going to be at the ranch in the afternoon. She had quickly cleaned a room across the hall from hers and was planning on having Missy clean the new "Rehab" room for Tinker. She hoped Missy got to the ranch earlier than promised, but had to take whatever she got.

Finally, the afternoon hit and Margo felt drained. She sat down wondering what to do. She had flown through all her work and was exhausted. "Why don't you go take a nap. I'll tell you when she gets here," Cade said.

"I'm tired, but I don't think I can sleep. Or I will sleep, like a dead person and you won't be able to wake me."

"Been there, done that, don't want a revisit. But go rest. You need it."

"Okay. Maybe a walk outside will help. I haven't seen Stormy today, I've been so busy."

"Sounds like a good idea. Guess I'll go talk to Tornado, if he's not too busy."

"Cade, I'm sorry. I have been very busy, as have you. We've gone in different directions with our work and it feels like we're passing ships in the night. It doesn't mean one of us can't change directions."

"I wasn't intent on throwing barbs at you. It just came out the way. Let's go see the horses then can we spend about a half hour tonight talking about something that's on my mind?"

"Sure."

While they were talking to their horses a car drove into the yard and a petite woman with short curly hair got out. She was wearing western boots, jeans, a plaid long sleeve shirt, open in front to reveal a white tee underneath.

Margo and Cade went to the barn door to see who had arrived and Margo ran out to greet Missy. There was the usual female war hoops—squealing and laughing—and then it settled down to racing around introducing everyone, showing off everything and then dragging a car load of stuff to the assigned room and putting it all away.

Cade figured his time with Margo was going to be put off and set his heart and mind to living with it. As it turned out, he was right. The two girls had locked themselves in Margo's room after dinner and the only thing he knew about them was an occasional hoot of laughter. He grinned about it, but missed Margo.

In Margo's room, Missy and Margo talked about everything the other had done since last seeing each other. Their weekly phone calls to each other had been forgotten as they rattled their tales to each other. Eventually, Missy brought up Delilah's name and it was hard for Margo to not want to hear some juicy little scrap of story as to her demise. The staff was without jobs now, but there just wasn't anything in town to work at except McDonald's, and they weren't hiring.

Margo felt glad for the way things had worked out in Delilah's case. She knew she shouldn't gloat, but she couldn't help it. She felt bad for the servers, but she was planning on hiring any of them that wanted to work for her and she knew she and Missy could get a pretty good business going with Mrs. Dietrich's help and the Banker's Auxiliary. Cade had really saved her.

When Margo stated that Cade was looking for a couple wranglers and a bookkeeper and moaned that it wouldn't help the servers from Delilah's catering business, Missy nearly leaped off the bed in joy. "Margo, Lois Metz is…was a bookkeeper. She used to work at the bakery in the office. Don't you remember her?"

Margo slowly shook her head trying to remember. There was no recognition of anything from the bakery. "Does she have kids, husband?"

"No kids. Her husband is looking for work, he's a Jack-of-all-trades, but he's growing and selling vegetables from his yard to tide them between odd jobs he gets."

"Missy. I'm…we're on a mission. Come on." She stood and grabbed Missy's hand.

They rushed down the stairs and as she let go of Missy's hand, she knocked on Cade's door. Cade opened it and stood there looking at two shiny faces. "Okay, I don't mind a bit of thunder from upstairs, or the occasional hoot, but I refuse to be invaded by two angels gone amuck."

Missy laughed and Margo shook her head. "Cade, Missy just told me Lois Metz is a bookkeeper. She's out of work since the bakery closed down, where she used to keep the books. She lives in Nowhere and her husband is a Jack-of-all-trades and is growing vegetables to help tide them over between his odd jobs. Cade, they could have a room upstairs and she could do the books for you while her husband became a wrangler and I suddenly realize I'm telling you what to do. I apologize. I got a little excited."

"Something you've become famous for. Missy, while this little tornado spins off over the horizon calling…Lois Metz, was it? How about you and I go get some cookies and coffee while we discuss what your life is going to be like here." He took Missy's hand and looped it under then over his arm and walked her to the stairs where he preceded her down. She knew he was teasing, though she didn't know how. But in the kitchen over cookies and coffee, Cade explained about Margo's tenacity and her penchant for rolling over him, and others, like a tidal wave then coming back like a tornado, sucking up the water and leaving dust in her wake.

Missy looked at him and laughed. "I guess that's why I run the vacuum from now on."

The next night, Margo and Cade sat on the sofa in front of the fireplace in his room. The pinewood walls lightly glinting in the firelight. The room was chilly but cozy and he had brought up a tray of cookies and coffee for their dessert. Cade threw a light blanket over Margo's shoulders and pulled her close, keeping his arm around her to add warmth.

"Okay?" he asked.

"Okay. What's up?"

"I wanted to tell you that I turned the ranch responsibilities over to Josh. I just don't need to keep the stress any more. I have other things I want to do, things I've wanted to do for a long time but haven't had the time.

"I talked to Lois Metz and her husband on the phone today. They are both coming on to the payroll. He's going to be a wrangler, knows welding, carpentry, mechanics and heavy equipment operations, plus several other things. I enjoy having good Jack-of-all-trades and her work as a bookkeeper is long in history and I think she'll enjoy working here. You need to fix up one of those suites upstairs for them. They'll be here next week. They are having a garage sale to get rid of most of their stuff and the house is up for sale. They own it, but they're going to leave it empty and hope it sells sometime soon.

"Back to my work around here. "I'll help in the work around the ranch when I'm needed, but hiring a couple more hands and with Missy coming on you'll be doing more with your catering business. But what I actually want to talk to you about has nothing to do with all that."

"Okay. What's up?"

"Do you know how much I love you?" He said it like he was just changing the subject from something that was going to be hard to talk about. She wondered what was going on.

Looking at his eyes, she found them dark and–mysterious? "Cade. You really do love me, don't you?"

"Immensely."

"Even with all my baggage? That's just crazy."

"Is it?"

"Oh, Cade. I'm too beat up to love. Don't waste your time and heart on me."

"It's too late, Margo. I already love you. I want to be your husband, friend, lover, and father of your children. Will you marry me?"

She opened her mouth and closed it tight, starred into the flames for a few moments then turned her head and looked into his eyes and saw only love looking back at her. Pure love. She felt the love emanating from his arms and instinctively knew that she would be safe with Cade. She would not see the monster that Jerry was hiding at the beginning, unleashed and uncontrolled after the quick wedding. Cade would not use her for a whipping post. Cade would love her, cherish her, protect her from everything. "Cade," she whispered.

He kissed her lightly. "Do me a favor?"

"What?" Her voice was still a whisper, having run down her throat, afraid to come out.

"Think about it for awhile. Consider it. I'm not Jerry. You're happy and safe here and you always will be. I want to spend the rest of my life here with you being my wife, friend, mate, and partner."

"Cade?" Her voice had almost made it out of hiding.

"Yes?"

"I love you. I do feel safe here. The safest I've ever felt, anywhere, I think. I love this ranch and if you're sure you want me, I'll marry you."

He didn't say anything. He didn't move and she wondered if she had said something that made him change his mind. Then, he kissed her passionately. "I love you. Thank you," he whispered.

She felt him shiver and asked if he was alright. He was, but Kellie's memory flooded his mind and he was beating it back furiously.

She was excited and, strangely, afraid. Finally, she had to leave because she needed sleep and spending any more time with him at that moment would mean more than she was willing to accept. She kissed him and stood up, pulling the blanket from her shoulders. He turned her into his arms and whispered, "I am loath to let you go."

"If I stay we'll get to know each other romantically and I'm not ready for that yet. Please, Cade. Understand. I'm not running from you. I have to get some sleep as my job requires and early rise and I am really tired. I love you, but let me go."

"One last kiss and you're free." He whispered it against her cheek. She put her arms around his neck and he pulled her up until she was on her toes. When he set her down, she was in the hallway and he had kissed her clear across his room. He let her go and watched her climb the stairs.

The days wore on and Margo and Missy were pretty inseparable. Cade was busy with his own work on the ranch and sometimes they didn't even see each other between breakfast and dinner. Those days, Margo missed him painfully.

Missy loved cleaning and was great at it. She seemed to consider the entire room and would start at the top, working her way down, washing windows and mirrors in each room as she cleaned.

Margo let her do all the housecleaning. It left her time to do the meal planning and set them up for efficiency and better timing. And as time went on Margo and Missy found they were very compatible in a great many things around the house. Margo didn't mind the monthly shopping trips. They were long, but interesting. Missy stayed home and made the meals for the hands and Josh assigned a couple hands to help in the kitchen.

One thing they found they both really liked to do was baking. Missy loved making bread. Any kind of bread you wanted, she could make it, from Apple to Sunflower Seed to Zucchini. She also enjoyed baking cookies, the more variety, the better and she even had a couple of favorites that became one.

Margo loved baking cakes and she could make spectacular cakes. With no training she was a natural at making elegant to funky cakes. Missy thought she should enter some cake decorating contest, but Margo just wanted to have fun, not worry about having to meet somebody's expectations on it.

Lois and Kirk Metz arrived and moved in to their suite upstairs one day then started work in their specific areas the next day. Cade had turned a smaller room on his floor into an office for Lois. Since Cade wanted everything on the computer, there wasn't a file cabinet. Everything was scanned and put on flash drives, and filed in card file drawers. Lois was grand at it. Hard copy documents were shredded and burned with other paper trash.

Kirk Metz went to work under Josh. Josh had lots of projects that needed Kirk's handiwork and his positive attitude. Cade was happy with the reports he got from Josh on Kirk and he was happy with Lois.

Tinker came home a couple of days after Lois and Kirk moved in. He met them and Missy, almost immediately as he arrived close to lunch. Everyone was so happy to see him Margo had to push her way into his room to give him a hug and drag him out for lunch. The others followed and had their own lunch. It was so good to have Tinker home.

Mrs. Dietrich's party was a success and she gave all the credit to Margo. Margo had worked constantly on it, and Missy was right beside her. The day before the party, Shirley Thompson came to the Double K to help with the last minute preparations; Margo was so pleased. Shirley would have a place in her heart, if not her company, forever.

As it turned out, Margo, Missy, Shirley, Chuck, and Paul, from the ranch were able to do the party to perfection without problem. The Grange actually had some decent dishes, flatware, and linens and it was easy to get it all put together. Afterwards, they tore down the entire event. First Margo organized it into levels. Collecting dishes, flatware, glasses and cups and saucers, then the linens, then the tables were flattened and put away. The guys took care of the main floor, flattening the tables and rolling them away, then sweeping the floors. Mrs. Dietrich took the linens to launder and the three girls stayed in the kitchen, sorting and washing dishes.

When they were finished, the garbage had been bagged and put out where it was ready for pickup and the grange building was spotless and after checking all the windows and doors, the last light was switched off, the door was closed and locked and Margo took the key to the bank down the street.

Shirley had left the grange in her own car and the two hands were riding in the back of Cade's truck while Missy and Margo were in the cab. Margo got out of the truck and walked up to the deposit box, dropped the key in and turned around to go back to the truck and Delilah was so close, Margo bumped into her. She leaped back, and slammed against the wall. A yelp escaped her throat and the two hands leaped from the truck to her rescue.

Chuck took Margo's hand while Paul pulled his phone and dialed 911. Delilah loudly laughed, with the sound of a maniacal witch and cold shivers ran down Margo's back. Missy was in the cab of the truck, staying right where she was told to stay by the hands that had run to Margo's rescue.

Margo climbed in the truck and Chuck asked her if she wanted him to drive. She shook her head and managed to croak out, "No, thanks."

When the two men were in the back of the truck, Chuck tapped on the fender and Margo backed out of the bank parking area and drove back down the street to the grange, then turned right and drove down the road to the ranch.

Missy and Margo were so scared they couldn't talk. Margo couldn't figure out how she drove because her hands were so cold and numb. Finally, she stopped in the middle of the road and started crying.

Chuck moved into the cab with Margo, Missy moved out to the back with Steve and Chuck drove the rest of the way.

When the truck stopped in front of the kitchen door, Margo got out and Cade came out, surprised to find her getting out of the passenger side, Chuck driving.

"Everything okay?" he asked.

"Yes. Delilah scared her, but she's alright," Chuck reported as he and Steve carted a load of pans into the house. Cade had Margo wrapped in his arms but when he saw Missy climbing out of the back of the truck, he let go of Margo and rushed to assist Missy. It was a long drop from the back bumper to the ground for Missy.

"Thanks, Cade. Could you reach in there and get me that canvas bag." Cade did as she asked and handed it to Missy, "You alright?"

"I'm fine. Margo is the one Delilah scarred," she said quietly. Cade wrapped his arm around Margo and pulled her into the house.

The flurry of activity ended, Margo insisting on helping, Cade standing by with two mugs of coffee, one very white and sweet, and as Missy went to visit with Tinker, Chuck and Paul left the house to drive the truck to the parking shed and then go to the bunkhouse, which by now, was very quiet and mostly dark. A dim light remained on in the bunkhouse and Josh heard Cade's truck go past on the way to the parking shed. He got out of bed, pulled on his jeans, and stepped outside. He met Chuck and Steve there and told them they could start work late, if needed, and thanked them for helping Margo and Missy.

Steve stepped inside and shut the door, Chuck and Josh remained on the porch. Chuck explained to Josh what had happened in town. "That Delilah. She's got no brains, plenty of stupidity and hate. She'd scare a grizzly to death."

"Margo okay?"

"Yes. But I know I wished I had my .45 with me."

"Probably best you didn't. Good job. It's late." Josh turned and opened the door and Chuck walked through the open doorway. Josh followed and went back to his room, leaving Chuck to find his bed.

One hand that Missy really liked was Tinker. He had been injured and had spent a great deal of time in the hospital and a rehab facility in Rapid City. Now he was spending his time in the bedroom suite behind the kitchen. Missy would empty the garbage from his room daily and take him cookies and coffee sometimes. But she saw him every day and he was fun to be around. Tinker always had a animal joke or funny story.

Missy was very petite, in every way but her heart, which was a huge and full of compassion. She even had compassion for Delilah Willglen. "Poor girl got raped when she was eight by her filthy father."

"Missy, where did you hear that from, Delilah?" Margo asked with disbelief.

"No! My mom used to work for family services. Delilah's family was in the system. Always had been. Delilah's mom was in the system, and so was her dad, even before they got married. When they got married, the system threw a party because now, instead of tracking two files, they only had to track one. That was the attitude then. I don't know what it is now, cause my mom is gone. Anyway, my mom used to tell me to be nice to Delilah. It wasn't her fault she was lazy. Her parents taught her that. It wasn't her fault she was sick in the head, her parents made her that way by bouncing her off the walls. Delilah was always covered with bruises and abrasions.

"Then when she was eight, her mom died. Apparently death by overeating. But my mom said it was because they were poor. I didn't understand it then, I do now. Did you know the worst stuff you can eat is processed foods? They're the cheapest thing on the market. I think they should outlaw processed foods."

Missy was silent while she was busy with something, then she started in again. "Margo, her daddy raped her when she was eight. Apparently, more than once before he was caught and she was safe from him. But she was still so young. She was afraid to be left without him and wouldn't talk to the authorities. She'd have been better if she'd been killed by that creep. How can a parent rape their child? It's disgusting! It's terrible! It's just plain wrong! What's wrong with people?"

Margo watched Missy go off on a verbal tirade over it and finally, when Missy collapsed on a bench in the dining room, Margo went to her and just let her cry. She sat nearby feeling useless.

Tinker hobbled out of his room on his crutches and saw Margo holding Missy. His eyebrow shot up and his eyes turned soft. "Hey, cowgirl. What's wrong?

Margo let go of Missy. "Nothing, Tinker. I just got a little over passionate about something. I'm okay," Missy said, wiping tears from her face with the back of her hand.

"You sure?"

"I'm positive. Thanks. Hey! You want some coffee?"

"That's what I came out here for. Coffee and I got a huge hankering for some cookies." He laughed silently and Missy got up to go get him coffee while Margo pulled cookies from a can and put them on a plate.

Tinker was tall and thin, and had as much compassion for Missy as Missy had for everything. Tinker didn't think there was anything Missy could do wrong.

When Missy had his mug of coffee ready, she turned to Tinker. "You want it here or in your room?"

"How about in my room? I got a chair in there, real comfy-like, with a twin right next to it." The smile on his face was pure joy, and Missy took the plate of cookies Margo handed her and lead the way to the Tinker's room. When they were out of sight, Margo silently whooped for Missy and Tinker, then ran up the stairs.

On July first, Cade asked Margo if she would marry him in December. When she agreed she was so excited she could only shake her head. Cade just grinned and scooped her into his arms and carried her upstairs. He didn't care what he was causing her to leave behind.

Margo was emphatic about no romantic episodes before they were legally married and Cade honored her wishes, but not without an occasional attempt to break her resolve. He failed each time. He loved her more.

The catering business had only a few parties but was basically out of business. She had October 31st booked for Mrs. Dietrich's Halloween Party and Cade was bemoaning that one. Now he'd have to go!

Cade came to Margo and asked her if she would like to learn more about the ranching business. As it turned out, he had a bunch of cattle needing to be branded. Everyone on the ranch was going to go out to the branding site and work on the various teams.

"Wait, Cade. You make it sound like some kind of huge game or something. Could you explain it a bit before you get me into it?

TWELVE

After hearing about the branding camp and how the cattle were quickly checked for injuries, signs of disease, branded, inoculated, tagged, and recorded, he explained that he wanted her and Missy out there making meals for the men. They wouldn't have time to make it all the way back to the main house every time they got hungry and tired. They were going to spend an entire week out at the camp. He wanted her to talk to Henry about cooking at the camp. "He can tell you what equipment we'll be taking, all kinds of things. He's done this for years so he's pretty good at it."

Margo calculated she would have three weeks to get ready for the branding camp and her mind raced with meal planning and logistics and she hadn't even spoken with Henry yet.

Tinker came out of his room, "Coffee break," he announced with a grin. The two girls laughed and while Tinker found a place to sit, Margo served him coffee and Missy brought fresh cookies. Tinker was almost to not having to use the crutches, but since he hadn't been cleared by doctor or physical therapist to abandon the crutches, he still used them.

Tinker was going to the doctor the next day and Josh had already assigned Chuck to drive him to Rapid City leaving after breakfast. Tinker had obtained an appointment for just before noon.

That night, Cade surprised Margo by asking her to marry him sooner than originally planned. She wanted to know how soon and he said, "within the month. We can get the license in a couple of hours, I know. I don't want to wait until Christmas. I want to make you my wife now."

Margo paced the room for a few minutes while she thought of all kinds of things related to getting married now instead of later. She started firing questions; he had answers for all of them.

"Okay. But what about all the things, like flowers, cake, dress, tux?"

"There's a shop in Cheyenne that I'll take you to tomorrow. I'm pretty sure you'll find something you like and I know I'll find the tux I want. It's a little western, but if you don't like it there's always 'Traditional Weddings' down the street."

"Tomorrow? I think Missy and I have a date with Henry tomorrow."

"It's okay. Henry will let you go."

"Cade, number nine?" she asked timidly.

"Not a chance. We'll get married before we leave for branding camp. Once done with that, I'm taking you on a cruise around the Caribbean.

"You gave me all of Kellie's clothes? What about the outfit you had for the wedding? I'm only asking to save time and money."

"Kellie's dress is upstairs. If you want it, you can have it, but I got rid of my stuff. So I have to go anyway. Please, Margo, find something different."

"It's alright, Cade. I'll find something different." She put her arms around his neck and he held her tight. "I can't believe I'm doing this so fast," she whispered.

Cade rushed Margo to Cheyenne along with Henry, Josh and Missy.

In Cheyenne, Cade tried on the tux he knew he wanted to wear and Margo thought it made him look too dudish. "Dudish?" he asked. He looked in the mirror again and decided she was probably right. She saw something she liked better and asked if he would try it on.

When he came out he was laughing. "Margo, this is Spanish Don's attire. I'm not wearing the sombrero."

"No. But I like that suit on you." It was black with silver embroidery and silver conchs running down the side of the pants. He looked good in it so he set it aside. Then he saw a white lace dress he wanted Margo to try on.

She did as he asked and came out of the dressing room looking like the queen he hoped he'd see. It was a long white dress, no ruffles, but plain and simple. It was satin covered in white lace. The bodice had little pearls and crystals all over it and the lower they went, the fewer they became. The store owner was delighted with how it looked on Margo. He wanted her to try a particular veil and, after placing on her head, Cade didn't like it. But he did like the crown in the display case. It was very petite, stood straight up in the front and then as it moved around the sides, it tilted outward until, in the back, it was almost flattened. It was covered in diamonds, not crystals or zircons. When he asked for that one, the store owner pulled it form the case, took the veil off the original headpiece and attached it to the crown, then placed it on Margo's head.

"Perfect," Cade said. Margo studied herself in the mirror. The dress had a long train and the veil, all white lace, streamed down her back and along the train until it ended just beyond the train. The top of the dress stopped just above her breasts, white lace going over one shoulder, the other bare. She liked it, tried to picture it with flowers in her hand.

"I like it."

Margo looked around for Josh and Missy. Josh had picked out attire much like Cade's only without the silver work.

Missy was chewing her lip over the dress she found in powder blue. Margo looked at it, asked her to try it on and while Missy was in the changing room, Margo talked to Cade about Missy's financial difficulties.

"Don't worry Margo. I'll handle it." He turned to the store owner, "we'll take that, just like it is, and the Don's tux."

While Cade dealt with the store owner, Margo was shown how the back tied up underneath into a bustle, making the train literally disappear. Then she removed the crown and veil, showed Margo how to remove the veil from the crown for the reception.

Margo loved the dress Missy had found and Cade quietly told Missy that he wanted to buy it for her because of the wedding. "It's an expense you wouldn't have if we weren't getting married." Missy relented and was very happy about it as she didn't have the money.

They found Henry at "Traditional Weddings". He wanted a traditional tux and had found a beautiful one for himself. When they found him, he had just come out of the changing room attired in his choice of tuxes.

They rushed back to the ranch, via helicopter and Margo caught up with work with Missy and Henry's help.

"Where are we in the branding camp thing?"

Henry laughed and shook his head. "Such a whirlwind." With a moment's thought, he was back into the swing of it.

"Now remember ladies, to ensure you bring all your gear for riding. You'll need your boots, both the western and the "muck-outs", your jackets, sweatshirts, gloves, hats, personal items and something to keep you entertained during the slow spots, which there are going to be, believe it or not."

They spent several days meal planning from first day to last day of Branding camp and managed to include a wedding in the middle of it. After that, Missy wanted to know if Margo and Cade were going on a honeymoon. While they worked on getting their gear ready, double checking and more, Margo explained that Cade was taking her to Mexico on a cruise ship. Two nights before they were scheduled to leave for the branding camp, Cade and Margo spent the evening in front of the fireplace talking about the branding camp and the wedding.

Missy was downstairs in Tinker's room. It wasn't as cozy as Cade's room, as it had no fireplace, but it had a huge couch and it was right next to the kitchen and the coffee bar so they had quick access to anything they wanted.

The two people had become great friends and Missy had missed Tinker the day he went to the doctor. He and Chuck had left shortly after breakfast and were apparently early for their appointment. The doctor saw Tinker early and Tinker graduated from the crutches to limited mobility. He could not ride a horse and no heavy equipment driving. He still needed to exercise the leg, but not abuse it. Tissues were still learning how to cling to the stainless steel bones and recovering from injuries. He was forced to sit anytime his leg started to ache and he was still using pain meds, even though they were only occasional and were extremely weak strength. He was advised that cold or hot weather would probably affect his leg so to be mindful of that and keep it warm on cold days and cool on hot days.

Tinker grumbled about it a bit, but on the whole, just accepted it and moved on. He tried to have an attitude of, 'grumbling and complaining won't change it', but once in awhile, especially when he was tired, a grumble would escape.

Missy didn't mind. She felt it showed her more of his personality and made their friendship stronger.

Missy told Tinker her fears and apprehensions about going on the trail. Tinker was able to talk her out of most of her fears, which were mostly bugs and the fact that she knew nothing about camping, riding, roping, bulldogging, or branding. She thought it would hurt the animal and no amount of persuasion was going to change her mind about that because they wouldn't cry if it didn't hurt.

Tinker took each one of her fears and gently talked about it. The bugs were no different out at the branding camp than they were right here at the main house and she could use all the bug spray she wanted as no one would mind.

"I thought you knew how to ride. Didn't Cade, Josh, or Margo ask you about it?" he asked.

"Well, I think Margo asked, I don't remember, but it was right in the middle of us getting me settled in and I don't think we really addressed it much and it isn't her fault anyway. I never learned, I never had time, and I think I'm too old to learn now," she replied with a little heat.

"Old girl, hum!" he answered waiting for her to snap at him.

"I'm not that old. Just not sure it's time to climb on some animal and learn."

"Okay, what about me. I have to eventually learn all over again, not how to make a horse go forward and backward or even sideways, which is actually the easy part, but I have to learn how to get muscles to do new things. It's not something I look forward to in that sense, but I'd like to get back on a horse and ride again. I feel bad about not being able to ride Rusty. Well, Rusty's gone now, so there's no point feeling bad about not riding him."

"Rusty your horse?"

"Yes. Red roan. He just looks … looked rusty standing there."

"Anyway, you get Margo to let you have some free time in the afternoons or mornings and I'll teach you how to ride on old Candy. She's a sugar, very old, but she'll let you ride her without any trouble. She's used to people putting on and taking off her bridle and saddle and climbing on and off all day long. You can learn at your speed. I'll show you something and then sit there and wait for your questions, give you some tips and then you can show off for Margo and be good to go. Can't hurt to know, can't hurt to ask."

"Okay. I'll ask Margo and I'll go to camp. Not sure I had a choice anyway."

"Well, you don't want to stay here all by yourself. Come on, Cowgirl, you'll have fun."

That night put Tinker permanently into Missy's heart and mind. She absolutely loved him and she went to bed wondering if Tinker could love her. Time would tell.

The time flew and it was the day of the wedding and Margo didn't care if she was ready or not, but she thought she was as ready as she could get. The decorations and flowers had been left for Missy, Tinker, Lois, and Cade and she was going to like them no matter what.

She made her own cake and had kept it simple because Cade had asked her to keep it simple. He knew she would work herself sick if he didn't request it so he made sure he asked her to keep it simple nearly every day. He actually hoped she would keep all of the wedding plans simple but when he found out Margo had released all but the cake to others, he relaxed immensely.

Before going down the stairs from his room, Cade went up the stairs. Missy opened the door to his knock, looked at Margo then left the room so Cade and Margo could have privacy.

Cade stepped into the room, leaving the door open. He looked at Margo. "You're beautiful. You're absolutely … beautiful." He leaned in and kissed her. "I have something for you. I'd like you to wear it, if it's appropriate."

"What is it?" She thought it was some garter, which she already had on, but she'd trade if it meant something to him.

"Close your eyes; turn around." He saw the mirror behind her. He was close and her scent was subtle and perfect for the day.

She did as he asked, making sure she didn't trip on the train and when she stood tall and quiet he placed a necklace on her and clasped it behind, then managed to get earrings in her ears without fumbling and hurting, then he stood behind her, put his hands on her arms and said, "Okay, open your eyes."

She did as he asked again and saw a necklace around her neck. It had three strands of aquamarines, each longer than the one above, and a marquise shaped aquamarine forming a pendent in the middle. The three strands looped through the huge bale, covered with more aquamarines, with four diamonds above and four diamonds below the marquise, as though to hold it in place. Aquamarine and diamond earrings dangled from her ears.

She turned back, retracing her previous steps, mindful of her long train and veil. "It's beautiful. I've never had anything so beautiful. Thank you." She stood on her toes, put her hands on his shoulders and pulled him down for a kiss.

A voice from the hallway came through the open door. "Sorry for the interruption, but it's time."

Cade was first down the stairs, Josh being Best Man also in a black Spanish Don's "tux", and then Missy came down the stairs in pink, she was the announcement that the bride was coming next. She had pink flowers in her short curly brown hair and looked to Tinker like a pixie. His heart skipped a beat and he knew he loved her.

When Margo came down the stairs after Missy, Henry was at the bottom to take her hand and lead her to Cade. First he gave her the bride's bouquet of one pink Stargazer Lily surrounded by white carnations and spider plants. He put Margo's hand in Cade's then turned and walked back down the aisle. They were married by the town Justice with the Dietrich's in the front row.

After they were married, they kissed and went downstairs to a spectacular cake Margo had made. Plenty of pictures of the cake, the flowers, the bride, the couple, the Maid of Honor, the Best Man, and the rings were taken by Mike.

Missy told Margo about the evenings she had with Tinker. Margo knew the day was coming real soon for Tinker to transfer back out to the bunkhouse and she really hated for it to come for herself, but she was more worried about Missy after listening to Missy talk about her evenings with Tinker. She felt in her heart that there might be love between them and she was afraid it might end with Tinker in the bunkhouse while Missy lived in the "big house". After Missy wound down, Margo looked at her, put her hand on Missy's shoulder to get her to stop her work and pay attention.

"Missy, I'm not going to force you to go out there if you don't want to. And I don't expect you to be a robot. I'll talk to Cade about it. If we can leave you here, I'll do that. I think you'll be bored to tears, but we've always got the 'com-links,' and it's not like we wouldn't be in touch."

"Margo, don't get Mr. Cade upset about it. If he wants all of us out there, he'll get all of us out there. I'm not going to make waves. Besides, Tinker has pretty much talked me out of my fears."

Margo laughed. "You called him Mr. Cade. I only call him that when I'm pouting."

"How can you pout at him? He's so perfect. He makes you happy!" Missy stated.

"He can make me mad, too. He's not perfect. He's a guy, and guys just aren't perfect."

"Oh, I hear that!" Missy laughed again. "Mr. Cade is just so easy going. It's hard to imagine him making you mad. It's hard to imagine him making anyone mad. That's why he just seems like Mr. Perfect to me."

"If he hears you talking like that, he'll become a monster!" Margo hissed with a smile.

Missy laughed and Cade came down the stairs. "Too late! Thank you, Missy." He grinned at their astonished faces.

"Cade, how do you do that?" Margo asked, embarrassed.

Missy looked at Cade and apologized.

"Thank you, Missy, but there's nothing to apologize for," he said as he shrugged into his coat. As he pulled on his gloves he said to Margo, "My queen, I love you." He opened the door and left, a grin across his face.

"Just like a man," Missy whispered after he left. Missy went upstairs to do some housework, laughing at the antics of her boss and her man.

In a small Wyoming town, in an old trailer house at the end of one of the few back streets, one crash led to another until everything inside the trailer was broken and littered the floor. At one point, had anyone been near enough to hear the commotion, the crescendo of cussing, abusive and foul language was insane. But since it was a place that demanded loneliness with its shabby exterior, sagging roofline, distant location, and overgrown yard, it went totally unheard and unnoticed.

THIRTEEN

L ater that same day in Nowhere, Wyoming, a trailer house
went up in flames and smoke. By the time the fire department
arrived, it was burned to the ground. They finished putting
out what little flame was still eating away at the mess and looked
around for bodies. Finding none, they finished with the mop up. The
chief would go to the public records department tomorrow and find
out who the owner was and notify them of the fire during the previous day. But there wasn't much concern as it was an old and rickety
thing that was better off gone than standing. Nobody inspected it
for arson, and nobody cared what caused it. When the flames were
out and the smoke gone, the foul-smelling charred ruins were left as
they were with little thought. The usual, customary warning sign was
posted near the road, advising all that the building was dangerous and
to stay out of it even though there was no building left. All the fire-
fighting gear was packed up and everyone left.

When they had all dispersed back to their homes, another house
fire started. This time the owner called in the alarm and vacated his
family from the house. It, too, was a total loss. The neighbors took
them in until they could arrange to live somewhere else.

The chief investigated this fire as if it was arson. This house was in
the middle of a block within a neighborhood filled with children and
families and in good repair. Finding an accelerant near the back door,
he thought he would go back to the first fire and check for accelerants

there, too. Maybe he was too hasty and given to pre-determined ideas to the old trailer house he hadn't even investigated. He thought he had been too quick to tack up the sign and walk away.

Arson investigators came out of Cheyenne, and he made the call. The second house was owned by one of his men. He and his wife were now homeless, and the real irritating issue was that someone didn't care that he and his wife were in their house when they torched it and could have killed or seriously injured someone. Or … maybe that had been the plan.

He called the county sheriff and took several rolls of film before he left the scene.

Near number six line station, Cade, Margo, and the rest of the Double K Ranch were setting up camp. Margo was delighted to see a small forest of thick trunk pine and fir trees around the station. Most of the hands had strung up hammocks between the trees, and Cade had strung up a hammock in a set of trees to the rear of the station.

The females were moved into the line station, the fire was set in the pot-bellied stove, and the water had been turned on. Missy and Lois were making beds for the three of them while Margo set up the chuck wagon.

Henry drove the wagon, with Missy and Tinker sitting beside him. Margo rode Stormy, and Cade spent most of the trip next to her on Tornado. Lois and Kirk knew how to ride and had been supplied with horses and equipment for the trip.

Cade, Josh and most of the guys were busy stringing lines for the horses, feeding horses, grooming horses, and setting up camp in one fashion or another and Missy was watching Henry instruct a new wrangler to use a shovel to scrape a spot of ground clean of prairie grass, set rocks around the edge in the shape of a large triangle and right at one edge lay in cinder blocks in the shape of a three-sided room about four feet long by two feet deep. A flat piece of sheet steel with a short chimney welded to one end of it was placed over the top blocks. Now there was a stove! He set a small fire under it and put a huge tin coffee pot full of water at one end.

When the coffee was set up, another fire in the corner was set and a steel rod tripod was setup. He hung a chain from it so it was set over the fire. A huge caldron was hung from the chain. An exact duplicate was set at the last corner.

Missy wondered about the other fires set over by the woods and hammocks. "What are those fires set for?" she asked, pointing at the fires by the "men's quarters."

"Safety and warmth! It will get cold out here tonight, and believe it or not, those fires will help keep us a bit warmer. Also it's a lot safer having a few small fires burning along your perimeter so you can see where you're going in the night and someone has to check on the horses and be ready to chase unwanted critters away." He looked at Missy and grinned.

Missy's eyes got huge. "Unwanted critters? What kind of unwanted critters?"

"Oh bears, coyotes, wolves, fox, squirrels, and chipmunks for starters." He was still grinning at her, and she began to figure he was teasing her.

She grabbed the shotgun out of the chuck wagon and took it to the line station. "I'll make sure the door of the station is locked tight tonight. I don't want any bears, wolves, or foxes wandering in there tonight."

Henry just grinned and headed back to the wagon for a stack of buckets directing the young man he was training. "Come on, son. We got work."

Missy followed Henry to the station and the little kitchen sink. "We'll need to fill these buckets about three quarters full and have at least one near every fire. That way we're ready if they try to get away from us and jump the dirt space around them. We'll also need one by the wagon to dip the stirring spoons into so they're not leaving food all over the wagon canvas when they're hung up. Margo and Missy can find a better spot for it if they want." Henry was talking to the young wrangler, but Missy jumped right in to help.

The first one was filled and set on the floor; then the second bucket went in the sink under the faucet, and Henry picked up the first and walked out. When the second bucket was about three-quarters full, the wrangler asked Missy if she could handle filling while he carried buckets to the fire pits. She took over the filling, set it on the floor, and put the next bucket under the faucet. Margo and Lois took the filled bucket out the door. When all the buckets were gone, Missy turned off the water.

Missy caught Henry's attention. He walked over to the wagon and Missy asked, "We made dinner at the house and brought it stored in coolers. When should we get it out?"

"Ladies, I know I'm running on empty. And just for future, you'll want to figure on dinner at dusk because we want to use all the daylight we can. Breakfast will be at dawn and lunch will be as they wander over here. We'll spell each other so the branding doesn't have to stop. We get a rhythm going, and we want to keep it going all day as it takes awhile to get that rhythm set. All right?"

"No problem," replied Missy.

Tinker, being pretty restricted as far as ranch work was concerned, was allowed to help out at the chuck wagon. He was there to help carry and tend, but he took every chance he could to keep Missy happy.

Missy climbed down out of the wagon and he helped her set up the tailgate as a buffet. They put a trashcan near the rear wheel, and Missy pondered how to get the cooler with all the soda in it out of the wagon.

"What's up?" Henry asked on approach.

"I was just trying to figure a way to get that cooler out of the wagon. The one that has all the cold pop in it."

"Easy. You just ask." He stepped around the end of the wagon to the side and spotted the cooler. Then he turned toward the woods and put two fingers in his mouth and whistled. He held up two fingers and waved back toward the wagon. Two men peeled out from the group and headed their way.

The girls stayed out of the way while the two men undid a couple of locks, swung the side of the wagon down until it formed a long counter, then hitched a chain to the outside corners. Tinker, already in the wagon, pushed the heavy cooler onto the counter and the two wranglers lowered it to the ground near the back wheel of the wagon. "Is this where you want it?"

"That's perfect. Thanks, guys."

The two men wandered back to the woods and the rest of the crew. Henry started pulling some large open pans out of the wagon. "You two ladies might want to get a bucket of water going for washing dishes." He looked up and saw three blank faces looking at him.

"Okay, camp cooking 101. Henry taught them how to wash dishes and cook using a campfire. It was very entertaining and educational and the ladies enjoyed his class. "You want me to get them over here to eat? I think they're staying away so they don't get in the way." Henry asked.

"Sure. We'll go get water. Oh! Do you think we have this set up good enough?"

"If there's food there, it's good enough. They don't expect Monaco's!"

"There's food." Missy took the lids off everything and set them aside. Henry looked into all the pots and then whistled and held up a fork, and the guys headed toward the wagon. Missy and Lois took the buckets into the station to fill them up.

Suddenly, three guys rode up dragging logs behind them. A couple of hands passed their plates over to others and walked over to move the logs in place around the fire; then they un-hitched the ropes so the riders could coil them and put their mounts away. The hands retrieved their plates and everyone sat down on the hard logs. It was much better than standing.

The three riders were now on foot, and they walked up and helped themselves to dinner. A few of the hands were still standing, but it was their choice. After everyone ate their fill, the dirty dishes were put in the empty pan, just like Henry had indicated would happen. The water in the cauldron was hot as steam rose from it and disappeared into the air.

Henry was herding a couple of new wranglers through the logistics of what to do with the dirty dishes and flatware, coffee mugs, etc. He included the girls because all the girls were new to branding camp regulations.

Margo loved the smell of the fire. It was sweet and memorable. She looked around the fire pit and saw Tinker and Missy sitting side by side on a log. Lois and Kirk were on the same log, just a few feet away. She leaned into Cade and offered some of the food on her plate. He just shook his head and patted his tummy, so she finished her food and stood up. She took his empty plate and fork and looked around to take anyone else's that hadn't moved yet. They had all deposited their plates and forks in the pan.

Missy was ladling hot water into the two pans. Margo went to the wagon and started putting the leftover food away. There was enough cold chicken for lunch the next day, and she could stretch the potato salad by baking a few more potatoes and then dicing them in and adding a little dressing. Beans were easy; just pop several cans and dump into a pot over the fire.

Coffee was being poured around the camp. Margo was wondering who was going to wash the mugs because they were done with the dishes and had thrown out the water. But as they finished, each of the hands took his mug to his sleeping area and hung it from a spot on the hammock or set it near their saddle. Mugs were reusable and didn't need to be washed daily, Margo supposed.

Margo took the potatoes that Missy had washed and put them in a grate on the stove, then dropped a cast iron pot upside down over the top of them. *Oven! Hope it works!*

She checked her watch for timing on when to check and hopefully pull them out of the heat.

Soon they were all sitting around the fire. When a guitar was strummed, Margo sat on the ground between Cade's knees and leaned back onto his chest. They listened to some of the guys singing western ballads quietly in the night. A few of the hands would peel off and go over to the hammocks and pull off boots and spurs and then quietly call it a day and go to sleep.

Cade had wrapped up Margo in his arms and was leaning on her, listening to the music as she was. Finally the guitarist stood up and wandered off to bed with the rest of the hands following, and Cade stood up pulling Margo to her feet with him.

"It was a long day today, my queen, and it'll be a longer one tomorrow. I need sleep. I'll miss you."

"Ditto."

"I love you." He waited while Margo took the potatoes from the fire and set them on a tray and carried them to the station. They couldn't leave any food out as something would get into it in the middle of the night. They didn't want to attract the critters—insect or other. Cade looked around to see the fires were low, and everything was as it should be. "Make sure you shut the door and keep it closed all night. I don't want any other critters joining you ladies in there tonight."

"Got it." She wrapped her arms around his neck and kissed him passionately. "Think that will hold till morning?"

"Absolutely not! I need more."

She laughed and kissed him again. He plundered her mouth with his. "That should do it!" He quickly opened the door, gently shoved her in, and hastily shut the door behind her before he could change his mind and drag her back out. He strode off to his bunk strung up under the trees and the stars.

Sleep did not come quickly for Cade as he thought about Margo and missed her so much it ached. Finally, sleep crept in like a ground fog, fingers creeping along in the dark, quietly overtaking everything in its path until Cade was breathing deeply and even and his eyes grew heavier and finally he was deeply asleep.

Morning came with the smell of fresh coffee. He nearly fell out of the hammock forgetting that he was several feet off the hard ground below. It was a cold dawn, he didn't want to get out of the sack in the first place but the day was coming with or without him and since he needed to get started on the work, he emerged from his warm cocoon moaning along with the rest of the sleepy hands awakened by coffee aroma and the sound of bacon and eggs cooking nearby. As the hands "rolled" out of the hammocks, a few fell to the ground and were helped up by those hands that had managed to not fall flat on their faces right out of the sack.

It wasn't long before all of them had washed their hands and faces in a pot of warm water provided by Margo's crew. They were all wondering over waiting for breakfast to be ready. Margo was dishing out by the platefuls, and as each hand came up, she handed out a plate of bacon, eggs, camp toast, and applesauce, done on an open fire. It smelled fantastic and was received extremely well.

Missy filled all the mugs from the coffee pot. At first, Tinker was slinging the coffee pot, as it was so big, heavy, and hot, but after he got it down to halfway, he set it down and Missy took over pouring.

It appeared that everyone was adjusting to camp and except for a few stiff muscles and joints that seemed to have settled out of place Cade felt ready to go and checked on his crew. "Everybody all right this morning?" he asked.

What first appeared to be utter confusion eventually turned into the obvious rhythm that Cade had told her about. First an animal was singled out of the herd, chased through a gate in the corral to a group of hands waiting to brand it. The first run of the day meant everyone waited while the first animal was placed. As soon as the first animal was sent down the chute, they went after another animal so that it went down the chute as soon as the other one left the first point. The first point was where the branding was done. When it appeared that the animal struggled and bawled enough, it was released to be chased to the next station. Animal one was now in the second station and animal two was in station one. Animal one stood in the second station while men held it there, slathered some gunky stuff over the brand it just received, injected it in the neck with a huge needle in a gun; and it was released into the herd again. Station three was the herd and inventory area. Lois was helping at the inventory area.

"Look, it appears there's something going on at all times at all three stations," Margo observed. That was the rhythm, and nobody was standing around too long waiting for someone else to get their part done. Margo could understand what Cade meant about the difficulty of getting the rhythm going and not wanting to stop it.

Cade called one of his men to take over his spot in the action and then walked over to Margo and the girls. "Hi! What's up?"

"We brought water for you guys. We're thirsty just watching you. Anyway, I'm advancing Missy's riding experience. Is that okay?

"Margo, you have been cleared to ride any horse you want. Second, you can teach anyone horsemanship because you know it quite well. The more you ladies can do around here, the more of an asset I've got on my hands and the less I have to worry about. Understood?"

"Yes, sir," Missy said.

"Okay, I have to get back. See you later. Thanks for the water!" He downed a cup of water, moved closer to Margo, and kissed her quick and turned to go back to the work.

"He's so cool!" Missy said.

"You ladies are sure a welcome sight," Josh said as he came up for a cup of water.

"Yeah, but I bet the water is more welcomed than us." Missy stated.

"Well, the water is easier to swallow, but you two are just as welcome and prettier to look at."

"Josh, you got a way with words, for sure," Margo stated.

He grinned as he passed out paper cups to the other men, and he dipped water from the bucket and then passed it back to the other two hands. Margo laid her reigns on the ground, put her foot on it and then took the bucket of water and ladle from the hands and started ladling the water into cups that Missy was handing out. When the hands had cooled their throats, they went back and sent a few more over. It was interesting watching the "changing of the guard" because it was easy to see that they all knew how to do the whole thing. There wasn't any group that was specialized in one particular thing and wouldn't go help on something else. Even the gardener and the hog and chicken masters were out there branding cattle.

Lois was busy with the inventory. She was in the third station where the animals ended their tour through the "flames of pain" as

Margo coined it. She sat on the fence rail or stood near the end of the shoot, protected by the men who kept the animals away from her and while they waylaid the animal long enough to do a quick inspection of its health, they would tell her information and she would tick it off.

Lunch went off without a hitch. Margo used paper plates and plastic ware, and it was easy to just throw it all in the trash. She had to wash the coffee mugs but didn't mind and was ready for it. The guys liked their coffee.

After everyone in the first lunch shift was through with their lunch, they went for a quick nap for a few minutes, or just a chance to kick back and stare into space, anything to relax for a few minutes. But they headed back to the branding area in time to relieve the next shift and only have been gone an hour. Margo and Missy were left in camp alone. Missy helped Margo wash coffee mugs and then Margo and Missy went for a ride.

"We have a ton of time before dinner has to get ready, and I'd like to go out riding in a different direction. We could go swimming in the lake if you want."

"I think I'd like to go riding, but I'm wondering if we should take a nap. I feel like I'm working all the time around here. That's an observation, not a complaint," Missy stated.

"I know what you mean, but I always enjoy riding. It relaxes me, and I'm ready to go if you are."

"Okay, riding it is."

They walked over to their horses and swung up in the saddles then moseyed around. After a little while they came upon a steer in the field, all alone. Margo called Cade on the phone and told him she found a lonesome cow. He told her to stay away from it and a couple of riders would be down to herd it up to be branded. Margo and Missy slowly rode a route around it and kept a wide birth of the animal. It didn't look real friendly. Once they were on the other side of it and riding down the hill to the grassland below, the animal made a noise, and Missy squealed out a startled sound. Margo looked over at Missy and noticed the animal was heading the other way. She could see the riders coming to herd the animal up the hill. But the animal turned and started running toward Missy and Margo.

"Okay, Missy, we gotta get out of the way or turn that animal back toward the guys. It looks more scared of us than the other way around. Come on." Margo headed Stormy toward the animal, and it turned, to her relief, and headed back up the hill. When Margo saw Missy beside her, she yelled for Missy to make space between them to cover more ground. They both kept well back of the animal, but they were effectively heading it up the hill. Finally, the guys came in and took over.

"Good job, ladies. We'll take it from here." Margo and Missy pulled up and then turned and headed back the way they had been going before.

"I don't know about you, but that was fun." Margo was energized.

Eventually, they headed back to camp laughing and feeling rather grand with themselves. They got dinner ready and then sat back and waited for the crew to come back.

At dusk, the men came back to camp, tired, dirty, and starving. The guys decided to go swimming in the lake to wash off the sweat and dirt before dinner. So Missy and Margo sat there waiting for them to get back when Missy said, "I wish we had a hair dryer." Lois headed for a shower and shampoo.

"We have a hair dryer," said Margo. "It's in the drawer in the bathroom."

"I saw that, but we don't have electricity," said Missy.

"Yes, we do. I don't know if it's turned on or not, but we have power to the stations."

"Well, let's go find out." Missy headed off to the station to check on electricity. She obviously found the hair dryer, the socket to plug it into, and the power on as Margo could hear the hair dryer on.

Tinker stopped by, gave Missy a bold kiss then, with towel in hand, walked down to the lake where the others had already gone.

"Margo, was that a cow or a steer we found?" Missy asked.

"Steer. Missy, I'm going to have to teach you the difference between the boys and girls out there. It might save your life," Margo stated. "What brought that up?"

"Tinker told me we did a good job with the steer today," replied Missy doubtfully.

"Look," said Margo. "A cow has an utter hanging down and gives milk. Those are the girls. A bull doesn't have an utter. They've got the male organs and are pretty obvious, but if you're looking at a bull from the side you'll see this … thing hanging down from his belly, about two thirds of the way back from his front legs. He's extremely recognizable from the back. Anyway, don't get near a bull. You don't even want to be in a pasture with a bull in it 'cause they are very aggressive. A steer is a guy that's been demoted to an *it*! He's lost his male organs, and he's a lot gentler as far as the animal goes. That's it for bovine anatomy 101 today."

"Not bad for a lady who calls them all cows," said Cade behind her.

FOURTEEN

"Cade!" Margo jumped and ran a couple of steps forward then turned in midflight to swing at Cade. He caught her fist in his hand and, laughing pulled her into his embrace and kissed the anger from her.

She wrapped her arms around him and sucked in his scent. He was all wet from a swim and smelled of English Lavender soap and clean. "Mmm. You smell good."

He held her in his arms, and when she looked up, he looked down at her.

"Is something wrong?"

"No. I just think my wife likes to tease me a lot. And sometimes I don't know she's teasing."

"Like when?"

"Like now when you're teaching Missy the difference between cows, bulls, and steers. You always called them cows to me before, exactly like when you called me and told me you found a cow, and now I find out you know the difference. I also know that you and Missy took a crack at herding that steer up the hill. The guys said you two were pretty natural at getting it headed in the right direction."

"Well, it came at us, and we decided that it looked more scared of us then we of it, so we chased it back the other way."

"Okay, that's fine, but you need to be careful of animals, especially if they look scared and they are several hundred pounds heavier than you. Any scared, cornered animal will try to defend itself. Cows and steers can do a lot of damage to a horse or man or another animal with their horns. So you remember that when you find a cow and start chasing a steer. I don't want to lose you. I love you."

"Cade, I love you, too."

He took his wet shirt and jeans over to his hammock and draped them over the ropes between trees and hammock.

The guys came back into camp, wet hair, much cleaner, wet clothes, washed out in the lake, still hungry and tired and looking for some place to string up a rope for a clothesline. Margo didn't think there was going to be much singing around the campfire tonight. She was right. While Margo washed and dried dishes, and Missy stoked the fires in camp, the men were already asleep in their hammocks Missy went into the station, and Margo stopped by Cade's hammock. He was asleep. She bent down and kissed his cheek. His arm snaked around her, but she knew he was asleep. "Good night, sweet prince," she whispered. She knew he wouldn't hear it, she barely heard it herself. She stood up and went into the station, laid down in her bunk, and was instantly asleep.

Much closer to town, another house went up in flames. This time the elderly lady that lived there was found charred in her bathroom along with her three cats.

While the firefighters were putting out the flames, another house on the opposite side of town went up in flames. Again, charred bodies, this time two people apparently died in bed.

Then a third house went up in flames, the family scrambling to escape just in time. All three houses were a total loss, and all three houses had the same connecting thread—arson. Cheyenne sent in their top fire investigators. The team scoured the ruins of each home, and the original and second fires from a few days earlier. They had to come up with answers fast because it was really out of hand now. If the arsonist kept up the events he was creating, they would have a town completely obliterated in a few more days.

While the arson investigators combed through ruins, the arsonist was free to roam about picking out new sites to torch.

The investigators determined that gasoline and balloons were being used to start most of the fires. The gas was poured into the balloons, the balloons hung from the ceiling. As soon as the flames raced across the ceiling, the balloons would explode, splashing their burning gasoline contents outward, and the raining fire would quickly ignite everything it landed on. The fires started in the kitchen, a burner left on high under a balloon on the ceiling. This gave the arsonist time to get out of the house and away before the balloon popped.

The fact that the arsonist was going into the houses with the occupants there told them they had a very bold arsonist, one that didn't seem to mind being caught by the occupants. The ME was advised to carefully check for drugs in the bodies to determine if they were being drugged prior to the arson.

The fires seemed blatantly random, and since it was apparent that the arsonist did not stand around watching his work to be accomplished, they knew they had an extremely dangerous arsonist to apprehend.

The Double K Ranch buildings were well off the road by more than ten miles. The cluster of buildings had originally ended up more or less by accident than good planning, but it was too late to rearrange the layout. However, it was handy and workable, and in the dead of winter worked sufficiently in spite of its inefficiency.

The arsonist had gone through all the buildings and only found the cats, pigs, and chickens at home. This seemed extremely strange to the arsonist, but the opportunity to collect all the valuables found was very rewarding. The fires were set and ignited, and the arsonist left. No alarms were given, no one was left scrambling; no bodies were going to be found as everyone was gone. If the cats could talk, they could tell Cade and Josh and the others who had set the torch to house and home.

The cats followed the trail that had been left a few days earlier to find comfort with their humans. Smart enough to find the way in the dark, the cats—nine total—leaped and jumped over tall grass, dodged snakes and gophers, and early in the morning, reached the crew just starting to stir at number six.

Jim was the first to be surprised by a cat leaping into his hammock and landing square in his stomach. He nearly landed on top of the cat as he leaped from his hammock in shock and surprise. It was still dark, but the sky was brightening with the rising sun, and he could see the cat on the ground nearby. He looked around and saw another cat leap onto Paul in his hammock. Jim's reaction was duplicated more than once as each cat from some unseen command found its human and leaped into bed with them.

As the crew was awakened, questions were being asked, quickly and without regard to who was asking.

Then Paul found singed fur on his cat and a blistered paw. "Oh, oh! Houston, we have a problem."

"What is it?" Cade and Josh asked nearly simultaneously.

"Look."

Cade pulled Margo aside and explained that the cats had followed them to camp and he was going to go back to the house to see why. Margo insisted on going with him. Josh needed to stay at the camp and Missy could cover for her, with Henry and Tinker's help. She didn't' want him going alone and he saw the warrior in her and the sense she was making.

She felt like Tornado in the respect that he could feel Cade's vibrations. The vibrations she was feeling were not good ones. They were black and off key, and she didn't like it.

Cade and Margo went back to the house in the truck to save time and when they got there it was light enough to see the damages. Everything was gone. Little smoke plumes rose from various places where coals were still hot, but it was all gone. The house, the barn, the animal houses, the bunkhouse. The equipment was burned, and sitting under a pile of charred wood and ashes.

There were a few chickens wandering around, some had just sat down and weren't moving, others were rumpled looking, like they were lucky to have escaped. Some hogs were rooting around looking for something to eat, but most were missing altogether. Cade told Margo to stay in the truck but she followed him out. "We're going together, Cade. I won't sit there and watch you get hit over the head, or be surprised from the rear while I'm watching you. We're going together and you can shut your mouth on the subject!" she whispered angrily.

He surrendered without comment and took her hand. She was right, in the first place, and he was glad for her company even though he didn't expect to have someone jump out of the ruins to attack him.

They didn't find any bodies except a hog and a few chickens, no humans were around and they got back in the truck and sat there in shock. Finally, he pulled his phone and called the Sheriff, reporting the fire, promising to stay and wait for them to get to the ranch.

Margo wanted to kill the jerk that torched her home. She could imagine what Cade was feeling. He'd lost the ranch, well everything except the ground and that was just ground. It was the buildings and people that made the ranch.

She cried. Cade wrapped her in his arms and let her cry and eventually he found tears of rage and hate, then fear and loss flowing down his cheeks, and finally, a resolve filled his heart and he prayed for what he had to do next.

"Margo, I love you. I need you. I'm going to rebuild the ranch. This ranch. We've got a ton of work ahead of us. Don't leave me. Work with me to rebuild the ranch?"

"Cade? Why would you ask. Of course I'll help you rebuild. I'm not going anywhere without you. What's first?"

She was all business, he thought. He needed that. "We've got our work cut out for us."

The Sheriff drove up and parked near Cade's truck, got out and Cade and Margo followed his example. "Looks pretty bad. Any injuries, death?"

"It's worse than bad. It's gone. Everything is gone. We lost a pig and some chickens, so far, but it may be worse in that direction, too. No human loss, so there's a blessing in the ruins."

"I have the arson squad notified already. They're on their way out. Where are you and the hands staying now?"

"Over at number six. If you squint, you can see it down trail from here."

The Sheriff looked down the trail the truck had left and could see a plume of smoke from the cooking fires and that was about all.

"You alright down there. I mean, water, electricity, food, clothing?"

"I'm leaving later today, tomorrow latest, to get supplies. Until then, we'll be alright. We've got a temporary camp down there, I'll have to build something more permanent until we rebuild the buildings here."

"Okay. You're better off than a lot of people in town."

"Sorry, Sheriff. We're a little bit off with the shock of this." Cade commented. God help him, he had enough to think about without considering people in town. But his heart swelled with compassion for those that had less than he.

"Are they getting the things and help they need, Sheriff?"

"Yes. I can get you some medical help if you need it. There's a team of Red Cross workers in town. I can made a call and a doctor and supplies will be here within the hour."

"Thanks, Sheriff, but we're alright. If you don't need us further, we're going back. We have quite a bit of planning to do before we go get the supplies we need." Cade was asked several more questions before he could leave.

"I know where to reach you Cade. Be careful."

Cade took Margo back to the truck and they went back to the camp.

He stopped because his throat seemed to close. He turned away for a minute, and all the hands could feel his anger, like a dark cloud moving over the sun. When he could talk again, everyone was sitting up and alert. He turned back before he spoke, and the hands could see the tears of pain in his eyes. "I've got good and bad news. Margo and I went back to the house this morning and we found a disaster. The buildings are burned to the ground. It was still smoldering, so it was done in the night. There is nothing left. Absolutely nothing! The trucks, the bulldozer, the stables, the bunkhouse, the barn, and the house, the chicken coop, and the hog house are all gone. Everything is charred. We lost a few of the hogs and chickens to the fire. The blessing; we didn't lose any people. Thank God, the hog and chicken masters decided to stay here with us last night. But the hogs and chickens and cats can't tell us who did this.

"I have contacted the sheriff. He and an arson investigation team from Cheyenne were out there before we left, and they may still be there as they've got a lot to sift through.

"Apparently, there is an arsonist running around town, and we were one of his victims. He has torched several houses in town. Also, it seems of the previous arson targets, we are the luckiest as none of us were there and all the animals were gone or escaped.

"Since I could account for the whereabouts of all of the hands, we are off the suspicious persons list; we are not homeless in that we have the shelter of the line stations.

"I don't think we are going to have to worry about the line stations, but I'd like us to consider staying together as much as possible and keeping away from the ones up in front near the main road except number one as it's hidden from the road, the others are too exposed.

"I don't have a problem if you want to stay here as we are, but it's going to take awhile for me to get something in here, so if you want to take a line station, go ahead. Just make sure you don't go alone, and let us know where you are going. Please stay as close as you can, and keep your phone on your person at all times."

Cade went to Margo, sitting on the back of the chuck near Henry. He wrapped his arms around her and just hung on for a minute. She gave him all she could, her love and support. When he went back to finish talking with the hands, he pulled her with him and kept his arm around her waist.

"Starting immediately, no one is to go up to the compound without prior permission from Josh or me. We will note the time you leave and the time you return. No one will go alone. Minimum of two at a time, and the reason for the log is to keep us all off of the suspicious persons list. I expect you to just accept my ruling on this, whether you like it or not.

"I would like you all to watch out for yourselves and each other. Guys, please pay close attention to our ladies. They will need your protection as well as the animals. I expect that statement came across very macho and will probably irritate the ladies, but I can't help it. I'm a protective sort of fool. We currently don't have a clue as to the reason or who is doing the arson, and I'm not sure at this point, if I ever want to know. I don't want to end up on death row."

"Josh, as soon as I get transportation back here, Margo and the girls can go to town and get themselves some gear. Tinker or you or Henry can go with them. I don't want them alone without one of us with them. Send them to Rapid City but keep them away from Nowhere."

Cade went back to the rest. "Margo, you are now the supervisor of all the women. Mostly as mentor but you will be working closely with Josh so make sure you are in communication with him at any instant. Missy, Lois, if you have a fear of something or a question about your future here, you talk to Margo. She has my blessing and the authority behind it. Does anyone have a problem with this—and I'm addressing this to the men, too?"

There were no dissenting noises.

Cade stopped for a few moments and stood with his back to everyone, his eyes on the distant mountains and his heart somewhere underfoot. Margo held onto his hand. Finally, he turned back around and continued.

"I will tell you this." He stood there, unable to talk for another moment, looking at the ground and the trees. Tears burned the backs of his eyes, and he had to fight desperately to keep them from escaping down his cheeks. Finally he looked at his people and continued, "I am glad you are all here. The reports from the fire chief are that there were bodies found in other fires in the last two days. They appear random and without planning. The town is in near panic, and while the sheriff's department is doing their best, it is in an investigative mode, not apprehend, and execute.

"I'm not advocating vigilante justice, but I don't want to lose any of you. I don't like losing what's gone now, but the loss of people and animals is what would do me in..... we will rebuild. I want you all to be prudent and safety conscious. Pay attention to where each other are. Check in often, follow the rules that we set up for this time and don't go off on your own for any reason. We don't know who we are dealing with, whether it is one or many, and until we do know, this is the best defense for ourselves and the ranch.

"I'm going to Cheyenne to buy some supplies and whatever I can get my hands on quickly to have protection from the weather and worse. If we have to become survivalists and live in tents, then we'll become survivalists! Does anyone have any comments, suggestions, or questions?"

He stood there, looking at them, waiting for reactions and questions and was a bit surprised to not hear any questions. Since there were no questions he walked away, pulling Margo along with him. Back at the chuck wagon, he pulled her into his arms and held on.

"It'll be all right, Margo. It'll be all right," he whispered. He kissed her and held her tight against his chest.

"I could go with you?" She looked into his eyes. Tears were blurring her vision, but she could see the tears filling his.

"I need you here to be strong for everyone. Josh needs his head cook. Let girls do their own thing. Each of them has a strong point, they all do. Let them run with it. You run with yours. I'm counting on you. You have your phone?"

"Yes. Call me and let me know where you are and that you're all right. Call me every day! Please?"

"I will, but we have tonight."

"Well, where?"

"Why do you think I hung my hammock up behind the station?"

Margo looked at him and saw the glitter in his eyes and just hugged him again knowing it was tears catching whatever light they could. Margo slept with Cade in his hammock behind the station, and while it seemed very short and she was so tired she could hardly wiggle, they managed to get some rest and still be ready for breakfast at six. Cade and Josh knew no one was going to want to climb out of the sack early and everyone was going to need to spend some extra sleep time after the emotional upheaval of the day and night.

At five thirty, Margo and Cade rolled out of the sack and went over to the fires and stoked them up for the morning breakfast and morning heat. Margo made the usual and with Cade's help, fed the hands as they came along. Cade was so concerned about his men he was having a real hard time. He made sure he talked to each of them, asking if there was something he needed to replace for them, anything special they needed or wanted. They stood there, each one separately with Cade and promised to stay and keep working at whatever needed to be done and they knew there was going to be plenty of work ahead. Cade got everyone's clothing, boot, and glove sizes. He was replacing clothing so they would have something besides what was in their saddlebags.

Margo was happy for Cade and proud of his crew. Margo collected the same information from Missy, Lois and herself as Cade had collected from his men. She gave him the information on both of them and he put it with the rest of the information he had collected.

"Missy is staying," she told him. "She got the heart of a lion and she's really cranked about this. She wants to get the sicko first. Lois has her husband who is planning on staying. They have nowhere else to go and decided if their house is gone, it's gone. They're grateful to you for giving them jobs."

Next Margo created a shopping list of supplies. It seemed like a list for a city instead of the ranch. Where were they going to put it?

When she was finished with it, she wondered how Cade was going to get this all done by himself. Could the hands survive without her, too?

Henry put together a list for tools and building materials. He knew they were going to need hammers and nails, rakes, shovels, and more.

Cade was armed with his lists, stuffed in his pocket, and went to Margo. "How about you? Do you need anything special, anything replaced?"

She shook her head and then remembered the necklace he had given her for a wedding present.

"Well, I had it insured, so I can replace it at some point. Anything else?"

She shook her head and looked into his eyes. "I could still go with you."

"Not going there again. I'll miss you so much it's going to hurt, but I need you here. Be my strong and beautiful queen, and take care of my empire until I get back. It's your ranch as much as mine, and you can think like that.

She looked into his eyes and said nothing that he couldn't feel from her and see in her eyes. Pure love flowed from her into him. It was easily returned. And she still wasn't thinking about money.

They heard the helicopter in the distance, and Cade hugged her tighter and kissed the top of her head then moved his lips to her lips and kissed her again then hugged her some more hating having to let her go. Henry and Josh walked up to Cade and shook his hand, and then Henry took Margo's shoulders and pulled her gently away from Cade.

Cade walked over, picked up his saddlebags, and took his wallet out and pushed it into his pocket and then checked for his phone, charger, and his lists. Then they all walked out into the grassland nearby and waited for the helicopter to land and pick him up.

Cade walked toward the waiting helicopter, saddlebags over his shoulder. Margo waved at him; he waved back.

When the noise of the helicopter was gone, camp was so quiet it was ominous. Josh stood near the cook fire and called everyone in to sit on the logs. Margo passed coffee, trying to get her emotions back in order by digging into work. She found Missy and Lois helping.

FIFTEEN

Okay, we've all had time to think about our situation and what we, as individuals, think we can and can't do. I need input. I don't have anything to add to Cade's information. What I'm trying to do is put together some plan … a working plan, a survival plan that we can, and will all follow; one that keeps us accounted for and watching out for each other without even thinking about it. And the hardest part I have to do is this, if you feel in your heart that you can't stay here with the bare minimum for survival until Cade get's stuff rolling in here, if you feel in your heart that you don't want to be part of rebuilding this ranch, I need to know it now. We will be dealing with enough problems as individuals and as a whole without putting up with constant or even occasional grumbling. If you've got an unhappy heart on the future of this place, you'll only start grumbling and that grumbling will undo all of us. It will fester and destroy us. I'll do my best to find you jobs someplace else, but we won't keep you here if you start complaining about anything."

"We need a plan like the snow line!" Margo stated. Josh looked at her, a huge question on his face. "You know, the line that's put up in winter. You don't even think about it. You just grab it and you know where you are even if you can't see. You just follow it and it takes you to the next stop."

"Yep, that's what we need!" Josh smiled. He had a start, a good start. "A snow line plan! It's got to include everything—animals, people, buildings, supplies, water, electricity, wood, fire, safety, absolutely every element of our lives, because this is it for now.

"In order to work as a team, the best team, black ops, SWAT, Delta, anyone ever put together, we have to ensure there will be no surprises. I need your individual strengths. If you need to be alone for an hour or so, take the time. But please don't go far..... we don't know what's out there." He continued after a moment of thought.

"We've got two men here that used to be in the special forces. If you two men will help us come up with a plan for security and safety and survival, I am sure we will all appreciate it."

Josh didn't realize it, but his request was quickly accepted by the two men, and it was dubbed the Triple S Plan—security, safety, and survival.

"Right now, I'd like a crew of four men to go up to the front gate and shut this place down from the main road. Shut it down so nobody gets in here without our permission. Let's make it four of you that want to stay there on guard duty for a while. Take all your stuff and your horses. We've got one truck, let's load it with supplies and take it up to number one to keep you for a while. I will be splitting up the crew as I will want four of you real strong men up at number one. You will be there to guard the entrance and stop and capture anyone who tries to sneak in. Call the sheriff at the first sign of a problem and be our eyes and ears at the gate. Split your shifts and spell each other. This is like war, people, and we are the only soldiers this ranch has at the moment." Four guys stood up and headed toward the hammocks and the horses. Josh watched without saying a word. He knew his men and what they were doing. He continued, "Everyone here has a talent or two to help us survive and move on from this current problem. We're going to have to rely on each other's talents and gifts, so let's figure out what we've got and plan on donating those talents to the whole and get on with it. Come on, let's think up some ideas. Lois can you keep a list for us somewhere?"

"Sure. Let me get it." Lois jumped up and ran into the line station to return a few minutes later with her clipboard and attached-with-a-string pen. She sat down again and was ready to write.

Ideas bubbled slowly at first and then seemed to grow with inspiration into a very good workable plan. They weren't fighting with high-tech smart bombs, but they weren't fighting with bows and arrows either, although Margo was sure someone in the group could probably make some very nasty, lethal arrows if needed. All the men had rifles and knew how to use them and would use them if needed. Some even had guns they attached to their belts or kept in their saddlebags. The girls were the only unarmed members of the crew and while Margo didn't know how to hold or shoot a gun, she was willing to learn. She already knew that she would kill to save herself. She'd already done it once.

"Any of you ladies want guns, knives, grenades, bazookas, or slingshots?" Josh asked.

Lois and Missy just shook their heads. Margo said she wanted a handgun. Josh told her he'd get with her later on the issue.

Four of the men had volunteered to go up to number One. They had water and electricity from the station.

Henry told them to call him if they had a problem with anything. He'd get there and mess around as best he could with no tools. Then he reminded them to climb the tower and let the windmill loose so the pump could bring water to the station from the well.

The four riders left, a truck loaded down with everything they couldn't carry and the camp could spare to follow the riders later. They had their rifles and guns and were prepared to act like pit bulls if required. Nobody was going to get past them.

True to his word, Josh got with Margo on the issue of a handgun. "Margo, do you know how to use it?"

"No, but I can learn."

"Are you sure you could use it if you knew how? I mean, are you willing to kill somebody to save yourself or someone else?"

"Yes."

"Well, okay. I'll put it on the list. I'm going to tell Cade because I don't want him killing me over this, so I'm going to let him know you want a handgun, and if he says absolutely no, then you'll have to convince him about it, I won't."

"Understood. But I have a question."

"Go ahead."

"Devil's advocate: if a guy asked you for a handgun, would you have put him off until later and would you be asking Cade for his approval?"

"Got me there. No, I would have dealt with it right then; and no, I wouldn't be asking Cade for permission. However, in defense of my macho way, I do have to answer to him as you're his wife and, like it or not, you are under my protection. I don't want him coming back here to kill me because I treated you like one of the guys and didn't confer with him on an issue involving you. Those in power usually have to sacrifice their own personal liberties for the good of those depending on them."

"What does that mean?" she asked without temper.

"It means that I can't allow anything to happen to you! If something happens to Cade, you're our only life source left. You alone would have the power to sell the ranch or keep it running and, in that respect, keep us employed, housed, and fed. Unfortunately, that demands that you think of us on the whole, as though you were our queen and we are your nation, and abandon all thoughts of only what you might want. You have a will of iron and enough emotional strength to pull all of us out of this fire. They need that, Margo. They need to see the steel of determination you have. They need to know, nothing is going to stop you and Cade from rebuilding this ranch. You can do anything you set your mind to do. Sometimes you have to talk yourself into something, but once you do that, you go for it and nothing or no one gets in your way of the final goal. We are going to need that from you now, more than ever. If you think I'm off base, talk to Henry. He has a way with the word better than I do."

"You're right about Henry and the word. I understand what you're saying. I don't like feeling as though I can't live as easily or freely as others around here, but I understand what you're saying and I won't be bothering you about this again. I never thought you were macho and never said it. I was not upset at you; I just wondered why I felt like I was cut out of the herd. Anyway, thanks for the time and explanation." She stood up, and Josh stood up beside her and threw his arm around her shoulder.

A short time later, Alex, the chicken-coop master and a couple more of the hands rode in the truck up to number one with the supplies for the guard-brigade at the ranch gate and then back to the ruins to see if they could collect any of the chickens and figure out a way of keeping them together and safe and then collect any eggs they would have laid over the past twenty-four hours. When Margo heard about it, she was glad someone had thought about it.

Gary and Jonesy had a similar idea for the hogs. If they herded them into a place of confinement and protected them from the wild hogs, they would be able to salvage some of the herd to provide meat later on.

The gardeners wanted to go and check out the garden to see what might be salvaged from it, and if it was relatively untouched, they would have veggies for a while. They wouldn't starve. Josh gave the go ahead and logged them out as going to the ruins and why.

When night fell, everyone except Cade and those at the front gate were back and accounted for. Josh had called the guys up at the gate, and they were doing great and thought it would be a good idea if Josh made a trip up there in a couple of days.

A couple of the hands had designated themselves as guards for the main camp and had gone to sleep under the trees early. When everyone else was heading for the sack, the self-appointed guards went back to work on guard duty. They took cell phones and charged them, swapping them out all night long.

They had gathered together near the cook fire, and finally when they were all in their beds sleeping and the guards were guarding, Margo had closed her eyes and fallen asleep, though she was sure she wouldn't be able to. She had curled up on Cade's hammock, and no one bothered her as they seemed to understand, even if she didn't.

Cade had called near noon, and he and Josh had their long discussion. When Josh hung up, Margo didn't think she was going to hear from Cade and was feeling a little low. She missed him so much.

Now it was after ten p.m., and she was feeling like he had forgotten her. She knew she could call him, but she didn't want to bother him, because she didn't know what he was into and if he was haggling some deal she didn't want to spoil it for him. When her phone rang, it startled her as it was on vibrate so it only hummed, but since it was still in her hand, it shocked her awake. She answered with a whisper. "Cade?"

"Hi, my queen. Did I wake you?"

"Yes. I miss you."

"I miss you. Are you all right?"

She rolled onto her side and put her pillow over her head so she wouldn't wake anyone up while she talked to Cade. "Yes. How about you?"

"I'm fine. Actually I'm better off than fine. I'm in a hotel for the night. I got a lot done, too much to bother you with tonight. Just feed the crew real good tomorrow morning. Josh will be whipping them into it tomorrow for me. There's a lot to be done and I know they'll get it done, but we have to do this real quick before they start giving up and bailing on us."

"Okay, without details, I understand the reason. We're fine and we'll be all right. Just do what you have to do. Are you coming home tomorrow?"

"No. Too much yet to do. But I'll be back as soon as I can. It might take a week or longer. I'll keep it as short as I can manage because I miss you way too much. How'd you get under my skin like that?"

They finally said good night and both closed their phones. Margo sat up on the hammock and heard her name called in a whisper. She turned her head toward the sound and saw Josh standing a short distance away, silhouetted against the campfire. He came over, and he asked if she'd recharged her phone lately. She said no, and he took it from her and plugged it in to one of the six chargers somehow attached to the station wall and a strip outlet. The guards were rotating everyone's phones at night so no one would be without a phone when needed. Josh told her to get some sleep, and she curled up on the hammock again and went to sleep. Dawn was fast approaching with more work for another day.

When the banker's home went up in flames, the only things saved were the owners. Both happy to be alive and both terrified and angry as irritated rattlesnakes. They were at the dry goods store before it opened, banging on the door for clothing as they only had what was on their backs. At least they had funds to handle the situation. Others did not.

Mrs. Dietrich, fuming at the blatant audacity of the insane moron that had torched their home pronounced that he had to be caught, and she, if no one else, was going to find the little bug and squash it all by herself, if that's what it took.

Her husband tried to calm her, but she was determined to gather as much support and stomp out the impudent arsonist, sooner than later. As soon as she could cover herself with appropriate clothing, she was going to devise some way of stopping this low-life. She was no longer waiting for someone else to do their job!

"Enough with investigations. We need to find this guy and hang him!" she shouted.

The storekeeper rolled his eyes. He knew Mrs. Dietrich was influential, but she didn't have that much authority. Yes, she could organize, she could probably garner the support of nearly everyone in town, and maybe all of the town's people, because when she turned her eye on you, you usually looked for the nearest floor tile to pull up and hide under. She was unwavering in her opinions.

When they both had changed into jeans, shirts, and boots, and looked nothing like the bankers he knew, he took the tags they handed him and put them on the banker's tab. He knew they would pay as soon as they could. They weren't the first people into his store in tattered, sooty clothing and having nothing left but fear in their eyes. He'd seen it far too many times of recent and he was going to join Mrs. Dietrich's fight. It was beyond time to find and stomp out this arsonist.

He noticed Delilah's truck roll by. Her truck was unmistakable. Three colors—red, white, and blue—and so beat up, it was a miracle it didn't fall apart right in the street. The fenders were all in rust colored primer, the bumpers were just plain rusty and bent, sticking out in various directions giving the truck the look of a bull. But then he thought about Delilah's bullish ways and wouldn't have been surprised to learn she had pulled the bumpers out like that on purpose. He looked at his watch as he locked the front door, made sure the closed sign faced out and tuned out the lights. He climbed the stairs to his little apartment above and thought he needed to clean it up a bit.

Who's got time? he thought as he dropped his jeans and rolled back into bed. *Maybe I'll get another couple of hours of sleep.*

The Dietrich's wandered town with anger in their eyes. They went from friend to friend all through town gathering support to find the source of the problem. Problem was; they had included the arsonist without knowing it.

Now there was joy in one person's heart. *Catch me! Catch me if you can! But you won't be quick enough!*

Before the next night was over, the sky was lighter over town, as though it were a huge city. The guards at camp saw it and woke Josh. He watched the sky, and when it seemed the brightness got brighter and larger, he woke Margo. She stood there with him and the guards watching. Josh and Margo walked out into the grassland so they could talk without waking the rest.

"Forest fire?" Margo asked.

"My guess; it's the town going up in flames. I hope no one else dies tonight."

"You think we could see it like that thirty miles away?"

"Yep," Josh replied.

Margo called Mrs. Dietrich's cell phone. It was answered quickly. "Mrs. Dietrich, this is Margo Knight at the Double K. Are you and Mr. Dietrich all right?" She could hear so much commotion and noise in the background she was instantly on alert.

"Yes, dear, but the town is burning to the ground. It's just awful. The buildings are so tinder dry they're catching on fire from each other. Oh! What a tragedy! I just don't understand this! Those poor firefighters can't possibly keep up with it! They're trying so hard and it's chasing them. This is just awful! I don't think there's a building that isn't burning now." Margo could hear her crying and then the line went dead.

She closed her phone and told Josh the town was burning to the ground.

They went back to their hammocks to try to catch some sleep. Margo felt awful about trying to go back to sleep with the town burning and all the people she knew there being left with absolutely nothing. She was awake until the sun started to lighten the sky and then she rolled out of the hammock and sent an arrow prayer to heaven asking protection, blessings, and help for the people of Nowhere, Wyoming. She didn't even know she did it. She was so tired she felt like a robot.

The day seemed to crawl, and yet she was busy all day and so tired. But Margo knew it was because she couldn't stop thinking about Cade and the town of Nowhere. And while she thought of him, she thought about the Double K and wondered how they were going to rebuild.

When she talked to Missy, she knew her friend was afraid.

While Missy and Margo were wandering alone, petting horses, or picking wild flowers in the nearby field, they felt safe with the rest of the hands.

"How are you and Tinker doing, Missy?"

"Oh! I guess it was just him being his everyday sweet, and I read it wrong. Since I don't have that much contact with him, he hasn't done anything to make me feel like he really wanted me or anything."

"Oh, Missy, I'm sorry. Can I do anything for you?"

"No. If it's to be, it'll happen."

"Okay." Margo was suddenly real sad and knew how lucky she was. She and Cade fell in love with each other almost instantly. They were both so happy, being able to draw on each other's strengths and just be happy being with each other.

The ladies started fixing sandwiches. While they were at it, Margo made a quick study of the inventory on the food again.

"We're going to need more bread and eggs, but the ice is all gone so I don't know how we are going to take care of the cold stuff," she discussed with Missy.

After the guys ate lunch, not using plates or utensils, the girls were left to wander and wonder.

"I wonder what the cave women did during their day," Missy said.

"Why?" asked Lois.

"'Cause we need to go on those lines a bit more. They didn't have refrigerators, so they must have had to do something that we aren't doing," returned Missy.

"Yeah, they didn't eat anything but raw meat." Margo laughed, and Missy started to cry. Margo was standing there holding Missy in her arms, and Tinker ran up and took Missy from Margo with just a look, silently and tenderly wrapping Missy up in his arms and letting her cry.

Margo had a huge smile on her face as she and Lois walked away. *Missy, he loves you. You just have to open your eyes and give him a chance, girl. . Now I just have to get my man back.*

The garden had survived, in part. They would still be able to harvest lettuce, radishes, some carrots, and string beans. They would build a garden closer to camp and plant corn, and other veggies for harvesting later in the fall. The rest of the crew was going to be busy finishing the branding, as Josh assigned everyone duties for the next day right then.

Lois was going to be busy with the branding, and Missy was going to be busy helping Tinker and the guys herd chickens and hogs and building pens for them with whatever they could find to use.

The second day of forced encampment started with a lot of noise—heavy equipment noise in the distance. Cade had warned Josh the day before and when they heard heavy equipment, Josh indicated to Margo that he wanted her to follow. They got in the truck and

THE DOUBLE (K) RANCH

Josh drove up ranch through the fields to where they found the heavy equipment.

Three trucks with two men each were digging a ditch from the main electrical feed on the road down the fence line to number Six.

Josh checked the permit for the project and each of the six man crew. The he called the electric company and obtained information on the permit and had them verify each of their men who vouched for each other. After taking a picture of each man, with his phone, Josh let them continue their work. The electric company had given a copy of the permit to Cade.

SIXTEEN

It took the line crew three days to complete the work and that included digging a ditch, laying the line and the inspection, then burying the line ditch and the final hookup to a huge box installed on the side of number Six. There weren't any problems and the ranch crew helped out where they could. When the line crew reached number six, they put in a huge circuit breaker box and a meter. Josh signed off on it and gave the copy of it to Lois.

The line crew made their own camp at night and ate their own food. They had come prepared, not knowing that there were people camping out in the middle of nowhere. The Red Cross and FEMA had descended, and they were bringing in temporary manufactured homes and supplies for the survivors, but things were rough.

The third day of life after fire brought the wholesale groceries truck, which arrived stuffed. It took most of the crew all day to offload it onto the ground. There was a huge refrigerator and an ice machine along with the groceries and the guys moved the fridge and ice machine and freezer into number six and plugged them in. Josh signed for the goods. The driver read it and gave a copy to Josh, jumped in his truck, and drove off following his original trail back out to the ruins and over the Double K Ranch Road.

The grocery truck was a welcome sight, but it took the entire crew several hours to sort through it and see what they had. All the perishables were put in the shade and covered in tarps until the refrigerator and freezer were plugged in and cold enough to handle the food. The ice machine was plugged in and Henry used the new tools to hook it up to water from the little sink. Cade had planned it well and had thought of every tool they might need for this project alone and ensured all of it was included. Henry ripped out the little sink, the counter and the stove from number Six and several guys shoved the freezer, refrigerator and ice machine as close to the wall as they could. There was barely enough room to open the machines without ripping out some of the bunks.

Several other tools were in the truck along with a huge supply of tarps and several "assembly-required" tool/storage sheds. The crew put the storage sheds together and had them lined up along number Six, as though they were going to march up to number Five. At least it was a place to put all the supplies!

Cade called that evening and they told him they got the supplies and the sheds for storing it all. "If anything is wrong with it, let me know, and I'll hit the store again before I leave Cheyenne. I should be back soon, but I'm still working on a couple of things. How is everything there?"

"Everything here is great. We locked down the ranch at the main road and have round-the-clock guards so nobody—sheriff, arsonist, neighbor, vandal, absolutely nobody, including jackrabbits—gets in without our permission. We appreciated the grocery delivery. The cattle were getting a bit nervous."

"Why?"

"Well, wouldn't you get nervous if there were thirty-some-odd hungry people looking at you constantly?"

Cade laughed and was glad there was a bit of humor in Josh again. It told him that all was fine. "Can I talk to Margo? Is she nearby so I don't have to end and redial?"

"You're going to ruin my phone with all the mushy stuff," he said with a chuckle. "Hold on."

He held the phone out to Margo. "You'll want this," he said.

Margo took the phone and told Cade about the town burning, the hogs, chickens, and garden. A short time later, Margo handed the phone back to Josh. "Thanks."

Six nights later, at dusk and everyone sitting around enjoying their dinner, even though it was only a dream now, Josh suddenly stood up and Margo felt his alert. A few others did too as they stood up and looked in the same direction, toward the ruins. Two evenly spaced, white round lights were headed, slowly, toward them across the grassland. Margo moved up close to Josh.

"You think it's Cade?" she asked as he picked up his phone and called the front gate. All he got was a recording that was sending him to automatic voicemail.

While he called Cade's phone, he said, "Don't know. Jim, you and Paul have your horses still saddled. Head out there, and check it out. Don't approach unless you know it's Cade, but go out there and pace him. A couple of you others, grab your rifles and take cover, in case we need it. Ladies, get in the station and keep the lights out and your heads down and away from the window. I'm not reaching the front gate on the phone, so I don't know what's going on." Now Cade's phone went to voice mail.

Everyone jumped into action. Josh and others kicked out the fires with dirt while everyone else went to their "muster stations," and when Josh was satisfied, he moved back into the darkness of the woods. The interior lights of the vehicle came on, and Josh could see Cade clearly. He walked out into the compound. "It's Cade!"

Everyone came out of hiding and waited at the cook fire pit for Cade to drive up. The two riders came up with him and everyone welcomed Cade back as he jumped down from his new truck. Margo hung back waiting for all the others to get their greetings in first. She heard Cade tell Josh and the rest that the back of the truck was full of groceries. They all started pulling stuff out of the back of the truck.

Chuck whistled in awe and said, "Hey, Boss. Did you know this bulldozer followed you home?" There was suddenly a great deal of laughing and hooting. Cade grinned. He knew his guys would love that beautiful machine on the trailer attached to the back of his new truck.

He looked around for Margo.

"I'm right here." She moved closer, and Cade wrapped her in his arms, picked her up, and kissed her desperately. When he set her down, her knees were weak. He pulled her over by his hammock, and they sat on it and talked about everything while everyone else ran around packing groceries into the proper spots.

They both reported on their time apart and between hugs and kisses caught up on all the news in both their lives.

Someone had restarted the fires, and Cade and Margo went back to the campfire and stood there, arm in arm, while Cade told the others of what he'd accomplished in the last week.

Because he had used his telephone several times on the thirty-minute trip to Cheyenne, a car dealer met him at the airport with a new truck, just like his last truck. He dropped the salesman off at the dealership, signed the papers, and headed off to a nearby construction company and bought a ranch worth of construction cabins. He'd ordered one trailer for him and Margo; one for Missy; one for Lois and Kirk, and four bunkhouse-style cabins that held eight people each for the guys; another cabin for Josh and Henry; a shower house complete with four shower stalls, four toilets, and four sinks; a laundry room complete with six washers and dryers; and the kitchen and mess hall. They were going to be delivered in a couple of days. They would have arrived earlier, but he had some special things built in, and he wanted it delivered all at one time so the delay was the custom building. "And I went to the wholesale store the next morning, paid four people to drive carts around the store and loaded them up, and sent it off in this direction. You got the refrigerator and freezer, right?"

"We sure did. We moved them into number six, plugged it in and filled it up. We can't tell you how much we appreciated those little items," Margo replied.

"It was the first thing on the cart." Cade laughed. "One of you heavy equipment operators, feels like firing it up first thing in the morning so we can make sure we have a nice flat place to set the trailers up?"

"No problem, Cade."

"I'll get with Josh in a few minutes, and we'll figure out a layout and be ready for the set up. By the way, Margo and Josh, Nick is on the way here to do the communication line feeds for number six.

"Ladies, we're probably going to move the cook fires and the wagon out of the way as we won't want it in the middle of our work, and we can reset it over yonder a piece so you'll be cooking in a new spot. We're going to be living here for a while so the first thing we'll be doing, after we get the new temp buildings set up is build a corral and a barn for the horses and ranch vehicles and tools and all that we'll need. Let's call it quits for the day as we'll be up early again tomorrow. I think we should have breakfast at five o'clock again, please, so we're ready to start work at six a.m. Can we have that, Margo?"

"You bet," Margo replied.

"Thanks. Are there any questions, comments, or helpful suggestions?"

"Welcome back, boss!" someone said, others repeated it, and everyone headed for their bunks except Cade and Josh. They got together at the campfire. The two men conferred over the building setup, and when it was decided a good plan, they both went to their hammocks and pulled off their boots, laid down, and Josh was asleep almost immediately.

Cade was busy with the wife he'd found in his hammock. They lay quiet and cozy under the blanket, holding each other and just enjoying being close for a while, whispering quietly.

"Cade?"

She felt his nod.

"Did you get the gun for me?"

"Yes."

"How much did this cost you?"

"The gun or the whole temp ranch?"

"The whole temp ranch."

"By the time we start living in the cabins and eating in the mess hall, a couple hundred grand, give or take a few thousand. Are you worried about it?" She shook her head. He seemed so casual about so much money.

"You got your big refrigerator and freezer running in the station. Where'd you set it?"

"Henry had some guys rip out the sink, counter, and stove—poor number six will never be the same. That poor little station is packed to the rafters with all the supplies you sent in a forty-foot trailer. Can you imagine our joy and surprise when this huge tractor trailer rig came around the curve at the ruins and then started bouncing down through the ruts to camp? We had to store some of it in the chuck and some went up to number one to keep those guy's supplied. I wouldn't be surprised to find some in number five and seven."

"I was a little afraid there would be a problem getting it all here, but I knew it would eventually get where it needed to be."

He was quiet for a while and then softly whispered, "I love you, my queen. Stay with me."

"Ditto, my liege." She yawned. "I'll be here, right beside you if you don't dump me on the ground."

She could feel him laughing. He leaned over and kissed her forehead. "Good night."

"Good night." She yawned again.

Five o'clock came quickly with dawn in hot pursuit, and Margo met up with Missy by the fire. Missy was stoking them and getting things ready for another meal over the open flames.   There was an excitement in the camp, and everyone was up and ready to go before breakfast was ready. Josh had them putting out their little perimeter fires, and then he had them move the logs from the cook fire and get the wagon ready to move as soon as breakfast was over, and the girls were ready to do the cleanup after the wagon was moved. It was decided to move the wagon to the end of the woods where the new fire could be built. It was a bit farther from the station full of supplies, but it was only going to be for a few days. They'd survive.

Breakfast was served and devoured, and Cade and Josh laid out the area for the new cabins. Tinker had the bulldozer running and scraping out the area required when the caravan of cabins stopped at the ruins. The drivers had been instructed to hold up there, and they did as they were told. Cade wanted to ensure that they came down in the proper order of setup, so he drove up and handed out numbers to the drivers. As they came down the dirt road toward camp, they pulled into the pasture and parked. After a short discussion with Cade, the first truck with cabin attached moved down to number six. Everyone was very cooperative, and it worked well. As the first trailer reached the camp area, Cade was back in camp, and he instructed the first driver where he wanted the cabin. All the other drivers left their tractor-trailer rigs where they were and came down to help with the set up of the first cabin.

Chuck had smoothed out the area very well with the bulldozer, and the setup went just as smoothly. The drivers leveled out the trailer with their piles of cinder blocks and one of the drivers suggested that if they were going to have the cabins for a long period of time they might want to consider making a foundation for them. Cade was interested, and the driver explained to Cade, Josh, Henry, Tinker, and Mike exactly where to set a foundation under the cabins.

While the first trailer was set up, Margo went to feed Tornado and Stormy a carrot and managed to give it to Tornado without him screaming and causing a scene. After he ate the carrot and came back to her, she asked him if he would let her ride him. He didn't object, and she led him over to the chuck wagon, climbed onto the tailgate, and Tornado obliged her by siding up along it so she could swing up onto his back.

He stood there waiting for her command. She talked to him constantly and petted his neck. "Okay, Tornado. Nice and slow for this early."

Tornado snorted and nodded. Margo held the reins as lightly as she could, and she lightly tapped his sides once with her heels. He moved forward a couple of steps and stopped. "What? What did I do to make you stop?" Tornado shook his head.

She tapped him again, and he moved forward and continued to move forward until she tipped the reins to the right and he turned, nice and slow, then he moved forward again. She was out in the field headed down slope to the bottomland, and she tapped Tornado again and said, "A little faster, please." Tornado obliged by loping into a canter. She felt exhilarated and sat easy in the saddle, feet just right in the stirrups, shoulders back. Then she turned Tornado to the left a bit and tapped his sides again, and Tornado took off, flying over the grassland like a streak. She lost her hat somewhere along the line but didn't even bother to look back to see where it landed. If she would have, she would have seen Cade walking out to watch her fly through the pasture on his horse, a twinkle in his eye and pride in his heart.

When he saw her hat fly off, he walked out to where it had landed and picked it up. She had taken Tornado in a long circle at full speed and stood in the stirrups, arms straight out, reins wrapped around the saddle horn as he flew along toward Cade. Tornado veered to the left instead of stopping in front of Cade, and then Cade whistled at Tornado. The horse stopped as suddenly as it could, turned, and raced back to Cade where he stopped and stood, barely breathing hard. Margo was nearly winded, but she was smiling. "Wow, it was like flying. He is so cool!"

"Come down."

There was no smile on his face or twinkle in his eye, and she was thinking now that he might be mad at her about this, even though nothing happened. She flipped her leg over the saddle horn and slid off Tornado to land gracefully on the ground. Tornado stood there as if nothing had happened, but he was looking at Cade.

"You lost your hat." He handed it to her.

"Yes, I did." She took it and put it back on her head.

"You were beautiful!" The smile bloomed across his face and eyes. He picked her up and swung her around. "Like a female warrior! What a sight! The two things I love the most, racing along like one thing. Anticipating what the other was going to do or wanted and just being one. It was beautiful. Do you realize, my wife," he stated, "that I don't have very many men that would do what you just did? Tornado

THE DOUBLE Ⓚ RANCH

is special and knows it. He doesn't let just anyone climb on his back and ride him like that. When I saw you climb up on the chuck wagon I knew what you were doing, and I watched, wondering if Tornado was going to dump you immediately or later at some other opportune time. But he obeyed you and was gentle, more with you than he ever was with me, and he let you ride him. You were beautiful!"

"It was so fun! I want to do it again."

"You will. By the way, here's your gun. We'll go practice as soon as I have time. I have this to contend with today." They walked back to camp, Cade leading Tornado with the reins in one hand and the other arm wrapped around Margo.

The trailers were all designed to look like log cabins and looked wonderful. Cade and Margo's double wide forty foot long trailer, Lois and Kirk's park model were set in and usable for the first night. There was space between the ends of the two trailers and Cade explained to the carpenters that he wanted a wooden "porch" between them and steps down to the ground below. He gave them a sketch of what he was seeing for a completed porch.

It took three days to get all the trailers set in and attached to electricity, water, and sewer boxes that would have to be emptied by the pumper truck once a month. The entire camp was set up in a horseshoe design with little number six crosswise at one end of the horseshoe and the huge kitchen and dining hall at the other end. Margo and Cade's cottage, which was the first one set in at a forty-five-degree angle cornered to the line station. Lois and Kirk's cabin was set up end to end with Margo and Cade's, and looked similar on the outside. Missy's was next with a walk through between them. Then one of the bunkhouses were set end to end with Missy's and another bunkhouse was set at a forty-five-degree angle to that with a walk through space between it and the next bunkhouse and the last bunkhouse was set at a 45 degree angle with that. The last cabin was Henry and Josh's, and it was closest to the kitchen, which made Henry very happy. The big double-wide, double-long kitchen building was set up at a forty-five-degree angle to the last bunkhouse with enough space between them for a walkthrough to the shower building and laundry building behind the bunkhouses. The small forest that was near number six line station was far enough away from the end of the kitchen/dining hall building that the equipment could drive through into the interior of the compound. Fortunately, the drivers had brought hammocks and strung them up between their trucks, having the foresight to know it was going to take a couple days to setup the trailers.

The feeling of safety permeated the little compound, and Margo had heaved a huge sigh when the drivers climbed in their tractor-trailers and left at the end of a long week. She was feeling safe again.

The next day, Chuck ran the bulldozer through the interior just enough to scrape the grass off the surface of the yard, then he actually built a new road around the end of the dining hall and up the back side of it, leaving enough space for the new little porch and stairs and the garbage can area at the backside of the kitchen, then around the corner of the kitchen, past the laundry and shower buildings; and a turn toward the ruins. While it took him most of the day, it was a great road when it was finished. He placed huge boulders at various places to ensure vehicles did not scrape the corners of the buildings or leave the road, causing unwanted widening of the road, hiding the sewer boxes but leaving them easy to access by the pumper truck. After a few days, trees were planted along the side of the road and the buildings, providing shade for future summers and instant eye appeal. Some of the guys unloaded and moved the storage sheds to a space behind the kitchen and then reloaded them.

Margo and Missy were delighted with the kitchen and dining hall. It was complete with double-wide fridge, double-wide freezer, two dishwashers, two clothes washers, two driers, two double sinks side-by-side, and an eight-burner electric stove with built-in grill/griddle, and four built-in ovens. It was actually a huge kitchen and mess hall designed for a construction site. Cade lucked out and found one that was decked out with the log cabin look on the outside. It apparently had been used, at some point for a logging camp, but Cade had all the new appliances put in. Along with the refrigerator in number six, they had no problem with keeping things cold. All the pots and pans, utensils and a huge coffee pot and toaster oven were included in the cupboards. Henry and Tinker helped put all the smaller appliances where Margo and Missy thought they would be best used. They even found an ice cream maker. Carpenters were available for quick carpentry work where and when needed.

Cade surprised them all by having four small refrigerators set into the front of the work island/stove and grill. This was for the cold drinks and was easily accessible to the hands from the dinning side of the room and eliminated the coolers on the floor.

Cade was very good at knowing what was going to be needed and ensuring the logistics to the project was set up and ready to go on a moment's notice, and he had remembered to put new mattresses in each of the beds or bunks, and packages of new blankets, sheets, and pillows on each bunk, tied down with string for the ride to the site. The line station was empty, and the hands moved the refrigerator and freezer from its temporary station to the kitchen beside the ice machine, gutted number six, and built in shelves; and it became a huge pantry and storage room. The cats were put on notice to keep all rodents at bay. The shower was still going to be used by the women and shelves and cupboards lined the concrete walls.

Lois set up office in her dining room and the carpenters built a "closet" between her trailer and Missy's trailer for storage of office supplies.

SEVENTEEN

The bunkhouses were four sets of two up bunks, which were on both short ends and the one long wall of the cabin. The last long wall, with the entry door was lined with closets, one for each bunk. They weren't much bigger than large lockers, but the guys didn't need walk-in closets. It was all very well space-utilized, and Margo was impressed. She was surprised they had no bathrooms until Cade took her to the shower building, and she saw that it had four shower stalls, each stall with a space inside to change clothes, then there were four stalls for the toilets and four sinks set into a long counter along the last wall. The carpenters built a "closet" between the shower and laundry buildings for mops and brooms and supplies.

Margo and Missy met in the kitchen the next morning and had to start breakfast feeling lost. So Margo suggested that they just make breakfast the best they could and worry about rearranging and storing stuff later. It was fairly easy making huge egg omelets and bacon and toast, and the guys enjoyed breakfast in their new dining hall. Everyone was talking about their new bunkhouses.

At five o'clock all the hands were present and accounted for, breakfast was ready when the door opened and the four gatekeepers walked in. They had locked the gate and left it to God, according to one of the hands. Everyone poured coffee from the new maker and then sat down at the long tables. The discussion about the great kitchen/dining hall intensified as breakfast went on but stopped long enough for Gus to stand and ask God's blessing on the food, the cooks, the hands, the new buildings, the animals, and last but extremely important, Cade.

Cade and Josh had their normal discussion over breakfast, and the others just enjoyed their meal and each other. They were used to Cade and Josh huddled together over meals.

Just before breakfast was completed, Cade asked everyone to stay put as he had something extra and he thought it would be nice to sit inside where they were.

When he and Josh were finished with their morning discussion, Cade told the crew that the next big project was going to be the "porch and over-roof" of the compound and then the barn. He was expecting the building materials to be delivered before noon so, as much as he would like to just leave the gate locked and under God's protection, someone was going to have to go back and keep watch with God on the gate. The four men laughed and nodded their understanding. They had set up their little rules and were very comfortable with what they had put together to guard the ranch. The meeting broke up for a few minutes while they left immediately for number one line station and everyone said thanks and good-bye to the guard crew and the morning meeting of the ranch hands continued. Chuck went with them as he had brought them in the truck and needed to get them back to the gate.

The building materials arrived on time, and the gate keepers had called down to advise that the supplies were on the way down. The rest of the hands had been given the morning for rest and relaxation and general cleanup of their personal areas until the materials arrived. Everyone took the morning to relax and enjoy except Tinker, Russell, and Patrick, the carpenters; and Steve and "Gross" the surveyors, who were all busy with Cade and Josh determining where the barn was going to be and measuring out the area so the foundation could be laid.

Josh told the gate to direct the delivery of the barn-building materials to the branding camp and they would get them where they wanted.

While they were making the porches, Josh got a call from the gatekeeper. Apparently there was another delivery of food, but it wasn't from the wholesaler and a female was driving. She wouldn't give them her ID and had a bad attitude. They were very suspicious and were watching her like a hawk while she waited for clearance. Josh knew that "watching her like a hawk" meant that there were at least three loaded rifles pointed at the driver's head and one loaded handgun ready to be pulled at the smallest reason. He told the gate crew to reject her delivery as they weren't expecting anything right now and to send her away.

That night at dinner, Cade and Josh discussed the attempted delivery. The gatekeeper stated that the driver was a woman with dark, short hair and stated she didn't have any makeup on, extra large, and had a very bad attitude making him think of the cook they had just before Margo.

Both Cade and Josh looked at each other and said, "Delilah."

"What is she trying to do?" Josh asked.

"I don't know, but I'm letting the sheriff know about our suspicions," Cade replied.

After dinner and the kitchen cleaning completed, they were all around the campfire in the compound of the branding camp. Margo and Missy brought out eight huge bowls of popcorn and they sat around telling ghost stories. The ghost stories were tailored to end in laughter instead of fear and screams, and Margo wondered if they had done that so the girls wouldn't have nightmares. At any point, they wound down as the hands drifted off to bed when the mood struck them.

Cade and Margo were the only ones left sitting at the fire. "Are you tired?" he asked.

"Yes, but it's a good tired. I'm not ready for bed yet. Are you? Tired, I mean."

"Well, same as you, I guess."

They sat there watching the flames for a while, and then Cade stood up and kicked the fire out, poured water on it, and pulled Margo up with him, and they headed off to their new bed.

...

A few days later, Margo and Cade received a visitor from the county. It was Inspector Carl, and he just wanted to stop by and chat. He had a lot of news about town, and the ranch was hungry for that information. He was hungry for one of Margo's pies and hoped to catch one coming out of the oven. He was indeed lucky as Margo and Missy were making pies.

Apparently, not a building was spared from the arsonist and not a single family was exempt from his wrath. One good thing about it was that all the junk around town was destroyed along with the good stuff. Nothing was spared, no discrimination. The bad thing: no one had anything of their own. They were living in donated housing, clothing, food, furniture, everything. No one had any vehicles, and he wouldn't have one if the county hadn't sent him a new one. There was a lot of posttraumatic stress syndrome, and his wife was having a severe case of it. He spent a lot of time running "home" to check on her.

When he was done chatting about town, he spotted the pies that Margo had pulled from the oven just before he arrived. She cut a piece of pie for the inspector, in a gesture of hospitality. It was an apple pie, just from the oven and she dropped a huge pile of vanilla ice cream on top of it.

"Margo, how much would you sell those pies for?" he asked.

He'd caught her off guard and she stammered for a minute. Missy finally spoke up, and Margo just looked at her with surprise in her eyes. Missy showed her the work she had been doing while Margo had made the pies and put them in the oven. The pies were calculated out for cost and profit. Margo nodded her agreement, and Inspector Hodges asked if he could buy one to take with him to the wife.

Margo had no box to put it in and explained to the inspector that all her foil pie tins had burned in the fire and she only had a few pie tins to make enough pies for the ranch's use. She carefully slid the pie from the pan onto a paper plate and wrapped a roll of foil around the pie, just under the edge to keep the pie from collapsing outward and then wrapped foil over the top. She was happy to sell him a pie.

"My wife is going to love this pie."

With all the news, the one thing Margo had not heard about was if the arsonist had been captured. She figured if he had been caught, she would have heard, but she had to ask.

"Inspector, have they caught the arsonist yet?" Margo asked.

"No, he hasn't been captured yet." He stood up, left the cash for the pie on the table, took the pie in a gentle grasp and carried it toward the door. "Thanks for the pie, Margo."

"He's going to tell everyone in the county we're selling baked goods," Margo said. Missy smiled.

"Wow! Can you figure this guy? Burning the entire town down! What is wrong with this idiot?" Missy asked.

"The idiot is ill and needs to be locked away for a very long time. I don't think anyone with a functioning brain cell will let him loose again," Margo stated.

"Amen to that! But personally, I hope they execute the cuss. I don't think it's possible to treat some fried brain cells that haven't figured out how to die," Cade said as he walked in. "I can't tell you how glad I am that we were all out here when he hit the old ranch site. God was with us that day."

Margo snuggled into Cade and Missy said, "Margo just sold the inspector a pie."

"I saw him getting in his truck with it. Seemed to be in a hurry to get away from here." Cade grinned.

A couple days later, Margo and Cade went out for a ride. Cade was tired. He'd been working for so long without a break, and he just wanted to take Margo for a ride, just a day with each other, away from the ranch and everything.

Margo packed a little lunch for the two of them, set up everything so Missy could handle it on her own, and they headed toward the old ruins and the front gate, via the back road around the lake his father had built. The road behind the lake was very rough and unused, almost overgrown in places, but eventually it came to the "triangle" as Cade called it. To the right was the asphalt road to the gate and to the left was the same asphalt road to the ruined ranch house. From here they could see the entire lake. Margo felt it was perfect for her restaurant bakery and told Cade her dream. He listened and asked one question. "Do you want a restaurant and bakery?"

She looked at him and said, "Yes."

Delilah sat in the temporary bar and grill up on the highway. The original building had been burned to the ground. They got the insurance and now had reason to rebuild and everything would be new. She sat at the bar and complained about how small and hard the little red stools were. Then when her drink was done, she ordered another and fingered the envelope on the counter, hidden by her arm. That was her check from Welfare. She had applied several times, been rejected, several times, but this time, because she lived in the burned out town of Nowhere, she was sure she had been granted benefits. Everyone else in town had been granted welfare. Everyone else in town had been granted everything they wanted.

She waved the unopened envelope in front of the waitress's face and said, "Put it on my tab. As soon as I get this cashed, I'll come pay off my tab."

"Can't do that Delilah. You've hoodwinked the owner twice now. I got orders to get money or have you arrested."

Delilah became indignant. She hadn't seen the four state troopers come in and sit down nearby. With vulgar language and a hot voice she started screaming at Hank, the owner behind the kitchen wall. She could see him back there by the stove and launched a stream of epitaphs that would cause a pimp to blush.

Delilah, sure the envelope held a check, ripped it open to wave in front of Hanks' eyes. She had stood up and rounded the counter to the kitchen, a trooper hot on her tail from a nod from Windy, the waitress. Windy cleared the area not wanting to be anywhere near the insane woman.

When Delilah saw only a letter of rejection she screamed, spun on her heels and looked at it again. With a second scream, Hank bolted through the back door, abandoning his café and everyone in it. *It's everyone for themselves,* he thought.

Two troopers left before they had even ordered their meal and by the time Delilah was delivered to the jail, she not only had handcuffs on, she had been gagged with the only thing available, duct tape.

The next morning, after breakfast, Cade was over in the wooded area by number six, behind Tornado, fighting with Tornado's tail, stuck in the tree. Apparently, Tornado had been flicking his tail around and some of his beautiful, long, black tail hairs were tangled in the bark of the tree. They were so tangled that Cade was working on it with a knife. He was so proud of Tornado, and he didn't want to cut Tornado's tail because he didn't want this huge, short mass on one side of his tail. It would take forever for it to grow out to its long, to-the-ground length, and he just wasn't into waiting for that to happen. So he was fishing one hair out at a time when Margo walked up to Tornado's muzzle.

"Hi, Tornado."

"Margo!" Cade yelled. "Don't give him a carrot. He'll kill me with his carrot dance."

Margo walked around to the rear of Tornado to see what Cade was doing. Cade looked at her for a moment and then told her to stay away from Tornado's back hooves.

Margo understood the reasoning for her to stay well away from Tornado's back hooves, but she couldn't figure out why it was all right for him to be right there. She knew he was tired. Maybe he wasn't thinking about the situation totally. He explained to her that he was close enough that if Tornado kicked him, it might hurt like hell for a while and bruise him, maybe break his leg, but the closer the better because he couldn't get much of a swing going before his hoof would strike. And since he was nearly through extricating Tornado's tail, it was pretty well moot.

He no more than finished his sentence than Tornado decided to take a survey of his own. He bucked and kicked both his hind feet out, catching Cade in the right hip and right wrist and knocking him about ten feet away. Cade fell to the ground like a tree. Margo screamed, and Tinker and Josh ran over to help Cade. Henry and Paul ran up, Henry grabbed Margo, and Paul took care of Tornado.

Tinker and Josh were hunched over Cade, who wasn't moving and Margo was pulling on Henry to let her go. He held her fast, telling her that Cade didn't need her right then. Missy and several hands ran up to see what had happened. Henry apprised them of the situation with Cade.

Paul moved in to the area with Josh and was asked to make a stretcher. Now Margo knew it was bad. Gus helped Paul make a stretcher for Cade, Josh stood and walked to Margo, held in Henry's hands.

"I think his hip is broken and definitely his wrist. We really need to call the LifeFlyte and get them out here to take him to the hospital."

Margo agreed, and Josh called the helicopter. Henry stayed beside her; he knew he had to get Margo into action. "Honey, go pack something for yourself and Cade; toothbrushes, that kind of stuff. You don't want to go without a change of clothes. You want Missy to help?

"Yes. Thanks, Henry." She went to her cabin to get something ready to go. Missy came in shortly and helped her put a change of clean clothes for herself and Cade in a bag, along with a few normally used toiletries, and then she hugged Margo and said it was going to be all right. Margo broke down and cried in Missy's arms. Finally she dried her eyes and closed the bag.

"You have your phone and charger?" Missy asked Margo.

"Yes."

"Well, let's go make sure you have Cade's, too."

They went out, and Cade was now fully conscious and on a stretcher made of a sleeping bag and a couple of ropes. It was only going to be used to get him to the helicopter. She stooped down and put her hand in Cade's. "How are you?"

"Hurts like hell."

"You just relax and let me do what I have to do for you, okay?"

"Okay, Margo, stay with me?"

"Absolutely, now relax. You're going to be fine. We'll just take our time and it will be fine."

She stood up and Henry put Cade's wallet and phone in her bag, Margo checked for her wallet. Then Henry put his arm around her and led her to the new road behind the shower building where they had set Cade down on his makeshift stretcher.

The helicopter landed a short distance away, and the engine was turned off and two EMTs carried a stretcher basket loaded with equipment over to where Cade was laying. Everyone moved away in order to give the EMTs some room. They took his vitals and checked his injury, cutting away his jeans.

One of the EMTs took information from Margo, then wanted to know how the injuries had happened.

"Kicked by a horse," Josh replied. Margo was starring at Cade, she was wondering if she was going to lose him. *How would I go on? What would happen to the ranch, to all the people that depended on Cade and her for their lives?* It suddenly hit her that she couldn't lose Cade and they had to go on, no matter what.

They gently transferred Cade into the Stokes's stretcher and put a needle in his left wrist and wrapped it in a gauze type of wrap to keep it and the line from being ripped out by accident. They hung up a clear liquid plastic bag on a short clip above his left shoulder. They covered him with a light blanket and laid a small oxygen bottle between his legs, and put some kind of packing over his right leg to keep it from moving and connected the safety belts over Cade to ensure he and his packing didn't fall out of the stretcher.

"Is anyone else going?" the EMT asked.

"Yes. I am," Margo stated.

The EMTs and a couple of hands picked up the stretcher and carried Cade to the waiting helicopter where the EMTs opened the door and slid the stretcher in. Margo and Josh walked along behind the stretcher and waited while it was loaded.

Margo turned to Josh and just looked at him, a million things running through her head, all of them disjointed and out of sync.

"It's all right. I understand. We'll make do while you're gone. Just go and be with him and make sure you call me several times a day. You know what it's like at this end not knowing what's going on with him."

"Yes. I'll call you often. Thanks for understanding, Josh."

"Not a problem. You ready?"

"Yes. Is there anything I need to do before I leave?"

"No. Just know he's going to be all right."

He gave her a hug and then took the bag out of her hand. He helped her into the helicopter after the EMT told her where to sit and he handed her the bag, then turned and walked back to the group on the road. The first EMT was at the helicopter controls and the second EMT made sure Margo had her seat belt locked and then he jumped in and sat down next to Margo, keeping tabs on Cade.

As the engine started, Margo asked the EMT if Cade was in pain.

"Yes, but he's getting a bit of morphine so he's all right. The less movement we can give him, the better he'll feel. He's going to need you through this as it isn't going to be an easy trip ahead. Be brave, strong, calm, and just keep him quiet, whatever it takes."

The helicopter flew over the ruins, and she looked down and prayed it wasn't an omen of their lives together. If Cade died, her life would be like the ranch ruins.

Cade seemed to be in excruciating pain the entire time. He reached out at one point and grabbed her hand with a viselike grip. She hung on as long as she could, letting him know it was all right. The EMT was constantly working around Cade, trying to keep him calm and relaxed as much as possible.

Hours later, having gone through the ER, x-ray, and all the forms, Margo called Josh.

"Cade's in surgery. After they took x-rays, they found that his ilium was pretty smashed, and they had to reconstruct it using pins. His right wrist is broken."

She called Josh again when someone came out of surgery about an hour later and said Cade was doing very well. They were still working on his hip. "Anyway, I'll call you when I know something, sooner, I hope, than later."

About an hour later, they wheeled Cade into recovery and started the vigil of making sure he remained stable and improving after surgery. The surgeon went out to the waiting room to find Margo. He found the waiting room empty, save one tall, slender woman, looking very tired.

"Mrs. Knight?"

Margo leaped to her feet, "Yes?"

"Mr. Knight is in recovery now and will be for several hours. He's doing very well. There's no need for you to sit here worrying about him. We've repaired his hip. His wrist has been set, and it's in a cast. He's going to be flat on his back for several weeks, and then he'll need to go to a rehab facility. He's going to have crutches for quite some time. It's not going to be fun, but he'll live and be just as good as new. Now I want you to go and rest. Do you understand?"

"Yes. When can I see him?"

"When I look at your face and see you've rested and he's out of recovery, then you can see him. Now stay here and I'll get someone to come see you about rest."

He turned and walked away. She collapsed into the chair she'd been in before and called Josh. She could tell by his voice that she had awakened him. She gave him the facts and told him that she would call him as soon as there was more news.

"I understand. Margo? Please go get some sleep."

"Yes, I'm going to bed now. I just had to know he got out of surgery and was going to be all right."

"Margo, have you seen him yet? Is he going to be alright? I know Cade. I've known him for a long time, he's like my brother, and for awhile, I felt like his dad when Henry and I had to pull him back from his depression. I don't know if I can do that again.

"Josh, you impress me as being able to do anything. I know you can do what you have to with Cade. He told me that you and Henry saved his life. If it hadn't been for the rough scrubbing you gave him years ago, he probably wouldn't be here. That's how much he loves you. He needs you to keep being that way, to keep the others from getting up and leaving. We can rebuild the ranch, but if he loses you and the others, he'll be down that trail you pulled him out of before. He can't go back there. I won't let him, and I need you and Henry and all the rest to help me keep him from that place."

"Okay. I understand. You're right. I know you're right. Bring him back to us, Margo. We need you to bring him back to us."

He ended the call before she could say anything. She closed her phone and stuffed it in her bag.

By the time she hung up her phone, she had followed the young girl down a couple of halls and down an elevator. Now she was in the lobby of some hotel/motel without a clue of how to get back to Cade.

She checked into the hotel. She was shown to a spacious and very clean room. As soon as she closed the door and locked it she went to the bed and pulled off her boots and then pulled down the spread and lay down. She turned on her side facing the window, two chairs, and a table with a lamp on it.

Margo was out like that lamp. It seemed like she was barely asleep when she woke up. It was nine thirty a.m. She had slept most of the night. She got out of bed and headed into the bathroom.

On her way through the lobby, the aroma of food attacked her senses and she stopped in mid stride wondering if Cade would forgive her for stopping to eat. Her stomach was feeling very empty and she was feeling her mind wandering constantly. She turned and found the restaurant nearly empty but open and functioning. She was led to a table in front of a window looking out on a garden with a small pond and fountain in the middle of it and handed a menu. She ordered coffee and plenty of cream, then scanned the menu. She decided on tomato soup and egg salad sandwich. When she finished, she paid and found herself at the hospital's information center. "Hi, I'm Margo Knight. My husband had surgery here and I know they moved him from recovery, but I don't know where they moved him to. Can you tell me, please?"

EIGHTEEN

S ure. Hold on a second and I'll get the information for you. What is the patient's name?" The receptionist was kind and perky. While she had a smile on her face and plenty of energy, she was still able to show compassion and understanding to those that walked up to her desk needing directions, information, even a shoulder to lean on.

"Kincade Knight," Margo stated and spelled it for the record.

The woman punched a bunch of keys on her computer and then looked at Margo. "Okay! And you're Margo?"

"Yes."

"Okay, Mr. Knight is in room four thirty-five. Go up the elevator to my left to the fourth floor, turn right, and the nurse's station should be right there. Please check in with them."

"Thank you."

She did as instructed and in short order found Cade's room. She walked in and found him in a bed that was totally flat, little rails ensuring he wouldn't roll out of the bed. Cade looked like he was floating on a cloud of soft pale green sheets. He looked quiet, pale, and fragile.

She moved to his side, took his left hand in hers, and he opened his sleepy eyes.

"Hi! How are you doing?" she asked quietly.

He closed his eyes and was asleep again.

The doctor came in and read his chart then looked at Margo. "How are you doing?" he asked.

"I'm much better. How is he?"

"His throat is a little dry. It'll feel better when we get a little liquid down it. He's responding very well. You and I can talk about his physical therapy and rehab a little later. But he's moving along quickly."

"He lives on the run."

"I understand. But I want you to understand, I want to see him for his checkups, which will be about once a month for several months after I release him from here, then you can take him to your local doctor after that. Do you understand?"

"Yes. I appreciate your understanding."

"Good. You look much better. You can't help him if you're laid up too."

"I understand."

The doctor left and Margo called Josh to tell him the most current events.

A few days later, Cade was much more animated and talking. He still had the IV. Pain was standard, but it was something the hospital staff worked on constantly, and it was apparently working as it was easier to control every day.

Margo and Cade were able to discuss the ranch and physical therapy, rehab and doctor's visits, and the new barn that the guys were building, and Margo felt like she was a part of his life and helping him and his business.

For that, Margo called Josh on a regular basis and let Cade talk to Josh. He had his own phone with him so he could call whoever, whenever, but she called Josh often while she was with Cade and would just hand the phone over so the two could talk.

The days passed slowly, Margo felt tired constantly and wondered if she was going to get sick. She ensured she ate good food, even wrote down dates, times, and food items eaten and where she ate them, but finally, one day, while talking to the doctor, she asked why she was so tired all the time.

He advised her to get more exercise. After a few minutes of contemplation, she went for a brisk walk through the parking lot, down some sidewalks that seemed to stretch out forever and returned, feeling full of energy and life again. She also took to buying and carrying a bottle of water with her constantly and counting how many ounces she drank a day.

She was feeling much better and when she walked into Cade's room one morning she saw him and instantly felt her love for him bloom again. "Hi!" she said quietly as she walked in. He was watching TV, but she could tell he wasn't really watching it.

"Hi." She watched him come alive as he became more animated.

"How are you feeling?"

"I'm okay. If I don't move, it doesn't hurt."

"Could be the meds you're sucking up."

"There is that, yes."

He watched her for a few moments, then smiled at her. "I love you, Margo."

"I love you, Cade. But it's you I love, not your money. Will you please be more careful from now on? I'm still angry with Tornado."

"You got me. You have all the rest, too, but you definitely have me. Why are you angry with Tornado?"

"Because of this."

"Oh," was all he said.

"You got me."

Josh sent Margo and Cade a picture of the barn with the crew, including the ladies, standing in front of it. Then he sent a picture of Tornado looking sad and missing Cade. Margo watched Cade for indications of anger or hate and was pleased to see his look of love when he saw the picture. Later that night, Margo asked Josh to give Tornado a couple of carrots and then take a picture of him after he'd settled down so Cade could have a picture of Tornado looking happy. He said it would be done. Josh seemed happy with the responses he was getting from Cade.

...

Occasionally, Missy would call Margo to ask about Cade, but then she would give her a short report on what was happening on the ranch. She was baking bread, pies, cookies, and cakes and a couple of the guy's would take them to town and sell them. They were doing a great business and Missy was afraid to stop making them. She was getting calls from people asking for specific items such as sunflower seed bread or peanut butter cookies. So she would package them, staple a tag with name and dollar amount, put them in a separate box and send them to town with the rest of the stuff. The guy's were going on Friday's only. It made it easier all the way around.

Margo was delighted. "Missy, don't quit. I'll be home soon and I'll help. Thanks. And thank the guy's too. We really appreciate it.

As time rolled on, Margo was really antsy. She was sure they would be able to go home in another couple of days. Cade was feeling very good, except when they made him move, which was still slow and painful. The doctor came in for a visit to check on Cade. He chased Margo out of the room to do the checkup. When she left the room, Cade was on his back; when they let her back in, he was on his side and still recovering from the painful event of moving. All they were waiting for was the doctor's farewell address. When Cade took a nap after lunch, Margo sat in the chair and fell asleep.

The doctor returned, bearing news. "He's doing wonderful. I'm going to let him go home, but you and I need to sit down and have a discussion on what he's going to need at home for a full recovery. Do you have time now?"

"I do, yes."

"Okay. Let's get started." He and Margo sat in a couple of chairs together next to Cade's bed. Their meeting with the doctor was informative, factual, and educational and they had the doctor's release for Cade. She knew she was going to be busy in the morning. She had a bed to order, set up a schedule with a PT, and ensure it was all ready and where it was supposed to be by the time she got Cade home.

...

Margo called Josh the next morning to check on the delivery of the bed she had ordered and to tell him that they were coming home as soon as the bed was delivered and ready for Cade. The physical therapist was scheduled to visit them the following day.

Josh called Margo as soon as the bed was delivered, but the only place it fit was in the great room of their house. He said the ranch was ready for Cade's return. Fortunately Cade and Margo had only been gone for about six weeks and everyone was looking forward to their return.

She spent the evening sitting next to Cade, and they talked about their dreams and their lives and their family of nearly forty. She wondered about the arsonist and the town and then with a yawn, she fell asleep in the chair next to Cade, her head lying on his mattress near his left hip. He lay there watching TV with the sound box next to his ear and his left hand stroking Margo's head. When the nurse came in, she asked Cade the usual checkup questions and took his vitals then left, not disturbing Margo.

Cade fell asleep not long after that, hand-in-hand with his sleeping wife in the chair. When he woke up at six in the morning, it was to another shift change of nurses, and Margo was missing from his room. He called her on his phone. She would be there shortly to take him home. All was set up and waiting for their arrival.

After they closed their phones, Cade went back to sleep. When he woke up next, Margo was working with a nurse getting him into a light sweatshirt and loose-fitting shorts for the ride home. Two male nurses came in and helped transfer Cade to the basket stretcher that the helicopter used to transport patients that couldn't sit on the seat. Cade wasn't real thrilled with going home in the prone position but had no say in the matter.

He was strapped down in the basket stretcher and left on a gurney in his room when the nurse came in and gave him one last injection. "This may put you to sleep. It's just a small amount of morphine. The vibration of the helicopter will bother you without it."

By the time he was transported to the heliport, he was asleep and unaware of being loaded into the helicopter. As soon as the engine was turned on, he woke up and looked for Margo. Margo was sitting in the front passenger seat, and Cade was somehow attached to the floor in the basket stretcher, behind her. The vibrations of the helicopter were irritating but not overly painful, but Cade was glad for the last-minute injection of morphine.

Margo kept an eye on Cade, who appeared to sleep all the way home. But Cade, deciding the view of the blades turning overhead was not the view he wanted, kept his eyes closed and relaxed as best he could, which was a lot better than he had anticipated after the nurse's declaration.

When they reached the ranch and started their descent, Margo looked back at Cade, and he was looking at her. She indicated that they were landing. He just nodded, and she went back to looking out the window in front of her.

They landed, the pilot turned off the engine, Margo signed a form to be billed, and he turned and instructed Josh and crew how to unlock the basket stretcher from the floor. Josh and crew removed Cade from the helicopter, transferred him to the new stretcher that had been ordered and delivered and then reloaded the basket stretcher to the helicopter. Henry helped Margo from the helicopter and took her bag.

Cade was home and delighted. He didn't mind "bunking" in the living room of the house and he progressed from being totally bedridden and doing isometric exercises with specific muscles to moving with a great deal of help. When he could walk five steps unaided, they had a party. Eventually, he was doing tai chi with Tinker.

Cade returned home at the end of October and he and Margo realized that one circle had closed on Halloween night. Tinker and Missy announced their marriage plans to everyone that night after a fun time of caramel apples for dessert. They wanted to get married on the day after Thanksgiving and Cade told them that if they wanted a cruise, he could make the arrangements for them. They asked him for a Hawaiian cruise and he told them he would make the arrangements.

A few days later, the Sheriff stopped by and discussed what was left of some poor woman in a car off the end of the service road on the ranch. The service road was quite a distance from the ranch house and by the looks of everything, it appeared the woman turned onto the wrong road and drove off the end. Her body had decayed to nearly skeletal remains, her purse revealing her name, Rayanne Sax.

When Cade heard the news he looked at Margo and said, "that was the woman that was supposed to come here as bookkeeper at the end of last year."

The information was added to the open file, and many more questions were asked and answered. There was an awesome amount of sadness when everyone realized someone had died on the ranch and they didn't even know. There was no way to have enough people to maintain the kind of security needed to protect every inch of the ranch.

The time between Halloween and Thanksgiving took on an entire new purpose and Margo found herself extremely busy. She wished the bakery wasn't going as it only added to the problem. Missy was baking cookies and bread constantly and Margo was forced to hire another person to do nothing but bake. She found a woman that used to work at the bakery with her and while the woman had survived the town burning, she was delighted at the prospect of moving out to the ranch. She was a great worker and would help Margo and Missy with the meals while cookies or pie were baking in the oven.

She started every day making bread at four o'clock, always worried about waking Cade. Margo had taken to sleeping on a couch next to Cade. Cade would sleep through all the noise, as he had become used to it and he had meds that he took every night that helped him sleep.

Tinker and Missy borrowed the truck and went to Beulah to visit her sister and kids. Tinker was glad to meet them and her sister wanted to come to the wedding. She was invited and Missy was delighted.

Tinker and Missy were married on Thanksgiving Day; Missy's sister and kids were in attendance, leaving almost as quickly as Tinker and Missy after the reception.

The ranch immediately missed Tinker and Missy but were happy for them. But Margo got things rolling when she asked the guys to build a small-one-bedroom apartment in the loft of the barn. Josh turned it around and had them build that small one-bedroom apartment on the ground at the end of the woods they had originally camped in for branding camp. It turned out much better and Margo was delighted. The new bakery cook had a place to call home at last and moved from Missy's cabin to the new cabin in the woods.

Candy helped Margo make the wedding cake for Missy and Tinker and Mike had taken several pictures of it so they could put it in a book for the bakery. Margo set up strict hours of operation and stuck to them. She had to or she would never have any time for Cade or anything else. She took up a split shift again, doing breakfast, cleaning up, then taking a couple hours rest, then doing lunch, another cleanup, and taking off three hours until it was time to get dinner going. She usually managed to bake a few cakes, some for the ranch, some for the bakery every night after she had dinner on the table.

Cade had become sufficient enough he could feed Tornado carrots, and Tornado would come from the barn around the corner of the kitchen and up to the rail in front of Cade's door every morning. Margo had put carrots in the refrigerator of their cabin so they could feed him.

Tinker was Cade's constant shadow before the wedding and after he returned. Cade actually enjoyed Tinker's company and knew that Josh had ordered it, but Tinker was so much help. He could advise on the little twinges of pain, the cramps, and the exhausted feelings after exercises. Sometimes the pain would be intense enough that Cade feared he was falling apart and had undone something. Tinker would calm him and explain that it was normal. He just needed to slow down a little.

While Cade had been in the hospital, the barn was completed, a chicken coop and pig pen were built, the gardener had remade the garden with a lot of help from all the hands and things were getting back to normal. The hands had gone on a chicken hunt to gather as many chickens as they could find and haul or herd them to the new coop. They were surprised after a few days of hunting to have collected all but about twenty of the original flock. Alex, the chicken master, was happy to have most of the flock back and figured a few died in the fire and a few more probably got eaten by wild critters. Russell and Patrick put together a new wagon for Alex to drag around collecting eggs. As soon as they were through making the wagon, they started making flats for the eggs.

Things were looking up for the ranch when some of the guys, still hunting chickens, came upon a small herd of pigs and hogs. They herded them back to the barn and some of the hands quickly erected a second "hog house," and then everybody joined in hunting pigs. One more chicken was found while hunting pigs, and it seemed to be real happy about regaining a new coop and being back with friends. Several more pigs and hogs were found, and Gary was careful to ensure that the pigs and hogs he was finding and herded back were his and not wild ones. When they were wild, they could destroy his herd.

One such poor young wild pig was slaughtered and roasted. It was very tasty and everyone enjoyed it immensely.

Finally Cade was cleared to ride Tornado again, and he couldn't wait to get on him. Josh ordered Tinker to continue as Cade's constant shadow because he knew Cade would go all out and hurt himself.

Christmas came and went without a blizzard or even a snowflake falling. Josh had ordered and received a pile of Christmas lights. There were several small fir trees cut and brought into the cabins. The hands of a particular cabin decorated their tree and then a larger tree was brought into the middle of the compound and along with a bucket, buried into a hole dug near the fire pit. The bucket was below the lip of the hole and someone threw water in it every day. Josh had a couple guys lighting the tree and on Christmas Eve at seven o'clock, the lights were turned on the big tree for the first time.

Everyone had gone out to the yard to watch the lights come on, Tornado was even present along with Stormy. Margo had tied festive ribbons in Stormy's mane and tail. Tornado was still boss but Stormy always gave him a run for it. He often let her win.

On Christmas day, Cade told Margo that Stormy was pregnant from Tornado. She was delighted.

That night, Margo lay beside Cade on their bed, and she asked him how he felt. He told her he was fine but tired. When she asked if he wanted to make love, he didn't reply, he just rolled over on to his side and wrapped her in his arms and pulled her close for a few moments.

Afterwards they lay there waiting for their breathing and heart rates to level out, and Cade laughed.

"Are you all right?" she asked.

"I'm fantastic!" He grinned. "How about you?"

"Fine. Why?"

"'Cause your pregnant, and I could hurt whoever is in there?" He put his hand on her belly and gently rubbed it around.

"I'm not pregnant."

"Yes, you are." He put her hands on her stomach. "It's not as flat as it used to be, is it?" He was right.

About a month later, Margo was sick in the morning and stumbled into the kitchen to make breakfast. All she wanted to do was go back to bed, but she turned on the ovens grabbed a saltine cracker and went into the restroom to vomit. After making sure she was presentable, she spruced the little restroom up, vowing to put a toothbrush and toothpaste in the cabinet, and went back into the kitchen. Henry was making coffee and after his greeting asked if she was all right.

As soon as she had put on the second batch of eggs, she ran into the restroom to vomit again. When she came out, more of the men were getting coffee, and Missy was taking care of the eggs and getting the food out of the oven to go to the table. She scraped the eggs onto a platter while Margo washed her hands.

When the food was on the table, Margo left without a word and went to her cabin and went back to bed. A couple hours later, she was back in the kitchen feeling much better and helping Missy to start the lunch menu.

"Margo, are you all right?"

"I think I have the flu. I've been sick for three mornings in a row and then I feel better about this time of the day. I am so tired that I sleep all night, which is not my style, and then I get up sick in the morning."

"You need to go see the doctor, and while you're there, take a pregnancy test. Looks like you're going to have a cute little baby in a few months."

"Oh, Missy, I don't want to be pregnant."

"Why?"

"I don't know. I just don't want to be pregnant right now."

"Sometimes, we don't get to pick the timing. Go tell Cade to get you to the doctor for a checkup. It wouldn't hurt in any case."

"Okay. But I hate doctors."

She went back to the cabin, and Cade was there doing some PT exercise with Tinker. She asked if she could lie on the bed while Cade did his exercises and, getting the affirmative, gently lay down on the bed while Cade continued to do his exercises. She was asleep in short order, totally unaware of everything after that.

NINETEEN

Cade went to the dining hall and ate lunch and told Josh and Tinker he was taking Margo to the doctor for a checkup. Tinker went with them to the doctor's office and waited while Margo and Cade went to the exam room.

Awhile later, Cade and Margo came out. Cade was beaming, Margo was still shaky and tired, and Cade announced that he was having a baby. Then had to amend it to they were having a baby.

Cade drove the truck home, practically crawling all the way. Tinker just sat there, patiently waiting because he knew what Cade was thinking. He was going slow because he didn't want anything to happen to Margo and the baby.

Tinker had a grin on his face by the time they reached the compound, and he got out of the truck and helped Margo out, then he went to his own bunk for a nap.

When Cade got Margo back into their own cabin, he helped her lie down on the bed and then stood there watching her, grinning like a huge cat that just ate the bird.

"You have a feather sticking out of the corner of your mouth," she said.

"What?"

"You have a feather … never mind. What are you grinning at?"

"You! My wife is having a baby! I'm excited! I'm happy! I can't help having a grin on my face."

"Go ask Missy if she'd mind doing breakfast and lunch for the next month or so. I'll do lunch and dinner. When the morning sickness stops bugging me, we can go back to before."

"Okay. I'll be back. Do you want anything? You didn't eat lunch or breakfast and you can't be sick now. I mean sick that you do to yourself."

"I know what you mean. I'm just too tired to push food in."

"I'll fix that," he said and headed over to the kitchen.

A woman called wanting to know if Margo was selling pies yet. She was told by a particular lady in town that Margo baked the best pies and she wanted to buy a chocolate cream pie and a fruit-filled pie.

Missy quoted her prices and asked when they were needed. A week out was all right, and Missy asked for the caller's phone number. After getting it, she told Margo they had a job. There was some excitement, and Missy got out the recipes for chocolate cream and then wondered if they could get something besides apples for the fruit pie.

The day of pie pickup had arrived, and Margo had called the front gate to inform them that Joan Hanon was coming to pick up some pies. Margo wasn't happy about the customer coming to the ranch, but she was very insistent with her old cracked voice. They were going to serve their guest a piece of apple and cranberry pie along with coffee. The pies were fresh baked, and the kitchen/dining hall smelled wonderful. The girls were so excited they couldn't sit still. Missy finally went into the restroom just as the guest arrived. But Missy no more than shut the door when Delilah Willglen walked into the dining hall.

Margo felt her blood go thin and just stood there frozen in place.

"Hello, Margo."

"Delilah. Did you change your name recently?"

"No, but I know I wouldn't have been given entrance to the palace using my real name, now would I?"

"We're not in the habit of entertaining liars, beggars, or theives," Margo replied.

"Well, it doesn't look so grand anymore. Too bad about the fire. Looks like it really sterilized Cade's place." She moved farther into the dining area and looked around. "Gone down a bit in status, huh? This place looks like a logging camp. Too bad it isn't in the woods." She turned back to Margo. "Oh! Don't even think about screaming for help, you little witch. Just come out the door with me and get in my car, and we'll be going someplace else and nobody will have to worry. Especially that rich cowboy you hooked and reeled into marriage. I figure he'll thank me for getting rid of you for him. Maybe he'll give me half his money just for the favor."

"Cade wouldn't give you the time of day, Delilah. You know that! Why would you think he'd give you half his money for any reason, never mind killing me? That just shows how silly you are. We know what you've been doing, Delilah!" Margo lied trying to stall for time, maybe even talk Delilah out of her plans, whatever they were, but she was so angry now she knew if she had her gun, she would kill Delilah, trained in firing it or not.

"What do you know about what I've been doing?" Delilah asked, pushing Margo along with her body.

Margo had to think fast. The first thing into her brain was Rayanne Sax. "We know it was you who killed Rayanne and made it look like she drove off the road at the cell tower. You told me one time you figured you could kill someone and get away with it because you loved CSI, and NCIS. So when the Sheriff came here to talk to us about the service road being on our property, Cade explained that he sold the property the road and cell tower are on to the phone company. It's not really Double K Ranch property." She lied again, weaving a story to irritate Delilah to a screaming fit. If she could get her there, she knew Delilah would tell all and be so angry she wouldn't be able to lift a hand to help herself. Delilah always froze when she got angry.

Delilah seemed to be on some kind of relaxing drug. She didn't get angry as Margo hoped for.

Delilah moved her hand, which was stuffed in a jacket pocket. Margo could see the shape of a gun in it, and she moved, like a zombie, to the door. Delilah moved in behind her and shoved Margo down the steps to her beat up little, red, white, and blue Datsun pickup.

Missy, in the restroom, saw the little rusted, red, white, and blue Datsun when it came around the corner of the dining hall windows just as she shut the bathroom door. She took out her phone and called Cade. Chuck was in the woods grooming a horse when Cade called him and he spotted the truck leaving the compound. He saw Margo sitting in the passenger seat, and when she looked at him, she mouthed a silent "help" out the window. He nodded at her and hoped she knew that they had been clued in on what was happening.

Cade had ended his call and called the front gate, and they were calling the sheriff. Cade, Josh, and the rest of the men climbed on horses and raced up through the pasture. While they were moving at breakneck speed, Chuck was following behind the little Datsun on his horse. He didn't care if Delilah spotted him. Perhaps he could be the distraction that the rest could use to advantage.

As Cade and his crew came up from Wandering Creek in the south part of the ranch, they could see the little red, white, and blue truck moving along the dirt road across the grassland, and Cade slowed his men down. He knew Delilah wouldn't think to look farther down in the field. He pulled Tornado to a halt and called the gate crew. "Is the sheriff here yet? Good, let him in and direct him to the ruins. If we can stop this by the ruins, we'll be done with it." The gatekeepers acknowledged and let the sheriff in telling him to get to the ruins.

Delilah drove her truck along the rutted trail to the ruins and as she drove she carried on a single-sided conversation with Margo boasting about how she burned her old trailer down and then a couple of other houses and eventually the town and how stupid the firefighters were because they couldn't figure out who did it and how it was done.

Just when Margo was giving up, Delilah dropped a bomb shell.

THE DOUBLE ⓚ RANCH

"How do they know I did it? That road is large crushed stone, so no tire prints. Gloves eliminate fingerprints and they found her ID and what about the $2,500.00 cash from her purse. If I did it, why haven't they arrested me?"

"I don't know Delilah. Maybe they were too busy trying to stop the town from burning down. You burned the ranch down, did you take anything of value from it first, or were you stupid enough to torch it without first ripping us off of all the valuables you could find?"

"Oh! You mean like your necklace?" She held up her hand now, Margo's necklace dripping glitter as the sun caught the stones and reflected their beauty.

When Delilah reached the ruins, she didn't just slow down, she stopped. "You see that charred mess over there?" She pointed at the ruins.

"What about it?" Margo answered with hate dripping from every word. She didn't need to turn her head and look at the ruins; she knew what they looked like. She never looked over at the ruins. Then Margo was looking at something else in the truck.

"That's my handiwork." Delilah stated with pride and a bit of insanity woven into the words. Margo had finally had enough of Delilah's boasting. But before she could move, a cat jumped over the back of the seat, landed on Delilah's shoulder and leaped onto the dash and crouched down with a mouse hanging from its mouth. Delilah screamed and was distracted by the cat, and Margo whipped out her left hand, grabbed Delilah's right ear and pulled her head down onto her own thigh. Her grip on Delilah's ear slipped, and Delilah sat back up, her hand going toward her ear. Delilah was screeching in pain and terror, and Margo quickly shoved Delilah's head against the door window and then quickly slapped Delilah on the back of her head as hard as she could. Delilah's head slammed into the window and then the steering wheel, and she let out a loud scream of pain, rapidly followed by a squeal of anger, equally as loud. Margo slammed Delilah's head against the side window, twice again, then grabbed her hair and pulled her down until it was on her thigh, and placing her left hand on Delilah's ear to keep it on her thigh, she started beating Delilah's face with her right fist as hard as she could. Delilah was screaming in terror and pain, and Margo was relishing the pain and fear she was inflicting.

"How's it feel, Delilah? How's it feel to hurt and be afraid? You are the nastiest female-mama-dog I have ever had the misfortune of knowing, and if I kill you, I'll be justified you stupid … brainless … twit!" The three words were emphasized with a punch to the nose, eye, and mouth. Delilah's face was bleeding, and Margo could feel a gash across her knuckles where Delilah's teeth had carved a nasty cut on them, but she continued to beat on Delilah. She was so angry she didn't care if she beat Delilah to a pulp. There was no mental help for Delilah. She was deranged and needed to be destroyed like the rabid, filthy animal she was.

Margo didn't realize it, but the truck was surrounded. Two sheriff's cruisers were blocking the exit forward, and Cade and some of the men were on the right side of the vehicle, while Josh and more men were on the left side, and there was Tinker and Chuck and a group to the rear of the truck. Cade sat on Tornado, grinning from ear to ear at Margo beating the stuffing out of Delilah and hearing Delilah squealing. He knew Margo wasn't pulling any punches. When he slid out of the saddle and handed his reins to Steve, he noticed all the men watching with grins all around, including the sheriff, who was standing with his arms crossed over his chest, greatly enjoying the scene unfolding in the truck.

Cade opened Margo's door and grabbed her wrist and pulled her out. She swung around and just missed his jaw with her bloody fist. She was still screaming at Delilah, and he really didn't know she had the vocabulary she was using, but it didn't surprise him. That was his warrior-princess!

When Cade pulled Margo from the car she managed a vicious kick to Delilah's jaw just before she was out of the truck.

Cade was busy with Margo as he continued to struggle with the extremely angry female in his arms. "Settle down, Margo." She continued to scream at Delilah who was refusing to come out of the truck, knowing nobody was strong enough to pull her out.

"Margo! Throttle back, simmer down, and be quiet!"

Margo was exhausted. Her anger and the physical exertion had so thoroughly emptied her fuel supply she slumped in Cade's arms. He set her down on Delilah's hood then checked her out. She was unharmed except the gash across her knuckles. While Cade checked on Margo, Delilah was screaming police brutality because they stood there, just grinning, and not helping her against that crazy woman of Cade's.

Delilah was screaming about police brutality and how she was the victim of Cade's witch. Cade dropped Margo's wrist and rounded the hood of the ugly little truck and bore down on Delilah with hate and death in his eyes. He reached into the truck and pulled the cat out of the truck, which dropped the mouse, which scampered around in the truck looking for a place to hide.

Delilah suddenly wanted out of the truck. Margo was very quiet now.

Delilah opened it and nearly exploded from the truck. While the sheriff watched Delilah screaming nonsense about suing Margo and Cade until she owned their fancy ranch and everyone on it, he heard Margo state that Delilah had her necklace. As soon as Margo said necklace, Delilah started twirling and shaking the necklace in a taunt at Margo. She had just given the sheriff all the evidence he needed for a conviction.

When Delilah twirled the necklace close enough, he snatched it from her fingers.

"Hey! That's mine! Give it back. Give it back!" she yelled louder.

The sheriff showed it to Cade. Two deputies grabbed Delilah and held on while she clawed the air trying to take the necklace back.

"That's Margo's all right." His eyes glittered a warning to Delilah, and she backed away in fear.

Then the sheriff pulled out a full can of gasoline and an open bag of balloons along with a timer from the small job box in the back of the truck. "Delilah, you're my arsonist."

"You bet I am," she said proudly. "And you'll have to admit, I'm the best one you ever had."

"Oh, I'll admit that you're the only arsonist I've ever had. I'll make sure the judge is aware of your pride in your work habits."

Cade couldn't believe how easily Delilah confessed. He knew she was bragging and didn't even realize she was confessing. His anger outweighed his pity for an insane, uneducated, woman who probably never knew love and was only taught hate and meanness. The sheriff had her confession, and it was done in front of thirty-plus people, all of whom would be happy and willing to stand up against her in a court of law. He looked around at each man and knew they had all heard Delilah's remarks to the sheriff.

"Delilah, why did you burn down Nowhere?"

"Because all you people are so stupid and selfish. All of you got welfare after I burned the town down, but did I get any welfare? All of you got clothing and food, shelter and even money, but I didn't get a thing, except a lot of crap no one else wanted. Besides, I started with people that did me the worst first. Like those that quit on me and caused me more work and worry. Nobody quits on me!" she yelled.

"Delilah, why did you burn the Double K Ranch? You fired Margo; she didn't quit."

"No, but that overly rich husband of hers fired me for no reason."

"As I understand it, Delilah, you were stealing him blind."

"He could afford it. Now, Sheriff, are you going to take me to town so I can put suit against the Double K Ranch owner and his hooker wife?"

"I am taking you to town. I'm putting you in jail, and you're going to stand trial for several counts of arson, first-degree murder, at least one count of grand theft, several counts of cruelty to animals, and more counts of child endangerment. Now you go with the deputies and behave yourself, and I'll make sure your cell is clean before I throw you in it."

"Wait a minute, Sheriff! You need to add kidnapping to that, at least two counts. Margo is pregnant! I want Delilah charged with two counts of kidnapping, with the intent to kill, because we all know she would never have let Margo go." Cade was in a rage. Margo had never seen him so angry.

"All right, Cade. I'll add the charges. I don't blame you. Would you like me to add trespassing to that?"

"Add every charge possible, Sheriff," Cade replied. "Even trivial ones."

The sheriff grinned and turned her over to the deputies that took her off to one of the cruisers and looked at Cade. "Margo all right?"

Cade looked at Margo. "Aside from a few bruises and bloody knuckles, my little hell-cat is just fine; pregnant, but just fine." He shook his head in disbelief and thanked the sheriff for his quick response and help.

"I figure I did this crew a favor. They looked pretty mean when I drove up."

"They were aiming to kill if needed. We're not vigilantes, but we're protecting our own."

"I understand, Cade. No problem here. Have a good day." He turned and went to his cruiser and got behind the wheel and turned it around, then rolled his window down and told Cade that he'd have Derrick and his wrecker come over and haul that pile of crap off the ranch and back to town.

"Wait! Sheriff, Delilah talked about the woman on the cell phone tower road. She said something about ID in her purse but $2,500.00 missing. I didn't hear anything about the woman's purse. Did you find it? Was there $2,500.00 in it?" Margo asked.

"No money, but we did find an empty bank envelope in her purse. I need you to come to the station. We'll need that little bit of information on paper. There was cash missing from her purse. We never published that because we wanted to use it to ensure we got the right person. We checked with the bank and Delilah nailed the amount to a penny. Guess we got our murderer, too."

Cade rounded the little Datsun and pulled Margo into his arms. "You did good, Rocky!"

Margo laughed and hugged him back. Then she climbed up on the hood of the Datsun with Cade's help, and Cade swung onto Tornado's saddle, slower than usual. He coaxed Tornado up next to the Datsun and slipped behind the saddle. Margo turned her back, and Cade slipped his arm around her waist and pulled her back onto the saddle. She swung her right leg over Tornado's head and the saddle horn and leaned against Cade. He wrapped his arms around her and tapped Tornado's sides with his boots.

Now that anger had chilled and love could swim back to the surface, he asked, "You okay?"

"I'm fine."

Baby?"

"Fine, too. Hanging on for dear life. I think it's a boy though."

"Why is that?"

"Because when I was beating on Delilah, he was kicking me in the side with each swing I took. Of course it was kicking Delilah in the head at the same time." Now Margo was grinning, and so was everyone else.

He held her hand to look at her knuckles. They were bloody, and he knew they would be bruised, too. She'd clean up well when he got her back.

"Glad you and the baby are safe, Margo. Good job," Josh said as he rode beside them. "You are a pleasure to watch, lady."

Josh kicked his horse into a canter and headed down the pasture. Tornado, unusually calm for his style, slowly wandered along toward the branding camp.

"What did you do to him? It's like he's stuck in first gear."

"He knows you're up here. Actually I've been fighting his will since I first saddled him this morning, so I'm a little surprised at him, myself. That quick ride up here just about did my ilium in. So right now, I'm not a bit unhappy about his slow speed."

"Cade, are you all right?" Margo was quickly anxious.

"Yep. Just going to go lay flat on my back for a couple of days ... I mean hours." He grinned.

She looked around, and Tinker was the only hand still beside them. All the others had made it back to camp already. "Tinker, is he ll right?"

"He seems to be fine Margo. I can't see him having any difficul-
 right now. He's still sore and a little slower than usual, but that's

expected. He wants to call it quits for the day; I'd let him. He still needs lots of rest and relaxation for a while yet."

"Guys, I'm still here. I can hear you."

They winked at each other and ignored him. "Do you think he's doing all right in his PT? I mean is he still doing it and getting enough?"

"Oh, he's fine in his PT. How's he sleeping at night?"

"Hold it! I know you're pushing this, but that's beyond. I'll risk the pain! He kicked Tornado in the sides, and the horse launched himself. Cade hung on to Margo and grinned as Tornado finished that last mile as though it were only a few feet. Tornado nearly skidded to a halt in the compound right in front of Cade and Margo's trailer door.

A small cat was sitting on the porch licking its fur. Margo recognized it as the cat in the truck. "I wonder whose cat that is. It saved my life," stated Margo.

"It's mine," replied Tinker. The cat stopped licking its fur and leaped up into Tinker's arms. Tinker settled it down onto the saddle horn, and it snuggled down as best it could for the ride to the barn. Tinker constantly stroked the cat as he rode along.

It didn't seem long before Margo felt like the Volkswagen she had predicted after her first visit to the doctor's office. Cade helped her move to everyplace. He wouldn't let her work in the kitchen because she was carrying his baby and she was starting to have a difficult time standing on her feet for long.

She was feeling huge and ugly and was at a point where she wanted the baby out of her belly and wondered if there was a way she could have a C-section. She even told the doctor that she felt like she was as wide sideways as she was forward and asked the doctor about it, and he turned her down. Too many unnecessary C-sections happening and she wasn't going to have one unless it was an emergency, he'd told her. He accepted no excuses and stood firm on the subject.

Going to town every week to see the doctor was a pain literally. The roads were bumpy, and the trip into town and back home were not fun nor did she look forward to it. What she really wanted was to be done with being pregnant and get on with being mom and wife again. About the seventh month of dragging around a bloated and growing belly, the doctor informed her that she was carrying twins. That explained why she was so large. Now two weeks before due date, the doctor instructed her and Cade that she needed to visit his office on a daily basis because she was close.

TWENTY

"Oh, joy!" she grumbled.

The next day she was sitting on a bench at one of the tables, rubbing her huge bloated belly, feeling the babies kicking inside when there was a splashing sound at her feet and her pants, shoes, and socks were soaked. "Oh no!" she said in amazement. "My water broke!"

Tinker had just walked into the kitchen when Margo had made her announcement and he stepped back out on the porch, opened his phone, and called Cade. Missy grabbed a towel she had nearby and rushed it to Margo's hands.

Missy, at Margo's direction had gone over to Margo's cabin and collected the items that Margo had asked for, shoes, socks, pants, panties, large suitcase, baby suitcase and had helped Margo into the lavatory where she was cleaning up and changing clothes. She was there with the mop cleaning up the water from the floor. She just got it in the bucket when Cade drove up outside. "Where is she?" he yelled as he leaped from the truck.

"She's in the kitchen, Cade," Missy yelled back through the open door.

Cade nearly ran through the door, saw her coming out of the lavatory. "Are you all right? Are the babies all right?"

Margo smiled and said she and babies were fine.

"The helicopter is on the way. The doctor might just make it here in time to catch it with us." He leaned over and kissed her forehead. "I so love you, mother of my children!"

"Just remember that when I swear to kill you for this and I'm ugly and naked in front of total strangers pushing and grunting and bleeding all over the place! Oh Cade! I can't do this. Why did I think I could do this?" Her face was blotchy, her hands were shaking, and she was a total mess. But he thought she was beautiful and loved her more.

"It's too late to change your mind now, and as I remember, you wanted them too."

"Yes, I did. That doesn't mean that I wanted to carry them and go through the part I get to go through now. We could have tried role reversal."

"Yes, we could have, but I'm lousy at giving birth. I don't seem to have the right plumbing."

"Smart butt! You had the right plumbing to get me here!"

Josh came in. "How's it going?"

At the first sound of the helicopter, off in the distance, Cade stood up, Paul came in and together with Josh moved in to form a cat's cradle. Margo stood up, and the two of them picked her up and carried her out in the cat's cradle.

Margo discovered she was so tired and her back was aching so badly that she didn't even care that they were hauling her around like some sack of potatoes.

Henry drove up with the doctor in the passenger seat. He'd driven up to the trail head to pick up the doctor, knowing that his little Volkswagen would have a real slow time of bouncing through the ruts.

The doctor joined the group and checked on Margo. When she told him her back was aching, he just patted her shoulder and said, "Good. Good! Won't be long now, Margo. Just relax."

Everyone was looking into the sky trying to see the approaching helicopter. Suddenly, Josh pointed and said quietly, "There it is."

Then he leaned over and kissed Margo on the cheek. "Good luck, Mama!"

"Thanks," she said.

The helicopter landed, and Paul and Josh picked Margo up and set her down on the seat. Then Cade climbed in beside her. The doctor climbed into the front seat and buckled in. Tinker handed the two little suitcases in to Cade, and he shoved them under the seat. When Tinker closed the door and moved away, the helicopter lifted off and headed to Sheridan with its precious cargo.

Fifty-three hours later, in the middle of the night, Josh's phone rang, and Cade announced the birth of three healthy baby boys. So identical that Cade couldn't tell one from the other yet. Margo was extremely tired and sleeping the entire ordeal off. At first, she had been upset with the doctor for incorrectly predicting the triplets, but after looking at their beautiful faces, she forgave him. Cade was drunk on pride and fatherhood. He'd been passing out little blue bubblegum cigars with a paper ring that said, "It's A Boy!" He sent a picture over the phone of the three babies crammed together in one bassinette.

Josh knew everyone would want to know, so he opened the door to his cabin and hollered out, "Triplets! Boys! Everyone is fine. More news at six!" Then he shut his door and went back to sleep.

There was a muffled cheer from the various cabins and then silence as everyone went back to sleep.

The next morning, Lois called a florist in Sheridan and ordered balloons from Tornado and flowers from the hands.

Missy started baking cookies for the homecoming. She was so excited she could hardly work. Mike painted another picture of Tornado for the mess hall and got his camera ready for the homecoming. He knew what he was giving Cade and Margo for Christmas this year.

Finally the morning came when Josh got the call from Cade saying that he and the family were coming home on the helicopter at noon.

When the helicopter landed, the pilot turned off the engine so the blades would stop turning and his baby passengers and parents could safely exit the aircraft. Cade jumped down and took one of the baby bundles in his arms. Josh and Henry went out to help Margo out, and Margo handed Henry a baby bundle and Josh another baby bundle. Tinker rushed out and helped Margo out of the helicopter and then pulled out the two suitcases. They all moved away from the helicopter, and Cade turned, baby still in arms, and waived his salutation to the pilot.

Everyone wanted to know which baby was which.

Cade shrugged his shoulders and said he didn't have a clue but Margo knew.

Margo, looking fresh and yet still tired, stood up, switched babies between Cade, Josh, and Henry. Josh was looking a little terrified, and Margo patted his shoulder and said it would be all right, the baby won't break, and just to relax, then she said, "The one that Cade is holding is first born and is Kinkade Jefferson Knight, since his first name is spelled differently than Daddy's, he's not a junior. The one Josh is holding is second born, and he is Kolt Joshua Knight. Henry is holding third born, and his name is Kody Henry Knight."

She watched Josh and Henry and saw the surprise and pride flash on their faces. They knew the reason their names were given, and they were proud. She wanted them to be proud.

Mike, always ready with a camera, jumped in and took a picture of the three men holding their "namesakes," and it was perfect. When Mike moved away, Henry laid the baby on his shoulder and patted his back.

"Hey, Kody, how's it going, little guy?" Henry whispered.

Routine grew rapidly in the compound again. It had changed a little for most and a lot for a few. Mornings found Margo to the kitchen at four, as usual, but she stopped each morning by the door to look at her beautiful boys, sleeping in a crib in what had been the dining room of their home.

Henry would show up in the kitchen and make coffee at four, as usual, but then he would go over to Cade's cabin and help him with the triplets.

By this time, Cade was bathing Kade; so Henry would take Kolt from the crib, pull off his sleeper and diaper, and lay him on the blanket on the floor. Then when Kade was through with his bath, Cade would trade Kade for Kolt. Kolt would go into the kitchen sink that had become the babies' bathtub, and Kade would get wrapped up in a towel and gently dried, powdered, and diapered then dressed in a tiny pair of jeans, a tiny plaid shirt and tiny socks. He'd be placed in his carrier, and Kody would go down to the floor to have his sleeper and diaper removed. He usually got an extra kiss from Henry during the process. When Kolt was done with his bath, Josh was usually there and would trade Kolt for Kody. Henry would take Kade in his carrier, along with the diaper pail, over to the dining hall for coffee and a visit with Mom. Josh would take Kolt and Kody in their carriers to the dining hall while Cade stayed back to clean up the morning bath, make the bed, and tidy the cabin before going to breakfast.

The triplets would be lined up on the couch, safe and warm and pretty much sleeping the morning bath off. Henry would be washing diapers, and Josh would get a mug of coffee for himself and one for Henry. They'd keep their eagle eyes on the boys and do the diapers for Margo.

If it was washday, Cade would take the clothes to the laundry and start washing clothes. The hands had reserved the washer by the door as the family washer. Nobody but Cade and Margo used it, or someone washing diapers for the babies.

Margo would pass out warm bottles to the three guys during breakfast, and they would each fuel up a baby for another hard day of growing, sleeping, and filling diapers.

Cade and Henry would fold diapers after breakfast while the rest of the men went out to the ranch work. When they were done folding diapers, they'd sit in the "lounge" area of the dining hall with the three boys lined up on the couch and Cade would read a book out loud for the boys or take a nap with them as he'd be worn out after all the work.

When Margo took a break between breakfast kitchen cleaning, and lunch preparation she'd come over and sit with Cade, hold the babies for a few minutes, then Cade would get up and go over to the cabin, put away the diaper pail and the clean, folded diapers. He usually took over a load of baby clothes and threw them in the wash. This put him back in the dining hall when Margo went back to work on lunch.

Afternoons found Margo napping on the bed and Cade doing PT with the boys in plain sight and Tinker as coach. When Margo went back into the kitchen, the babies moved to the lounge and Cade and Tinker would go off to the showers and clean clothes, come back, and spend the evening with Margo and Missy in the lounge area with the babies.

They spent a lot to time planning the new ranch house. They decided the first order of business had to be where to build it. Cade pointed to a spot on the map, and it was where Margo had envisioned it many weeks prior.

Cade seemed to have a concern about getting it built as soon as possible as he wanted to be living in it with his family long before the babies were walking. It wasn't long before Cade realized that his dream of living in the new house before the babies were walking was never going to come true.

Two weeks to the day, another portrait was brought into the dining room. It was a picture of Cade, Josh, Henry, little Kade, Kolt, and Kody. The picture taken of the three men holding the three baby namesakes was finished and was perfect. Three tiny versions of Cade were in the men's arms, and while Cade asked it to be put on the wall, the babies gurgled and cooed as it was put in place, as though they knew the picture was of them and were happy with it. Cade stood in front of the picture with first one son, then the next, and the next, letting them look at it.

The portrait wall became crowded with small portraits of individuals that Mike captured on film and then painted in oil. It was a bit like having a private art show in the dining room. Everyone enjoyed it, and it became tradition at dinner to see if you could find the new portrait on the wall.

The ranch prospered and grew in spite of anything that anyone could have done. Cade was happy but hopping and so was everyone else working at the ranch.

It was a mild winter with no blizzards and only a couple of snow falls that hung around for a couple of days at a time. Cade was delighted as he really didn't want to spend another winter in the branding camp.

Delilah's trial arrived and the entire town wanted into the courtroom to watch, but being a small courtroom, only a fraction was allowed in and since Margo and Cade were witnesses, they were ensured a seat.

Delilah became unruly and obnoxious several times during the week-long trial. Each time she got out of line, the judge would have her removed, but not before she shot her mouth off, bragging of one thing or another, or attempting to verbally intimidate someone testifying against her.

The jury was dismissed to deliberate and they nearly walked out of the courtroom and turned around and walked back in. It took them fifteen minutes to elect a foreman, vote, and return to the courtroom. Guilty of every charge brought against her, Delilah was sentenced immediately. That was another surprise. She received four counts of kidnapping in the first degree, ten counts of murder, in the first degree, several counts of cruelty to animals, in the second degree, endangering minors in the first degree, trespassing, theft, and something that amounted to just-plain-meanest-and-harassment. Her sentence was three life sentences, served consecutively. When she died, the judge stipulated that she was to be buried in the prison cemetery, never to be released from behind the guarded gates again.

Amazingly, Delilah was led from the courtroom, silent and without any resistance. There was more noise from the courtroom spectators than from Delilah's demise. Margo was sad, even though she knew Delilah deserved everything she received, it still left her feeling depressed and pitying Delilah.

Cade put his arm around her shoulders and took her to the truck. They climbed in and left the small town of Sundance and headed back up into the woods and hills to home.

The boys' birthday approached, and Margo and Missy created a party. Margo made the birthday cake. It was a train, complete with peppermint candy wheels, butter-mint candy windows, a boxcar with horses "painted" on the side, a gondola full of Boston beans, and a caboose, red of course. She set it all on a foil-covered board and laid the rails in icing. Plastic horses roamed the fields near the winding rails and she made hills from more cake decorated to look like lush, rolling pastures. A ramp up to the boxcar was made from cake and frosted brown with grooves between the boards. When she set it on the floor with the boys, everyone was looking on, and Mike was taking pictures. The boys sat there, looking at the cake, then at Dad, then at Mom, and finally at each other. They seemed afraid to touch it. Finally Kolt reached out and took a wheel off the engine and put it in his mouth. It was a bit too much, so Cade had to rescue the wheel from Kolt's mouth, but that started the other two vandalizing the train of wheels and windows. Apparently the windows were more fun to eat because they left the wheels alone and ate all the windows. At some point, Kolt plucked the top of the caboose off and shoved it into his mouth accomplishing the feat of getting most of it all over his face, hands, neck, and chest and just enough in his mouth to like it. Now he smeared gooey cake on his two brothers, and they had to eat it off their arms. Before they could vandalize the train further, Cade, Josh, and Henry picked the bandits up and hauled them to the nearest sink to clean them up before jailing them in the highchairs. Margo rescued the train, and everyone enjoyed birthday cake.

There were balloons to keep the boys happy and entertained while the adults enjoyed cake and ice cream, and of course the boys got their first taste of that creamy, cold stuff. Before long, they were fast asleep with visions of great-tasting trains and cold, creamy stuff dancing in their heads.

Margo had triplet daughters, Kayla, Kola, and Kallie, and before they finally moved into the new house at the lake, she was pregnant again. It was well past time as little number six had become over grown in several different ways and Cade refused to expand again, this time with twins. With the triplet boys at fifteen months and the triplet girls just starting life, they moved, lock, stock, and barrel into the new house, settled in, and for the first time in nearly three years that Cade and Margo really felt at home.

They knew the tranquility wasn't going to last long, but they didn't care. They just relaxed and enjoyed what they had and thanked God for their family and all their riches, whatever they were.